# With Tender Loving Care

*from the auxiliary of*
## CHILDREN'S MEDICAL CENTER DALLAS, TEXAS

printed by
Taylor Publishing Company
Dallas, Texas

First Printing 10,000 Copies
October 1979

Library of Congress Catalog Card
Number 79-89290

This book is dedicated
to
Jeane Doonan Powell
a loyal friend of
Children's Medical Center

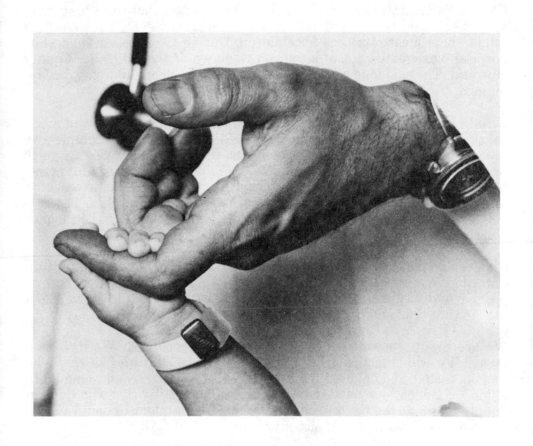

# With Tender
# Loving Care

# PREFACE

Dear Readers,

Children's Medical Center was founded on the fact that the young have very special needs. An epidemic in Dallas in 1913 evidenced the need for unique health care services for children. During that crisis, a makeshift hospital was created out of a tent on the lawn of the old Dallas County Hospital. The epidemic passed, but the obvious need of children's care remained.

Firmly supported by community leaders, our Center has grown in medical skills and reputation. In 1967 we opened the multi-million complex we occupy today. CMC is committed now, as it was so many years ago, to provide complete pediatric health services to patients ranging from newborns to 18 years of age. Our Center is the principal pediatric teaching hospital of The University of Texas Southwestern Medical School at Dallas, and is affiliated with Baylor School of Nursing and TWU School of Nursing, to provide top quality training in many pediatric areas.

Children's Medical Center has grown from its infancy into a mature institution. We, the auxiliary, are proud of what the Center has accomplished, and, as a member of the CMC team, we are pleased to have had a part in that vital and outstanding service to the community.

We are proud, too, of our contributors to the cookbook. We have had many. We want particularly to recognize our six faithful testers who cooked, tasted, and endured for over a year. A special recognition goes to Mike McCaddon, our outstanding photographer. Mike runs the Central Supply Room at the Center; he gave his time and talent to picture what we could not describe in a thousand words.

Faithful Testers:

Mrs. Don Addington
Mrs. Corrine Calder
Mrs. Don McIllyar

Mrs. Ed Crow Miller
Mrs. Robert Mullins
Mrs. Arthur White

Thank you all.
Sincerely,

Mrs. T. P. Votteler, Mrs. Ralph Wood, Jr.
Co-Chairmen

# TABLE OF CONTENTS

We have devised these fun graphics merely as a guide for you, dear readers. You may wish to delete some or add as you work through our book — anyway — have fun.

 FOOD PROCESSOR

 EASY

 EXPENSIVE

 INEXPENSIVE

 FREEZES

 LENGTHY

 IN-A-HURRY

# APPETIZERS

# APPETIZERS

### HOT ARTICHOKES

*They will definitely be impressed with this toothsome concoction!*

2 8½ ounce cans artichoke hearts
Lemon Pepper marinade
2 3-ounce packages cream cheese, softened

1 stick butter, softened
1 jar chopped chives
Parmesan cheese

Butter bottom and sides of a 8x8 inch Pyrex dish. Cut artichoke hearts in half. Place artichoke halves in bottom of dish and sprinkle with lemon pepper. In a separate bowl mix cream cheese, butter and chives. Spread this mixture on top of artichokes. Sprinkle with Parmesan cheese. Bake at 375° for 20 minutes. Serve hot with toothpicks to the side to spear artichokes for hors d'oeuvres. Serves 8.

### HOT ARTICHOKE DIP

*All the testers loved this one!!*

1 16-ounce can artichoke hearts
1 cup mayonnaise
1 cup Parmesan cheese, grated

Dash of garlic powder
Paprika

Drain artichoke hearts and mash well. Add mayonnaise, Parmesan cheese and garlic powder. Mix with a fork or spoon. Sprinkle paprika on top. Bake at 350° for 30 minutes. Serve with Waverly Wafers. Serves 6 to 8.
*Hint:* Excess grease can be drained from the sides with a paper towel.

# A QUICKY, BUT GOODIE APPETIZER

1 package Knorr cream of leek
   soup mix
1 7-ounce can minced clams,
   drained

1 pint sour cream

Mix all ingredients and chill at least 2 hours. Serve with Fritos. Serves 6 to 8.

# CHIPPED BEEF DIP

*Doubling this recipe will fill one chafing dish and this can be done the day before and reheated.*

8 ounces cream cheese
2 ounces green chilies, diced
2 tablespoons minced dried onion
   flakes
½ pint sour cream

½ teaspoon garlic salt
½ teaspoon pepper
2 tablespoons milk
½ jar chipped beef, shredded
Crumbled bacon

Cook all ingredients, except bacon, in a double boiler until cheese melts. Serve from a chafing dish with crumbled bacon sprinkled on top. Serves 10 to 12.

# SPICED BOLOGNA

*Since roast beef has become so $$$ you may wish to substitute this on an informal buffet table.*

**4 pound stick of bologna (pierce in a number of places with your meat fork)**
**½ cup chili sauce**

**Juice of one lemon**
**½ cup melted butter**
**2 teaspoons Worcestershire**

Mix the sauce, lemon juice, butter and Worcestershire sauce, pour over bologna. Refrigerate overnight, turning once or twice. Remove from marinade; bake in 250° oven for 4 hours, basting a number of times with marinade. Cool, slice thin, serve with thin sliced party size bread, or Parkerhouse rolls and a zippy mustard.

# CAVIAR MOLD

*Caviar (the red kind) from your reliable chain grocery store is not as expensive as you might think. Be daring try it!! We promise you will be glad!!*

**1 envelope unflavored gelatin**
**½ cup milk**
**1 cup mayonnaise**

**1 3-ounce jar caviar**
**Juice of one lemon**
**½ pint whipping cream**

Dissolve gelatin in milk and heat to melt. Cool. Mix mayonnaise, caviar and lemon juice. Add cooled gelatin. Fold in whipped cream. Pour in a greased mold and chill. Serve with Melba toast. Serves 8 to 10.

# CAVIAR PIE

*Another version of the caviar appetizer. The cost is not as great as you might imagine, and it is an impressive treat to serve.*

9 ounces cream cheese
Lots of grated onion (at least ½ onion)
1 cup mayonnaise
1 tablespoon Lea and Perrin's Worcestershire sauce

2 drops Tabasco
3 ounces caviar
2 eggs, hard boiled
½ cup parsley, chopped

Whip cream cheese, grated onion, mayonnaise, Worcestershire sauce and Tabasco in mixer. Spread in a 9 or 10 inch pie plate and chill until set. Drain caviar and spread on top. (Lump fish may be used instead of caviar.) Chill. Sprinkle with grated hard boiled eggs, then chopped parsley. Chill and serve with Melba toast rounds or crackers. Serves 8 to 10.

# CHEESE AND BEAN DIP

*Good appetizer for cold weather, maybe with our Stacked Enchiladas for a Mexican dinner.*

1 6-ounce garlic cheese roll
1 10¾-ounce can bean and bacon soup, undiluted
1 cup sour cream
2 tablespoons green onion, sliced

Generous dash of Tabasco
½ teaspoon salt
1 teaspoon chili powder (or more, if desired)

Cut the cheese roll into chunks. Place the cheese and soup in a sauce pan and heat slowly on a low fire for approximately 30 minutes. Stir in remaining ingredients. Heat an additional 5 minutes. Serve with crackers or chips. Serves 12.

¢

## CHEESE AND CHILI SPREAD

*Simple, but tasty!! Mucho bueno!!*

½ pound sharp Cheddar cheese
¼ cup butter, softened
½ cup sour cream

1 package green onion dip mix
2 tablespoons green chilies, chopped

Let cheese come to room temperature. With electric mixer or food processor, beat all ingredients until smooth. Chill for 1 to 2 hours. Makes 2 cups. Serve with crackers or Melba rounds. Will give pleasure to 6 to 8 folks.

## CHEESE SPREAD

1 pound Cheddar cheese, grated
1 16-ounce can Spam, chopped
1 cup mayonnaise

1 cup catsup
2 dill pickles, chopped
1 onion, chopped

Combine all ingredients and mix well. Good on biscuits, rolls, etc. Serve with soup and salad for a lunch or light supper.

## BLUE RIBBON CRAB DIP

*We think crab anything should be served with lightly or non-salted chips or Melba rounds.*

1 8-ounce package cream cheese, softened
½ cup mayonnaise
1 teaspoon Worcestershire sauce

Drops of Tabasco
2 teaspoons onion, grated
¼ teaspoon Lawry's salt
¾ cup crab meat, fresh or frozen

Combine all ingredients. Serves 6.

# CURRY DIP

*The 24 hours mellowing makes all the difference in the flavor.*

2 garlic buds, crushed
1 pint mayonnaise
6 tablespoons catsup
2 tablespoons Lea and Perrin's
   Worcestershire sauce

6 teaspoons curry powder
4 tablespoons onion, grated
2 teaspoons Tabasco
Salt and pepper to taste

Mix all ingredients and let mellow 24 hours before serving. Excellent with raw vegetables or as a salad dressing. Serves 8 to 10.

# HA'PENNY SNACKS

*These cheesy crackers are nice to have on hand. They keep for several weeks in a tin.*

1 cup flour
½ cup butter or margarine
½ pound sharp Cheddar cheese,
   grated

½ teaspoon salt
2 envelopes Lipton's onion soup
   mix (cup of soup size)
Sesame seeds

Blend flour and butter. Add remaining ingredients and mix well. Form into ½ inch roll. Wrap in foil and refrigerate for 1 hour. Slice in fairly thin slices and put on cookie sheets. Sprinkle with sesame seeds. Bake at 350° for 8 to 10 minutes. Store in airtight containers. Makes about 3 dozen. May be frozen.

## "HOT MIX"

*Delicious as a dip with Fritos or Doritos — also as a picante sauce for Mexican food or eggs.*

2 4¼-ounce cans chopped black
   olives
2 tomatoes, chopped
1 onion, chopped
Chopped jalapeño peppers (to
   taste) — begin with 2
   tablespoons

Garlic salt
¼ cup olive oil
¼ cup cider vinegar

Place vegetables in a dish. Pour vinegar and olive oil to cover the chopped vegetables. Add garlic salt and refrigerate at least 2 hours. Serves 6 to 8.

## HUNGRY MAN'S DIP
### (or should we say Person's?)

*College boys seem to believe this is what good boys are awarded. You won't have any left over.*

1 large onion, chopped
½ green pepper, chopped
½ stick butter
1½ pounds ground meat

1½ pounds Kraft's Velveeta
   cheese, cubed (¾ of a 2 pound
   box)
1 can Rotel tomatoes

Sauté onions and green peppers in butter. Remove vegetables, add meat and sauté until meat loses its color. Drain off fat. Add cheese and tomatoes, stirring while the cheese melts. Add onions and green pepper. It may be made the day before and reheated. Serve in a chafing dish with chips. Serves a lot of hungry people.

# BOURSIN STUFFED MUSHROOMS

*Our men folks loved this easy, terrific before dinner party thing.*

**12 medium mushrooms**
**Melted butter**

**1 5-ounce container Boursin**
**cheese with garlic and herbs**

Preheat oven to 350°. Wipe mushrooms with a damp cloth. Remove stems. Brush outside of caps with melted butter. Fill cups with cheese. Arrange on a cookie sheet and bake for 15 to 20 minutes.

# JIFFY DIP

*For something so simple, this is really good.*

**1 8-ounce roll braunschwieger**
**1 cup sour cream**

**½ package Bleu cheese salad**
**dressing mix**

Mix all ingredients. Chill and serve with chips. Serves 4-6.

## COLD OR HOT MARINATED MUSHROOMS

*This quick, simple appetizer will enhance your reputation as a cooking wizard!!*

**1 package Good Seasons Cheese Garlic salad dressing mix**

**3 4½-ounce jars whole mushrooms, drained**

Mix the salad dressing according to directions on the package.

*For hot hors d'oeuvres,* heat the dressing, add the mushrooms, simmer for about 15 to 20 minutes.

*For a cold appetizer,* mix the dressing and marinate the mushrooms for 30 minutes or all day.

Serve either with toothpicks as an appetizer or condiment with dinner. Serves 6 to 8. Our tester thought these may be even a bit tastier the second day.

## TOASTED PECANS

*These little gems make good holiday gifts.*

**¼ cup butter**
**1 tablespoon garlic salt**
**4 teaspoons Worcestershire sauce**

**½ teaspoon Tabasco sauce**
**5 cups pecan halves**

Melt butter over low heat. Add remaining ingredients and mix well. Spread into a large flat pan and toast in a moderate 350° oven for 30 minutes, stirring frequently. Drain on paper towels and store in an airtight container.

# MINI-QUICHES

*These are good "do-aheaders" for a dinner party, or neat to give as a holiday gift from your kitchen freezer.*

1 package dinner flake rolls (12 rolls)
1 cup small cooked shrimp or 1 cup ham (25¢ size pieces)
1 egg, beaten
½ cup Half and Half

1 tablespoon brandy
½ teaspoon salt
Dash of pepper
1⅓-ounces (2 triangles) Gruyere cheese
Paprika

Grease two dozen 1¾ inch muffin pans. Separate each dinner roll in half. Press into muffin pans to make shell. Put a shrimp or piece of ham in each shell. Mix egg, cream, brandy, salt and pepper. Divide evenly among shells — about 2 teaspoons for each. Slice the cheese into 24 small triangles. Put one on top of each appetizer and sprinkle with paprika. Bake at 375° for 20 minutes or until lightly brown. Cool. Allow 2 per person; 3 for those hungry men.

These can be frozen. To serve, place frozen appetizers on a baking sheet and bake at 375° for 10 to 12 minutes.

# MOCK PATÉ

*If you don't tell it's not honest-to-goodness paté, we won't.*

12 ounces cream cheese
1½ pounds Oscar Meyer liver sausage

½ cup red wine
1 tablespoon brandy

Soften cream cheese and mix all ingredients. Serve with Melba toast rounds or other crackers. Serves 20 to 24.

# MANHATTAN MEATBALLS

*Meatballs:*
1 pound ground beef
1 pound ground pork
2 cups bread crumbs
2 eggs, beaten
Salt
Parsley

½ cup onion, chopped
*Sauce:*
1 10-ounce jar apricot preserves
½ cup barbecue sauce (hickory smoked)
¾ cup red wine

Mix all ingredients for meatballs. Shape into small balls using your melon ball cutter. Bake at 350° for 15 minutes or until brown. Combine all ingredients for sauce. Pour over meatballs and bake at 350° for 30 minutes or longer. Will serve 20. May be prepared the day before and reheated.

# PIROSCHOKY

*This is a European goodie that is great to have in freezer for pop-in guests or holiday gifts.*

1½ pounds ground beef
1 medium onion, chopped
3 hard boiled eggs
½ teaspoon salt

½ teaspoon pepper
½ teaspoon dill weed
2 cans Butterflake rolls
1 raw egg

Brown meat and onion in a skillet. Drain. Add chopped hard boiled eggs. Season to taste with salt, pepper and dill weed. Separate rolls. Using ¾ of a roll for each, flatten rolls one at a time in the palm of your hand. Place a heaping teaspoon of meat mixture on roll, wrap dough around meat and seal with egg whites. Brush with egg yolk and repeat with remaining rolls and meat. Bake at 375° for 10 to 15 minutes until golden brown. Yields about 2 dozen. Can be served with hot clear beef or chicken broth.

Piroschoky can be prepared ahead of time and baked, then frozen. Remove from freezer and heat until piping hot.

# POPCORN

*Who doesn't like popcorn? Can you eat only one handful? Try this for a new twist on an old favorite. Teenagers thrive on it.*

**Popcorn**  **Lawry's seasoning salt**
**Melted butter or margarine**

Pop corn. Pour melted butter over popcorn. Sprinkle with a liberal amount of the seasoning salt. Hm-m good.

# QUICK AND EASY DIP

**1 package Good Seasons Cheese**  **1 8-ounce carton sour cream**
   **Italian or Cheese Garlic dry**  **1 8-ounce package cream cheese**
   **salad dressing mix**

Blend the ingredients well. Chill several hours and serve with fresh vegetables, chips or crackers.

# RYE BREAD DIP

*So simple, so different and so-o-o tasty!!*

**1⅓ cups sour cream**  **2 teaspoons onion, chopped**
**1⅓ cups mayonnaise**  **1 teaspoon parsley**
**2 tablespoons Beaumonde salt**  **1 round loaf rye bread, unsliced**
**2 tablespoons dill seed**  **(preferably from the bakery)**

Mix sour cream, mayonnaise, salt, dill seed, onion and parsley the night before serving. Scoop out round rye bread in chunks. Put dip in center of the bread and use the chunks to dip. Serves 6 to 8.

## SAUSAGE DIP

*This is number one on our list for an Open House appetizer. Serves a bunch.*

2 pounds hot pork sausage
2 pounds Velveeta cheese
1 13-ounce can evaporated milk

1 package Good Seasons Garlic salad dressing mix
1 2-ounce jar pimientos

Fry sausage, crumble and drain. Meanwhile, melt cheese in top of double boiler. Mix evaporated milk, garlic mix, sausage and pimientos, stir in melted cheese. Serve in a chafing dish with chips for dipping. Serves 20.

## CAJUN SHRIMP

*This is good for a party of 15 to 20.*

5 pounds shrimp
1 pint Hellmann's mayonnaise
1 small jar Louisiana Creole
   Mustard

Juice of 1 lime

Cook and clean shrimp. Mix mayonnaise, mustard and lime juice. Add shrimp and marinate overnight. Serve in cold, iced bowl for appetizers.

## SHRIMP DIP

*All the men folks who tasted this for us gave it an A + +.*

1 8-ounce package cream cheese
2 tablespoons lemon juice
2 tablespoons onion juice
2 tablespoons catsup

½ cup Hellmann's mayonnaise
¼ teaspoon garlic salt
¾ pound cooked shrimp, coarsely chopped

Beat the first six ingredients until smooth. Add the shrimp. Prepare at least two hours prior to serving or prepare the day before. Serve with Fritos or Doritos. Serves 8 to 10.

## SHRIMP MOLD

1 10¾-ounce can tomato soup
8 ounces cream cheese
2 teaspoons unflavored gelatin
¼ cup water
¾ cup celery, diced

½ cup green onions, chopped
2 4½-ounce cans shrimp
1 cup mayonnaise
½ cup sour cream

Warm tomato soup with cream cheese until dissolved. Dissolve gelatin in water, add to soup and cheese mixture and cool. Add remaining ingredients and mix well. Pour into greased ring mold and chill. Put parsley sprigs, dusted with paprika, in center. Serve with round wheat wafers. Serves 8 to 10 generously.

*Note:* Check our observations section on canned shrimp.

## SMOKED OYSTER DIP

*Oyster lovers, this is just for you!!*

8 ounces cream cheese
¾ tablespoon onion, minced
1 tablespoon Worcestershire
  sauce

1 3¾-ounce can smoked oysters

Cream the cream cheese until light and fluffy. Add onion and Worcestershire sauce. Dice oysters. Add oysters and a little of the oil from the can to the cheese mixture. If necessary add milk to desired dipping consistency. Serve with potato chips. Serves 6.

# SWEET AND SOUR DIP

*Of all the appetizers (we never could spell Hors' whatever) we tested, this is the most unusual. We thought it most appropriate with wine — you try it and judge.*

1 6-ounce jar Colman's hot mustard

1 9-ounce jar Kraft horseradish sauce

1 small jar (approximately 10 ounces) apple jelly

1 small jar pineapple preserves

1 8-ounce package cream cheese

Combine first four ingredients in a blender or food processor, adding mustard by thirds or it might be too hot for your taste. Blend well. Pour over block of cream cheese and serve with crackers. This makes a lot, but it will keep well in the refrigerator.

# SWEET AND SOUR TIDBITS

*Another gem for a large gathering.*

1½ pounds ground round steak

1 12-ounce bottle chili sauce

1 8-ounce jar grape jelly

Roll meat into tiny balls. Combine chili sauce and jelly in a sauce pan. Heat to a slow boil. Add meat balls and simmer for 45 minutes. Serve from a chafing dish with toothpicks. Serves 20.

# ZUCCHINI CHIPS

*Greasy, but sure 'nuff good!!*

**2 pounds zucchini**
**½ teaspoon salt**
**½ cup Bisquick**

**1 teaspoon Lawry's seasoning salt**
**Vegetable oil**

Wash zucchini thoroughly. Cut in thin slices. Sprinkle with salt. Place in a mixing bowl and cover with waxed paper. Take a brick or some other heavy object wrapped in a paper towel and place it on the waxed paper. Toss the zucchini three times in 1½ hours. The object is to try to remove as much moisture as possible. After 1½ hours, drain, toss zucchini in Bisquick and seasoning salt and shake off excess Bisquick. Fry for a few minutes in hot, deep vegetable oil until golden. Drain and serve with lemon wedges. Serves 4 to 6.

# SOUP, SALADS, SALAD DRESSING

# SOUPS

### BLENDER AVOCADO SOUP

*This is a pretty beginning, especially for a summer dinner party.*

1 ripe avocado
1 10¾-ounce can chicken broth
2 tablespoons lemon juice

1 cup light cream
Salt and pepper to taste
Dash or two of cayenne pepper

In a covered blender or food processor on a high speed, blend avocado, chicken broth and lemon juice until smooth. Stir in cream and seasoning. Chill thoroughly. May be garnished with thin slices of lemon and another dash of cayenne. Serves 4 to 6.

### BEEFYTOM SOUP

*We like cold soups for company. They are simple and can be made ahead. Serve them as first course before guests are seated and it gives you an opportunity to finish any last minute dinner details.*

1 46-ounce can V-8 juice
1 11½-ounce can condensed beef
  consommé

1 teaspoon Tabasco
1 teaspoon Worcestershire sauce
¼ cup white wine (optional)

Mix all ingredients together. Serve hot or cold. If adding wine, do so just before serving. Serves 8 to 10.

## CORN CREOLE

2 large onions, chopped
½ bell pepper, chopped
1 stick butter
6 12-ounce cans White Shoepeg
  Corn
3 14-ounce cans tomatoes

1 teaspoon salt
1 teaspoon pepper
Worcestershire sauce to taste
Tabasco sauce to taste
Cayenne pepper to taste

Sauté onions and bell pepper in butter. Add corn and simmer for 8 to 10 minutes. Add remaining ingredients and cook for 1 hour. Serves 8 to 12, generously.

## BEVERLY'S GAZPACHO

3 10-ounce cans Snappy Tom
1 10¾-ounce can beef consommé
1 32-ounce can Hunt's tomato
  juice
⅓-½ cup fresh lemon juice
2 cucumbers
1 green pepper
1 onion

2-3 tomatoes
1-2 teaspoons sugar
Salt and pepper to taste
Accent to taste
Tabasco to taste
Lea and Perrin's Worcestershire
  sauce to taste

Blend all ingredients in a blender or food processor and chill. Serves 8 to 10.

## BLENDER OR FOOD PROCESSOR SOUP

1 10-ounce package frozen peas, corn or spinach, cooked and drained
2 cups milk

1 onion, sliced
1 tablespoon butter
1 tablespoon flour

Mix all ingredients in a blender or food processor. Heat and serve. Serves 3.

## CHICKEN-CHEESE SOUP

1 large package chicken breasts (approximately 4)
6 cups of water
3 chicken bouillon cubes
3 carrots, grated

4 ribs of celery, chopped
3 shakes of lemon pepper
3 shakes of Lawry's seasoning salt
1½-2 cups cubed Velveeta

Boil the first five ingredients until the chicken is tender. Cool and debone in bite size pieces. Add seasonings and cheese according to taste. The more times this is heated, the better it tastes. If two or three days have passed, add ½ cup chicken broth to thin the soup. Serves 6 to 8.

# CHICKEN-RICE SOUP

*Grandmother couldn't make it any tastier from scratch.*

1 fryer
Salt and pepper
1 box frozen Green Giant Rice
  Pilaf

1 can Swanson's chicken broth

Simmer fryer in stew pot with salt and pepper until tender — approximately 45 minutes. While fryer simmers, cook rice pilaf according to directions on box. When fryer is done remove from pot, discard skin and bones and break cooked chicken into bite size pieces. Put chicken pieces into a clean pot, add cooked rice pilaf and 1 can chicken broth. Heat. Serves 6.

# GOOD CORN SOUP

2 16½-ounce cans cream style corn
1 tablespoon margarine
¾ teaspoon curry powder

5 tablespoons sherry
1 cup Half and Half

In a blender, blend corn, one can at a time, until smooth. Pour into a pan with the remaining ingredients. Simmer for 15 minutes. Do not boil. Serves 6.

# COLD CUCUMBER SOUP

*Grand way to begin a meal. Tuck on top a tiny piece of parsley that has been dusted with paprika. Cool and refreshing in taste and appearance.*

1 cucumber, peeled
1 cup sour cream
Salt and white pepper to taste

1 10½-ounce can Campbell's green
  pea soup (without ham)
¾ can cold water

Put cucumber, sour cream, salt and pepper in blender or food processor. Stir soup and water together and add to cucumber mixture in blender. Blend for a few minutes. Chill thoroughly. Serves 6 to 8.

# CRAB BISQUE

1 cup flaked crab or lobster
1 10-ounce can condensed tomato
  soup
1 10-ounce can condensed green
  pea soup

1 soup can hot milk
½ soup can of dry sherry

Soak the crab in sherry for a few minutes. Combine tomato and pea soups and heat to boiling. Stir in slowly the hot milk. Add crab and sherry. Continue cooking, but do not boil. Makes 6 cups. Do not freeze.

# CRABMEAT SOUP

*Your guests will think you worked for hours to whip this up!!*

1 10¾-ounce can mushroom soup
1 10-ounce can asparagus soup
1 soup can milk

½ soup can sherry
1 small can crab meat

Gently heat all ingredients together, adding more milk or sherry to taste. Fresh or frozen crabmeat may be used instead of canned. Serves 8. Can be prepared in the morning.

# CURRIED SOUP

*Very subtle first course for any meal.*

1 10-ounce can green pea soup
1 10-ounce can chicken broth
1 soup can bouillon
3 teaspoons curry powder

Dash of onion salt
Dash of cayenne pepper
Dash of garlic salt

Mix all ingredients together and heat. To serve cold, add 1 pint of Half and Half. Serves 6.

# GOOSE AND DUCK GUMBO

*Don't despair when hunting season opens. The following will solve your problem of what to do with the feathered prizes your Nimrod bags.*

3-4 geese or ducks
2 large onions, coarsely chopped
3 stalks of celery
1 tablespoon salt
1 teaspoon pepper
1 bay leaf
1 cup flour
1 cup bacon drippings (no substitutes)
4 stalks celery, chopped
2 large or 3 medium onions
1 clove of garlic, crushed
½ of 15-ounce bottle of Doxsee's clam juice

1 8-ounce can tomato sauce
3 tablespoons Worcestershire sauce
1 tablespoon salt (or more, if necessary)
1 tablespoon pepper (or more, if necessary)
3-4 drops Tabasco (or more, to taste)
2 cups frozen okra (or more, if you like)

Place first six ingredients in a heavy kettle with 3 quarts of water. Cook until tender — approximately 1½ to 2 hours. Cool, remove meat and strain stock. Cool thoroughly. Put flour in a heavy skillet and add drippings. Mix to make a roux. Cook over a medium heat until the color of a brown paper bag. Add celery stalks, onions and garlic. Stir and cook until golden and tender. Add warmed stock, a little at a time, stirring until smooth. Add remaining ingredients, adding okra last. Simmer for 1 hour. Serve over rice.

If you have a few stray frozen shrimp or crabs, or really feel generous, add a small can of lobster to gumbo. It will enhance it. This makes a lot and freezes wonderfully well.

*P.S.* Our hunters never knew it, but we also slipped in some of their doves and quail.

# EASY GUMBO

2 medium onions, chopped
1 garlic button, crushed
1 pound okra, sliced
1 pound ground meat or 1 cooked
  boned chicken or 1 pound
  flaked crab meat

¼ cup bacon drippings
1 20-ounce can stewed tomatoes
1 tablespoon chili powder
½ cup raw rice
Salt and pepper to taste
Worcestershire sauce to taste

Brown onions, garlic, okra and meat in bacon drippings. Add remaining ingredients and simmer for 30 minutes. Serves 4.
This recipe freezes well. If chicken or crab meat is used, do not brown, just add after okra, onions and garlic are browned.

# MEXICAN SOUP

*Great for a winter luncheon. Serve with a green salad, oil and vinegar dressing, hot soft tortillas — Ole'!!*

2 pounds of chuck
5 cups of water
1 cup onion, chopped
1 garlic pod, crushed
2 tablespoons margarine
1 tablespoon wine vinegar
Dash of Worcestershire sauce
Dash of Tabasco
½ teaspoon pepper
1 teaspoon salt

1 teaspoon cumin
1 6-ounce can tomato paste
1 large fresh tomato, chopped
4 soft tortillas, cut in squares
*Topping:*
1 8-ounce carton sour cream
1 cup avocados, diced
1 cup Monterey Jack cheese,
  grated

Simmer the chuck in the water for 1½ hours, covered. If necessary remove from the broth and cut into bite size pieces. Meanwhile sauté onions and garlic in margarine until limp. Return to broth and add the remaining ingredients. Simmer over a slow fire for at least 1 hour. Just before serving, add tortillas. Serve in bowls and pass additional bowls of sour cream, diced avocados and Monterey Jack cheese. Serves 4 to 6.

# POTATO SOUP

*Hearty and filling for a one dish dinner.*

3 large Idaho potatoes, peeled and sliced
3 large onions, peeled and coarsely chopped
2 chicken bouillon cubes
¼ teaspoon salt
Couple shakes of pepper
Water
3 tablespoons butter or margarine
1 cup milk
Sliced Polish sausage or weiners to suit taste

Place potatoes, onions, bouillon cubes, salt and pepper in a large kettle. Add just enough water to cover vegetables. Cook until tender and mash. Add butter, stir until combined; add milk and stir. If you want the soup richer, add Half and Half. For a really hearty supper dish, slice weiners or Polish sausage, heat in a skillet and then add several slices to soup when it is being served. Serves 4 generously. This can be prepared the day before needed.

# SHRIMP SOUP

*One of our tester's favorites.*

1 10¾-ounce can tomato soup
1 10¾-ounce can mushroom soup
1 11-ounce can cheddar cheese soup
1½ cups milk
½ cup sherry
1 10-ounce package frozen shrimp or 2 cans small shrimp
1½ cups Half and Half

Combine all ingredients and heat. Serves 8.

# SUMMER SOUP

*A good beginning for a summer meal.*

5 cups tomato juice
1 cup sour cream
¼ cup onion, grated
2-3 tablespoons lemon juice
1 teaspoon grated lemon rind
Salt to taste

White pepper to taste
¾ cup minced ham
1 cucumber
1 small cantaloupe
Fresh basil, minced

Whip first seven ingredients in a food processor or blender until smooth. Stir in ham, cover and chill. Cut cucumber and cantaloupe into balls. Sprinkle with minced fresh basil. Chill for 4 hours. Put soup in bowls and garnish with cucumber and melon balls.

# TOMATO AND SHRIMP SOUP

1 cup canned jellied beef
  consomme
¼ cup cucumber, finely diced,
  seeded, and peeled
½ cup tomatoes, finely diced and
  seeded

1 tablespoon wine vinegar
1 teaspoon olive oil
¼ tablespoon fresh green onion,
  chopped
½ cup cooked shrimp, diced
¼ cup avocado, diced

Mix all ingredients together several hours before serving, refrigerate and serve very cold. Garnish with croutons or sour cream if you wish. Serves 2 to 6 according to cup size.

# CREAM OF TURTLE SOUP

*This goes with a special dinner party for four. Serve in demitasse cups. For an added touch, just before serving, add a dollop of unsweetened whipped cream with a light touch of paprika.*

1 10-ounce can turtle soup
4 egg yolks (use whites to make
  Forgotten Peppermint Cookies)
½ teaspoon curry powder

1 tablespoon dry sherry
Salt
Pepper (freshly ground is best)

Bring can of soup to a boil. In the meantime, in the top of a double boiler gently heat egg yolks, curry powder and sherry. Watch carefully or yolks will hard boil. Slowly add boiling soup to warm yolk mixture. Cook and stir over hot water until soup thickens. Season to taste with salt and pepper. This can be held over warm, not hot, water for 30 minutes or so. Serves 4.

# ZUCCHINI SOUP I

*This can be halved to fit exactly in blender or food processor.*

2 10½-ounce cans Campbell's
  chicken broth
2 10½-ounce cans Campbell's
  cream of potato soup
3 small or 2 large zucchini, seeded

3-4 small green onions
1 pint sour cream
¼ teaspoon white pepper
¼ teaspoon dill
2 shakes cayenne pepper

Put soups in blender. Cut unpeeled zucchini in chunks and add to soup mixture. Add remaining ingredients and blend. Chill. Serves 10.

# ZUCCHINI SOUP II

1½ pounds zucchini (3 medium),
   remove seeds
½ cup green onions, chopped
6 cups chicken broth
3 tablespoons butter

1½ teaspoons wine vinegar
¾ teaspoon dill weed or tarragon
4 tablespoons cooking farina or
   cream of wheat
½ cup sour cream

Cook zucchini and onions in chicken broth. Put through blender and return to broth. Add remaining ingredients, except sour cream, simmer 15 minutes. Stir in sour cream just before serving. Serve hot to 6 or 8.

# SALADS

## MOLDED APRICOT SALAD

*The Sprite gives this a sparkly, sunny taste!*

1 3-ounce package lemon jello
1 3-ounce package apricot jello
1 17-ounce can apricot halves
1 8-ounce package cream cheese
2 bananas
Juice from apricots and enough
   Sprite to make 3 cups liquid

*Topping:*
1 cup pineapple juice
2 tablespoons flour
1 egg yolk, beaten
½ cup sugar
½ pint whipping cream

Dissolve jello in boiling liquid. Put apricots, cream cheese and bananas in blender and mix. Combine with dissolved jello and chill until set. Add topping before serving.

*Topping:* Dissolve flour, sugar and pineapple juice in bowl. Stir in beaten egg yolk and stir until thickened. Whip cream and fold into egg mixture. Spread over congealed salad. Serves 12 to 14.

## COLD GREEN BEAN SALAD

1 10-ounce package French style
green beans
1 8-ounce can water chestnuts,
drained and sliced
½ cup ripe olives, chopped

1 small can artichoke hearts,
drained and coarsely chopped
1 cup fresh mushrooms, sliced
½ cup green onions, chopped
Italian dressing

Cook and drain green beans. Toss all vegetables with your favorite Italian dressing. Refrigerate several hours before serving. Serves 4 generously.

## COLD/HOT BEAN SALAD

*Excellent summer salad and different.*

1 15-ounce can kidney beans,
drained
1 bunch green onions, chopped

Mayonnaise
Tabasco

Place beans and green onions in a bowl. Stir in enough mayonnaise to coat beans and onions lightly. Sprinkle Tabasco over mixture and stir. Taste and add more Tabasco until it is hot enough to suit your taste. Marinate in refrigerator at least 4 hours. Serve cold. Serves 4.

# DELIGHTFUL BEANS

*The chestnuts give it a good crunchy texture. We vote to prepare it as an accompaniment to smoked turkey or baked ham.*

2 16-ounce cans French style
  green beans, drained
1 10 ounce jar salad olives
2 8-ounce cans water chestnuts,
  sliced
¼ cup fresh parsley, chopped
1 cup fresh green onions (tops
  included), chopped
4 cloves garlic, chopped
¾ cup oil
½ cup lemon juice
1 cup fresh mushrooms, chopped
  or sliced

Combine all ingredients and refrigerate for at least two days for flavors to enhance each other. Serves 8 to 10.

# BROCCOLI SALAD

*Good for a buffet or holiday table.*

2 10-ounce packages frozen,
  chopped broccoli
1 10-ounce can consommé
1 envelope unflavored gelatin
½ cup cold water
2-3 hard boiled eggs
2 teaspoons salt
2 teaspoons lemon juice
2 teaspoons Worcestershire sauce
¾ cup Hellmann's mayonnaise
Couple dashes of Tabasco

Cook broccoli until just tender. Drain very well. Heat consommé. Mix gelatin and water, add to heated consommé and stir until dissolved. Mix in broccoli and eggs. Stir salt, lemon juice, Worcestershire sauce, mayonnaise and Tabasco together and add to the broccoli mixture. Place in one large mold or several small ones. This can be made the day before needed. Serves 8 to 10.

# CABBAGE SALAD

*A crispy accompaniment for seafoods, soups or ham.*

1 medium head of cabbage, coarsely chopped
½ medium onion, finely chopped
¼ cup vegetable oil
⅛ cup white vinegar (more if you like it tangier)
1 teaspoon Sweet and Low or other powdered artificial sweetener

1 teaspoon salt
¼ teaspoon black pepper (white, if you have it, looks prettier)
1 teaspoon crushed dill

Steam the cabbage until just done — 3 to 5 minutes. Mix the remaining ingredients and stir into the hot cabbage. Chill. Serves 4 to 6.

# MARTY'S DILLED CARROTS

*A tangy, piquant real dilly of a way with carrots.*

2½ cups carrots
1 tablespoon parsley (more if fresh)
¼ cup fresh green onions, chopped
¼ cup Green Goddess dressing

¼ cup Italian dressing
½ teaspoon pepper
¼ teaspoon salt
½ teaspoon sugar
1 tablespoon dill weed (more if fresh)

Cook carrots. Cut in julienne strips. Combine remaining ingredients and add to carrots. Chill at least two or three hours before serving. Stir several times while chilling.

# CHICKEN SALAD INDIENNE

*We thought this was a really fresh approach to an old standby.*

½ cup mayonnaise
½ cup Marzetti's cole slaw
   dressing
2 cups cooked chicken

1 can mandarin oranges, drained
1 cup seedless green grapes
1-2 hard boiled eggs, chopped
Salt and pepper to taste

Cut chicken in bite size pieces. Combine mayonnaise and cole slaw dressing. Mix with chicken, fruits and eggs. Chill. Serves 3 to 4.

# COUNTRY CLUB PINK SALAD

*Luscious and lovely!*

1 8-ounce package cream cheese
1½ cups miniature marshmallows
1 9-ounce jar Maraschino cherries,
   drained

1 can fruit cocktail, drained

Beat cream cheese in Mixmaster. Chop marshmallows, a few at a time, in blender. Chop cherries in blender. Mix marshmallows and cherries into cheese. Add fruit cocktail. Pour into a mold and refrigerate. Serves 4 to 6.

## SCANDINAVIAN CUCUMBERS

*Excellent for a cold summer luncheon or dinner.*

3 small unpared cucumbers, thinly
  sliced
½ cup sour cream
1 tablespoon sugar
2 tablespoons parsley

2 tablespoons tarragon vinegar
1 tablespoon onion, finely
  chopped
½ teaspoon dill weed

Combine all ingredients, except cucumbers. Mix well, then fold in cucumbers. Chill for 2 hours.

## FROZEN FRUIT SALAD I

2 cups water
1½ cups sugar
10 large marshmallows
1 10-ounce package frozen
  strawberries

1 20-ounce can crushed pineapple
1 29-ounce can apricots, drained
  and chopped
4 bananas, sliced

Boil together water and sugar. Add marshmallows. Remove from heat when marshmallows have melted. Add partially thawed frozen strawberries, pineapple, apricots and bananas. Freeze salad and slice to serve.

To make this a festive Christmas salad, freeze in lightly oiled bundt pan. Just before ready to serve, place on cake stand and place artificial holly around base.

This can also be put in paper cupcake containers or in muffin tins to freeze. Suggest using electric knife to slice. Serves 10-12.

## FROZEN FRUIT SALAD II

⅓ cup nuts, chopped
3 tablespoons cherries, chopped
1 9-ounce can crushed pineapple,
   drained well
1 pint sour cream

¾ cup sugar
2 tablespoons lemon juice
⅛ teaspoon salt
1 banana, diced

Combine all ingredients and freeze. Remove from freezer a few minutes before serving.

Paper cupcake cups can be filled with mixture and frozen in muffin tin. Fills 10 cups. Then it is easy to use only as many as you need!

## FROZEN FRUIT SALAD III

*Pretty for Christmas dinner.*

1 8-ounce package cream cheese,
   softened
1 8-ounce can crushed pineapple,
   drained

1 16-ounce can whole cranberries
1 package Dream Whip
½ cup nuts, chopped

Combine first three ingredients and mix well. Prepare Dream Whip and beat until stiff. Add nuts and fold into fruit and cheese mixture. Pour into a pan, bowl or smaller containers and freeze. Remove from freezer ½ to 1 hour before serving. Grease molds or pan with mayonnaise for easy removal. To keep it from becoming soft at room temperature, 1 package of unflavored gelatin can be added.

# GOOSEBERRY SALAD

*Pretty and crunchy!!*

1 3-ounce package lemon jello
1½ cups boiling water
1 cup canned gooseberries,
   drained

1 cup celery, finely chopped
1 cup pecans, finely chopped
1 orange, peeled and sliced

Combine jello and water and then cool. Add gooseberries, celery and pecans. Put in cup-like molds. In the center of each mold, place a section of fresh orange. (Interesting when you eat the salad.) Serves 8.

# GREEN GAGE PLUM SALAD

1 3-ounce package lime jello
1 cup boiling water
1 #2 can peeled green gage plums
1 cup plum juice

¼ cup mayonnaise
1 3-ounce package cream cheese
1 cup pecans, chopped (optional)

Break cream cheese into bits. Cut up plums. Combine all ingredients except plums and mix well. Add plums and pour into mold. Chill until set. Serves 6.

## ITALIAN SALAD

*Serve with the Spinach Lasagne recipe.*

1 head Romaine lettuce
4 ounces fresh mushrooms, sliced
2 ounces Swiss cheese, grated
1-2 tablespoons sesame seeds,
  toasted

Italian dressing
Salt and pepper to taste

Toast sesame seeds on cookie sheet in oven until lightly brown. Mix all ingredients together and add dressing. Serves 4 to 6.

## MACARONI SALAD

*This would be nifty for a picnic or boxed lunches.*

2 cups cooked macaroni, drained
  and cooled
½ cup sweet pickles, chopped
½ cup celery, chopped
1-2 cups cooked ham, chopped
½ cup Cheddar cheese, diced

2 tablespoons onion, chopped
2 hard boiled eggs, chopped
Salt and pepper to taste
4 tablespoons salad dressing
  (approximately)

Combine all ingredients with enough salad dressing to moisten. Chill and serve. Serves 8 to 10.

## FESTIVE POTATO SALAD

*When it is picnic time or for a buffet after a game this is most suitable. We strongly advise you to make the day before to allow the seasonings to do their thing.*

3 cups potatoes boiled, peeled, diced
2 tablespoons vegetable oil
1 tablespoon vinegar
1 teaspoon salt
½ cup ripe olives, chopped
1½ cup cabbage, finely shredded
¼ cup dill pickle
½ cup carrot, grated

2 tablespoons pimiento, minced
2 tablespoons green pepper, chopped
*Dressing:*
⅔ cup mayonnaise
2 teaspoons onion, grated
1 teaspoon prepared mustard
Black pepper to taste

Peel, dice the hot potatoes. Blend the oil, vinegar and salt together, pour over potatoes, mix lightly, cool. Gently add the olives, cabbage, pickles, carrots, pimientos and green peppers. Mix the dressing, pour over potato mixture. Taste, you may wish to add more salt. Cover and *refrigerate* overnight. Serves 6.

## POTATO SALAD

*A different approach to an old family favorite.*

6 large boiling potatoes
1 cup celery, diced
1 cup green onion (tops, too), chopped
2 tablespoons fresh parsley, minced

Scant ½ teaspoon celery seed
2 teaspoons salt
¼ teaspoon pepper
2 cups sour cream
4 ounces blue cheese
¼ cup white wine vinegar

Boil and peel potatoes. Cut in 1 inch cubes. Combine potatoes with celery, green onions, parsley, celery seed, salt and pepper. Combine the sour cream, blue cheese and vinegar and toss with the potatoes. Chill, covered, for several hours. Serves 6 to 8.

# REALLY RED SLAW

*Delicious with any fish or beef dish.*

4 cups shredded (not grated) red
  cabbage
*Dressing:*
½ cup mayonnaise
2 tablespoons lemon juice

1 teaspoon onion, grated
½ teaspoon celery seed
½ teaspoon salt
½ teaspoon pepper
1 cup bell pepper, chopped

Mix dressing ingredients and add to cabbage. Serve on lettuce. This slaw should really sit for 24 hours to gain full flavor. Serves 8 to 10.

# RICE-ARTICHOKE SALAD

*My, my, but we liked this one; you will too, if you like a touch of curry.*

1 package curry flavored rice
½ cup green pepper, chopped
4-5 green onions, chopped
8-10 pimiento stuffed olives

1 6-ounce jar marinated artichoke
  hearts
½ cup mayonnaise

Cook rice according to directions, omitting butter. Cool. Add green pepper, onions and olives. Drain artichokes, saving the marinade. Mix mayonnaise with the reserved marinade. Add to the salad, toss and chill at least 12 hours. Serves 6 to 8.

## SALMON MOLD

1½ tablespoons unflavored gelatin
1 cup cold water
1 can tomato soup
1 3-ounce package cream cheese
1 cup celery, chopped
1 small green pepper, chopped
1 small onion, grated

½ teaspoon salt
Juice of 1 lemon
1 tablespoon Lea and Perrin's
  Worcestershire sauce
1 15½-ounce can red salmon,
  boned, drained and mashed
1 cup mayonnaise

Soak gelatin in cold water for 5 minutes. Heat tomato soup and melt cream cheese in it. Stir and add celery, green pepper and onion. Stir constantly and remove from heat. Add gelatin to mixture and stir until melted. Cool thoroughly. Add salt, lemon juice, Worcestershire sauce, salmon and mayonnaise. Put in mold and chill. Serves 6.

## NEW ORLEANS SHRIMP SALAD

1 cup cooked rice
1 cup shrimp, cooked and peeled
½ cup raw cauliflower, diced
¼ cup onion, minced
¼ cup green pepper, chopped
¼ cup celery, chopped

¼ cup stuffed olives, sliced
½ cup mayonnaise
¼ cup French dressing
½ teaspoon salt
1 tablespoon lemon juice
Lettuce

Combine all ingredients and toss lightly. Chill thoroughly and serve on lettuce leaves. Or stuff avocados or artichokes. Serves 4.

## SWEET AND SOUR SLAW

1 large crisp head of cabbage
2 large Bermuda onions
1 large green pepper
1 cup sugar
2 tablespoons sugar

1 tablespoon salt
1 cup vinegar
1 teaspoon dry mustard
1 teaspoon celery seed
¾ cup oil

Slice cabbage, onions and green pepper. Place in alternate layers in a large crock. Sprinkle 1 cup sugar on top. Place remaining ingredients in a pan and heat to boiling. Pour over cabbage and cover immediately. Put in refrigerator and let stand for 4 hours. Later, mix thoroughly.

## TOMATO SURPRISE SALAD

*We will be surprised if you don't love this one!!*

2 packages unflavored gelatin
½ cup cold water
1 can Tomato Bisque
1 3-ounce package cream cheese
1 cup celery, chopped
½ cup chives or onion, chopped

1 cup mayonnaise
2 6½-ounce cans tuna
2 tablespoons Worcestershire
  sauce
1 tablespoon lemon juice
Dash of Tabasco

Dissolve gelatin in cold water. Heat bisque and stir in cream cheese. Cool and add remaining ingredients. Chill until set. May be prepared the day before serving. Serves 8.

# MUSHROOM SALAD

½ pound fresh mushrooms
3 stalks celery
½ green pepper
3 green onions
*Dressing:*
¼ cup safflower or walnut oil

¼ cup white wine vinegar
2 tablespoons fresh dill, chopped
1 teaspoon chervil
¼ teaspoon salt
¼ teaspoon sugar

Wash and clean vegetables. Pat dry. Put vegetables through food processor using slicing blade. Place in salad bowl.

Mix dressing ingredients well. Pour over mushroom mixture. Cover and refrigerate for 2 hours. Makes one quart of salad. Serves 2 to 4.

# PINEAPPLE SALAD

*Delicious! Very rich!*

1 16-ounce can crushed pineapple
  (do not drain)
1 box instant vanilla pudding
  (unmade)

2 cups miniature marshmallows
1 package Dream Whip

Stir pineapple and vanilla pudding until dissolved. Add remaining ingredients and mix together. Chill. Serves 6 to 8.

# TUNA MOLD

1 10¾-ounce can mushroom soup
1 8-ounce package Philadelphia
  cream cheese
2 envelopes unflavored Knox
  gelatin

2 7-ounce cans tuna
Juice of 1 small lemon
1 4-ounce jar pimiento, chopped
1 cup mayonnaise
1 cup celery, finely chopped

Heat mushroom soup, add cream cheese and stir until melted. Dissolve gelatin in cold water and add to soup mixture. Drain, flake tuna and add to soup mixture. Add remaining ingredients. Cool to room temperature and pour into a greased mold. Refrigerate until set, unmold, surround with carrot curls, ripe olives, radishes, etc. Serves 8 to 10.

# DI'S WILD TUNA SALAD

*This is the perfect answer for a ladies' luncheon. Serve with little pimiento cheese sandwiches and our Ellen's Crunchy Cookies — simple, but most suitable!!*

1 6-ounce package Uncle Ben's
  Wild and Long Grain rice
1 cup mayonnaise
½ cup sour cream
½ cup celery, chopped
1 cup cashews, chopped

2 tablespoons onion, chopped
⅛ teaspoon salt
⅛ teaspoon pepper
2 7-ounce cans white tuna (water
  packed)

Cook rice as directed on package and cool. Add remaining ingredients and chill overnight. Keeps several days and gets better every day. Serve on lettuce cups. Serves 8 to 10.

# WATER CHESTNUT TUNA SALAD

*This is a grand answer for your bridge, sewing, or card club luncheon.*

1 7-ounce can white, solid tuna
1 8-ounce can water chestnuts, sliced
1 tablespoon onion, grated

1 teaspoon lemon juice
1 teaspoon soy sauce
½ teaspoon curry powder
½ cup mayonnaise

Combine all ingredients and mix well. Refrigerate two hours or longer.

# 24 HOUR GREEN SALAD #1

*There are many versions of 24 hour salad. We think these two are really great!!*

1 head lettuce
1 package raw spinach
1 box frozen peas, uncooked
1 pound bacon
6 hard boiled eggs, sliced

*Dressing:*
2 cups mayonnaise
1 pint sour cream
1 bunch green onions, sliced
1 envelope Hidden Valley Original Recipe dressing mix

Break lettuce into bite sized pieces. Remove stems from spinach and break into bite sized pieces. Cook bacon until crisp and then crumble. Layer lettuce, spinach, peas, crumbled bacon and sliced eggs in a 9x13 inch container. Mix dressing ingredients well. Spread over layered greens, etc., sealing to edges. Cover tightly and refrigerate for 24 hours before serving. Serves 14 to 16.

# 24 HOUR GREEN SALAD #2

*This is a great recipe for a large group of people. Do it in a large oblong wooden bowl.*

Romaine lettuce
2 cups celery, chopped
1 cup radishes, sliced
1 box frozen peas
1 small can water chestnuts, sliced

1 bunch green onions, chopped
1 quart jar Hellmann's
   mayonnaise (no substitutes)
Swiss cheese, grated
3 hard boiled eggs

Layer first six ingredients in a large oblong wooden bowl. You may also add anything else that has a "crunch" to it, e.g. carrots, sunflower nuts, etc. Cover entire salad with Hellmann's mayonnaise and a little sprinkled sugar and seal to edges of bowl. Cover with saran wrap. Let sit overnight. Before serving, cover with grated Swiss cheese and sliced eggs. Serves 12 to 16.

# VEGETABLE SALAD

1 16-ounce can French style green
  beans
1 16-ounce can LeSuer Green Peas
1 16-ounce can Peg corn (white
  kernel)
1 4-ounce jar pimientos, chopped
1 cup celery, chopped

1 cup green pepper, chopped
½ cup onion, chopped
1 cup sugar
⅔ cup vinegar
½ cup Wesson oil
Salt and pepper to taste

Drain canned vegetables. Mix all vegetables. Heat sugar, vinegar, oil, salt and pepper. Pour heated mixture over vegetables and marinate overnight in the refrigerator. Keeps several days. Serves 10.

# SALAD DRESSINGS

## BLUE CHEESE DRESSING

4 ounces Blue cheese
¼ teaspoon garlic powder
¼ teaspoon salt
¼ teaspoon pepper

1 teaspoon Lawry's seasoning salt
3 ounces cider vinegar
21 ounces mayonnaise
8 ounces buttermilk

Crumble blue cheese into bowl and add a small amount of mayonnaise. Add seasonings. Alternately add vinegar and mayonnaise. Add buttermilk until it is the right consistency.

## EGG YOLK DRESSING FOR SPINACH

*Your spinach salad will love you for this!!*

1 egg yolk, slightly beaten
1½ teaspoons Dijon mustard
4 teaspoons red wine garlic
  vinegar

¼ cup salad oil
2 teaspoons onion, grated
1 garlic clove, pressed
Salt and white pepper to taste

Whip together lightly egg yolk and Dijon mustard. Gradually stir in vinegar and oil, then onion and garlic. Add salt and pepper to taste. Toss well to coat leaves lightly. Do not drown them. Serves 4.
Use on spinach and fresh mushroom salad. If rings of purple onion are used in salad, omit grated onion from the dressing.

# HOUSE DRESSING

*Too simple, but so good!!*

1 teaspoon salt
3 tablespoons sugar

⅓ cup vinegar
1 cup salad oil

Combine salt, sugar and vinegar in a jar and shake well. Add salad oil and shake before serving.

# SARA'S BLUE CHEESE SALAD DRESSING

*Excellent on salads, head lettuce or as a dip for vegetables. Keeps well.*

½ pound blue cheese
4 tablespoons lemon juice
1 cup Wesson oil

1 pint mayonnaise
1 13-ounce can Carnation milk

Combine ingredients by hand, not blender or mixer. Makes 3 pints.

# FRENCH DRESSING I

1 cup oil
½ cup vinegar
Scant ¾ cup sugar

2 tablespoons salt
½ cup catsup

Combine all ingredients and mix well.

# FRENCH DRESSING II

*Delicious on green salads, grapefruit and avocado. This keeps indefinitely.*

1 clove garlic, pressed
1 cup salad oil
½ cup white vinegar
½ cup sugar
½ cup Heinz catsup

1 tablespoon Worcestershire
  sauce
Juice of 1 lemon
Salt
Paprika

Combine the ingredients in a quart jar or decanter, shake and refrigerate. A fancy "Christmastime" liquor bottle can be used for this dressing when used as a gift.

# SWEET AND SOUR DRESSING

*A welcome change for fruit salad.*

⅓ cup catsup
⅓ cup honey

⅓ cup Italian dressing

Combine all ingredients and mix well. Good on fruit or green salad.

# THOUSAND ISLAND DRESSING

⅔ cup Hellmann's mayonnaise (no
  substitutes)
3 tablespoons milk

1 tablespoon chili sauce
1 tablespoon sweet pickle relish

Combine ingredients and mix well. Serve on head lettuce or chef's salad.

## WATERCRESS SALAD DRESSING

*Good on salads and a new twist for cold seafood.*

2 cups watercress with stems
2 tablespoons lemon juice
2 cloves garlic, peeled and sliced

Dash each of salt and pepper
1 cup mayonnaise

Rinse and remove the leaves of watercress from the stems. In the blender or food processor container place the lemon juice, garlic, watercress, salt and pepper. Blend well. Remove from the container and stir into the mayonnaise. Cover and refrigerate.

# SAUCES

## AGITATE AND BAKE

1½ cups ground oat flour*
1 cup grated Parmesan cheese
½ teaspoon Lawry's seasoning salt

¼ teaspoon pepper
¼ teaspoon garlic powder
2-2½ pound chicken

Combine all ingredients. Store in a closed glass jar. This will make enough coating for 1 chicken.

*Place 1½ cups old fashioned Quaker oats in blender and buzz up or use your food processor.

# BEEF MARINADE SAUCE

*Dandy for that backyard barbecuing.*

2 tablespoons butter
2 tablespoons Heinz 57 Beef Sauce
2 tablespoons A-1 sauce

2 tablespoons soy sauce
2 tablespoons whiskey

Melt butter. Add the remaining ingredients in order listed. Pour mixture over steak or beef. Let stand for at least four hours before cooking meat.

# MARINADE FOR BEEF TENDERS OR A VENISON ROAST

½ cup coarsely ground pepper
¾ teaspoon cardamon
1 tablespoon or more tomato
  paste

½ teaspoon garlic powder
1 teaspoon paprika
1 cup soy sauce
¾ cup cider vinegar

Make a paste of pepper, cardamon, tomato paste, garlic powder and paprika. Spread this paste on the meat. Pour over it the soy sauce you have mixed with the vinegar. Marinate overnight in refrigerator. Let stand at room temperature 3-4 hours before cooking. Roast at 350° 1 hour. Adjust time according to size of tender and degree of doneness desired.

# MARINADE FOR FLANK STEAK, CHUCK ROAST
## (Or Almost Anything)

⅓ cup soy sauce
⅓ cup salad oil
1 tablespoon instant minced onion

3 tablespoons red wine vinegar
2 tablespoons chopped chutney
⅛ teaspoon garlic powder

Mix all ingredients and pour over meat. Let meat marinate for at least 4 hours.

## JERRY'S HOT SAUCE

*This sauce is only for the true "muy caliente" lovers — it is HOT, but tasty with meat, pinto or kidney beans, etc.*

2 16-ounce cans stewed tomatoes
2 medium onions, chopped
6 jalapeño peppers, seeded and chopped
1 cup carrots, sliced
2 tablespoons wine vinegar
2 tablespoons lime juice

½ teaspoon garlic salt
¼ teaspoon Picapepper
2 drops Tabasco (more if your hospitalization premiums are current)
Scant ¼ teaspoon dried parsley

Drain juice from tomatoes. Pour juice into pan and add chopped onions. Place over medium heat to simmer. Chop tomatoes in small pieces and add with the remaining ingredients to the tomato juice and onion mixture. Taste and add more seasonings if you wish. Simmer all, stirring occasionally for 1 to 1½ hours.

## LEECE MUSTARD SAUCE

*Delicious as a spread on sandwiches with ham, chicken, etc. Use as a sauce on cold chicken or ham. It is HOT!!*

3 eggs, well beaten
3 tablespoons flour
1 cup light brown sugar

½ cup consomme
1 cup cider vinegar
2 small cans Colman's mustard

Beat eggs. Mix flour and sugar, adding them to the eggs, consomme and vinegar. Cook until thick, stirring often. Add 2 small cans of Colman's mustard, dissolve in a small amount of water.

# CAPTAIN SANDERS BATTER FOR FRIED CHICKEN

*Since this isn't quite like the Colonel's, but we think just as good, we demoted ourselves.*

3 cups powdered milk, mixed
1 or more cut up fryers
Cooking oil
1½ cups or more of Bisquick
1 tablespoon Lawry's seasoning
  salt

1 teaspoon lemon pepper
½ teaspoon garlic salt
½ teaspoon Accent
2 eggs
½ cup bottled club soda

Prepare three cups of powdered milk according to directions. Cover and soak chicken in mixed powdered milk mixture for at least 1 hour.

Pour two inches of oil in a heavy skillet or kettle. Place on stove to heat.

Mix Bisquick and seasonings. Beat eggs well and gradually stir in club soda. Place Bisquick in a large, brown grocery store bag; dip chicken pieces in egg mixture and drop in bag. Shake vigorously and place in *HOT cooking oil. Fry until golden brown. Great balls of fire, Rhett Butler, that's good!!

*Hot — when one drop of cold water boils in the oil.

# CHILI SAUCE

*If you use those pretty quilted glass jars these will make super Christmas gifts.*

1 peck tomatoes (scald off skin)
1 dozen onions
2 bell peppers, chopped
8 hot peppers (long green ones)
3 tablespoons salt
1 tablespoon allspice

1 tablespoon whole cloves
1 tablespoon cinnamon
1 quart vinegar
4 cups sugar
1 6 ounce can tomato paste

Blend the tomatoes, onions, bell peppers and hot peppers in a blender. Tie the spices in a bag. Put these ingredients in a large vessel with the vinegar and boil for 1½ hours. Add the sugar and boil for 1½ hours more. Add the tomato paste. Seal and process while hot. Makes 8 to 10 pints.

## MEAT SAUCE

1 cup mayonnaise
¼ cup French's prepared mustard
1 teaspoon leaf oregano
¼ cup onion, chopped

⅓ cup sour cream
⅓ cup chili sauce
1 tablespoon horseradish
⅛ teaspoon cayenne pepper

Mix all ingredients well with a fork. You may want to strain to remove chili sauce seeds for extra smoothness. Let stand for several hours before serving. Makes about 2 cups. Refrigerate. Serve with hot or cold meats, poultry or fish.

## SAUCE FOR POT ROAST OR SWISS STEAK

*This helps on the less expensive cuts of beef.*

4 tablespoons bacon drippings
1 cup onion, chopped
1 bell pepper, chopped
½ cup celery, chopped
1 clove garlic, crushed
1 teaspoon chili powder
1 bay leaf

1 tablespoon Worcestershire
   sauce
2-3 drops Tabasco sauce
Pinch of thyme
½ cup tomato sauce
¼ cup sherry
1 cup tomato, chopped

Sauté onion in bacon drippings. Add bell pepper, celery and garlic. Sauté until limp. Add chili powder and bay leaf and bring to a boil. Reduce heat and simmer for 15 minutes. Remove bay leaf. Add remaining ingredients and stir well. Simmer while you are searing pot roast or swiss steak on both sides. Pour sauce over meat and bake, covered, for 1½ to 2½ hours, until meat is fork tender.

This sauce may be made the day before. If your roast is small, use only half of the sauce. Store remainder in refrigerator. It will keep up to two weeks.

# SEASONING SALT FOR SMOKER TYPE COOKERS

*This is our favorite for smoker type cookers. We always have some on hand. Makes a nice remembrance for neighbors at holiday time.*

6 tablespoons salt
3 tablespoons black pepper
2 tablespoons Accent

2 tablespoons garlic powder
1 tablespoon paprika
2 tablespoons dry mustard

Place all ingredients in a clear pint jar. Shake well.

Use this for chickens or turkeys. It is best to rub fowl with Wesson oil, then generously sprinkle salt mixture over birds.

# SPICED TEA, INSTANTLY

2 cups Tang
1½ cups instant tea
1 package Lemonade Mix

1½ teaspoon cinnamon
1 teaspoon ground cloves
1 cup sugar

Place all ingredients in large glass jar, screw on cap, shake vigorously. Use 2 teaspoons mix to 1 cup hot water.

**BREADS**

# BREADS

### APRICOT-NUT BREAD

*We like to bake these in small loaf pans, cool, cover with plastic wrap, tie with a bow and give as gifts.*

2 cups dried apricots, chopped
1½ cups Dr. Pepper (boiling)
1 stick butter or margarine
1½ cups sugar
1 egg, unbeaten

2¾ cups sifted flour
1½ teaspoons soda
½ teaspoon salt
1 teaspoon vanilla
1 cup pecans, chopped

Pour boiling Dr. Pepper over apricots and set aside. Blend soft butter or margarine with sugar. Add unbeaten egg and cream until light and fluffy. Sift flour with soda and salt and add half of the flour mixture to creamed sugar. Add apricot mixture and remaining flour. Blend well. Add vanilla and pecans. Pour into one large greased and floured pan. Three small pans can be substituted. Bake at 350° for approximately 1 hour for large loaf, 45 to 50 minutes for small loaves.

### BANANA PEPPER CORNBREAD

*This is not difficult and fills out a meal of leftovers beautifully!*

1½ cups self rising cornmeal
2 eggs
⅔ cup salad oil
1 8½-ounce can cream style corn

3-4 semi-hot banana peppers
   (remove seeds and mince)
1 small onion, chopped
1 cup sour cream

Mix all ingredients except sour cream. Pour half of batter in a greased 8 inch iron skillet. Spread sour cream on top. Spread remaining batter on top of sour cream. Bake at 400° until golden brown.

# BLUEBERRY MUFFINS

*One of our favorite holiday gifts. We buy tall glass containers with cork stoppers, use a festive ribbon—presto, happy holidays!!*

⅔ cup shortening
1 cup sugar
3 eggs
3 cups flour
2 heaping teaspoons double action
  baking powder

1 teaspoon salt
1 cup milk
1 can blueberries, drained

Cream shortening and sugar. Add eggs, one at a time. Sift together flour, baking powder and salt. Add dry ingredients alternately with milk. Fold in blueberries. Bake in muffin tins at 375° for 15 to 20 minutes, or until golden on top. This mixture will keep in the refrigerator for two or three weeks. Makes two dozen.

# BLUEBERRY-NUT BREAD

*A good Christmas gift or any time.*

2 cups flour
½ teaspoon baking soda
1½ teaspoons baking powder
½ teaspoon salt
⅔ cup sugar
1 egg, beaten
Juice of 1 orange and enough
  boiling water to make ¾ cup
  liquid

2 tablespoons butter or margarine
Grated orange rind
1 cup fresh or frozen blueberries
1 cup pecans, chopped

Sift together dry ingredients. Make a well in them and add the beaten egg. Stir the margarine into the orange juice and boiling water and add to the batter. Add the grated orange rind, blueberries* and nuts. Mix slightly. Pour into one large, two medium or three small loaf pans. Bake at 350° 1 hour for large, 45 minutes for medium or 35 minutes for small loaves.

*If frozen blueberries are used, take them directly from the freezer; do not let them thaw.

## BUTTERMILK BISCUITS

2 cups Wondra flour
½ teaspoon salt
4 teaspoons baking powder
½ teaspoon soda

5 tablespoons Crisco shortening
1 cup buttermilk
vegetable oil

Mix dry ingredients. Cut in shortening and add buttermilk. Stir until moistened, then roll out on well floured surface. Cut and dip each one in oil and then stack them by twos. Bake at 300° to 350° for approximately 20 minutes. These freeze well. Just put them in a freezer after you dip and stack.

## BUTTERFLAKE ROLLS

*A pastry cloth helps when rolling out rolls.*

2 packages yeast
¼ cup warm water
½ cup sugar
½ cup shortening

3 eggs, beaten
1 cup warm water
4½ cups flour
2 teaspoons salt

Dissolve yeast in ¼ cup water. Cream sugar and shortening. Add eggs, yeast mixture and 1 cup water. Stir in flour and salt. Let stand in refrigerator overnight. Roll out thin like a jelly roll, spread with softened butter and then roll up like a jelly roll. Pull the roll so it will be the same thickness the entire length of the roll. Cut the roll in ¾ to 1 inch slices, dip in melted butter and place butter side up in greased muffin tins. Let rise for 3 hours. Bake at 400° for 10 minutes. Makes approximately 2 dozen.

## CASSEROLE RYE BATTER BREAD

*Batter breads are so easy to make because of the no kneading technique.
Your family will be so impressed with your efforts as a baker one of
them may volunteer to clean up the kitchen — well, maybe . . .*

1 cup milk, scalded
¼ cup brown sugar, packed
2 teaspoons salt
¼ cup butter or margarine
2 packages active dry yeast

1 cup warm water
2 tablespoons caraway seed
3 cups flour
2 cups rye flour
1 teaspoon caraway seed

In the large bowl of electric mixer, pour scalded milk over brown sugar,
salt and butter. Cool to lukewarm. Dissolve yeast in warm water. Add to
milk mixture. Add 2 tablespoons caraway seed and about half of each
flour. Beat at medium speed for 2 minutes or until smooth. Add remaining flour and beat until well blended. 1 to 1½ minutes. Cover bowl and let
rise until double in bulk — approximately 45 minutes. Stir batter for ½
minute. Turn into well buttered 2 quart casserole, brush top with milk
and sprinkle with caraway seed. Bake at 350° for 45 to 50 minutes. Turn
out on rack to cool.

## CHEESE STRAWS

4 sticks pie crust mix
2 jars Old English Sharp cheese
1 3-ounce shaker of Kraft
  Parmesan cheese

⅓ stick butter or margarine
6 tablespoons cold water
Dust of cayenne pepper

Mix all ingredients until the dough is smooth. Put through a cookie press.
Bake at 400° for approximately 10 minutes. Makes enough for a small
army.

## CUSTARD COFFEE CAKE

*This is grand served warm for a coffee, and a snap to do. The cheese makes a custard on the bottom, it's good!*

1 package of Duncan Hines
  Yellow Cake Mix
1½ cups of Ricotta cheese
4 eggs, beaten

⅔ cup of sugar
1 teaspoon vanilla
Powdered sugar

Mix cake according to directions on box. Pour cake mixture into 9x13 inch greased, floured pan. Mix the cheese, eggs, sugar and vanilla. Pour cheese mixture gently over top of cake batter. Bake 50 to 60 minutes in 350° oven. Sift powdered sugar over top while cake is still warm.

## CINNAMON FRUIT BISCUIT CRUNCHIES

*The younger members of your family will flip over these!! Good treat for their spend-the-night company breakfasts.*

1 10-ounce can refrigerated Big
  Flaky biscuits
½ cup sugar
½ teaspoon cinnamon

¼ cup butter or margarine, melted
10 teaspoons plum, strawberry,
  peach or other preserves

Preheat oven to 375°. Separate biscuit dough into 10 biscuits. Combine sugar and cinnamon. Dip both sides of biscuits into melted butter, then in sugar mixture. Make a deep thumbprint in the center of each roll. Fill with 1 teaspoon preserves. Bake on ungreased cookie sheet for 15 to 20 minutes or until golden brown. Serve warm or cool.

## DATE-NUT BREAD

1 cup dates, chopped
2 teaspoons baking soda
2 cups boiling water
2 cups sugar
3 tablespoons shortening

2 eggs, beaten
2 teaspoons vanilla
1 cup walnuts, chopped
3 cups sifted flour

Combine dates, baking soda and boiling water. Cool. Cream sugar, shortening and eggs. Add date mixture, vanilla and walnuts to creamed mixture. Gradually add flour, mixing well. Fill two 1 pound coffee cans half full and bake for 45 minutes to 1 hour at 350°.

An easy way to remove from can is to open the other end of the can and push outward! Delicious plain or with cream cheese.

## EASY JALAPEÑO CORN BREAD

1 package Dromedary or Jiffy
  corn bread mix
1 stick margarine, melted

5 jalapeños, seeded and chopped
½-¾ cup sharp cheese, grated
⅔ cup cream style corn

Mix the above ingredients together. Pour into corn stick pan, a square pan or muffin tins. Bake at 375° for 30 minutes. Serves 4.

# FLOYERS
## (Greek Nut Roll)

1 cup pecans or almonds, chopped
2 tablespoons sugar
Cinnamon and cloves to taste
1 pound Fillo Strudel Leaves*
½ pound butter, melted

*Syrup:*
1 cup water
1 cup sugar
¼ cup honey
1 teaspoon lemon juice
Few pieces lemon and orange rind
Cinnamon stick
*available at specialty grocery stores

Combine nuts, sugar and spices. Cut sheets of Fillo in half (12x8 inches). Place sheets on top of each other and cover with a damp cloth. Take one sheet, brush it with melted butter and put 1 teaspoon of nut-sugar mixture at lower end of strip. Turn in sides and roll lengthwise. Put on buttered pan. Brush with butter. Continue until all are rolled. Bake at 325° for 20 to 25 minutes until golden brown. Makes about 60 rolls. Remove from oven and pour syrup evenly over rolls.

*Syrup:* Bring all ingredients to a boil and cook for 10 minutes. If rolls become soft, reheat in hot oven for a few minutes.

# HUSH PUPPIES

*This delicious, different recipe makes a large volume — 'nuff to feed an entire Indian Guide campout or a passing herd of grazing teenagers.*

1 cup flour
2 cups corn meal
1 tablespoon salt
1 teaspoon Cavender's Greek Seasoning

2 teaspoons baking powder
1 teaspoon black pepper
3 eggs
1 large onion, chopped
1½ cups milk

Mix dry ingredients. Add eggs, onion and milk. Stir until well mixed. Drop by teaspoons into very hot oil. Fry until golden brown. These are a bit different in that they are light and puffy in texture and have a great flavor. You can halve this recipe. Halve three eggs? Well, you just use two and perhaps a bit more corn meal, all will be well, OK?

# FRENCH MUFFINS

⅔ cup shortening
2 cups sugar
2 eggs
3 cups flour
3 teaspoons baking powder
1 teaspoon salt

½ teaspoon nutmeg
1 cup milk
*Topping:*
Melted butter
Sugar
Cinnamon

Combine shortening and sugar. Add eggs. Then add dry ingredients alternately with milk. Pour in muffin tins. Bake at 350° for 20 minutes. Remove from muffin tins, roll in melted butter and then in a combination of cinnamon and sugar. Makes 24 muffins. May be frozen and then reheated.

# JANE'S SPOON BREAD

½ cup yellow corn meal
2 cups milk
3 tablespoons butter

1 teaspoon salt
3 eggs, separated

Sift corn meal into milk. Stir constantly over medium heat until mushy. Add butter and salt. Beat until melted. Cool mixture. Beat egg yolks and fold in. Beat egg whites stiffly and fold in. Pour into 1½ quart, well greased pan. Bake at 375° for 20 to 25 minutes. Serves 4 to 6.

## LUSCIOUS CINNAMON ROLLS

*Make these on the day you have to wait for the repairman. Pop half in the freezer and enjoy on a lazy Saturday morning.*

| | |
|---|---|
| 1 loaf Rhodes frozen bread dough (no substitutes) | ½ cup pecans, chopped |
| | 1 teaspoon ground cinnamon |
| 2 tablespoons butter or margarine, melted | ½ cup whipping cream |
| | ¾ cup sifted powdered sugar |
| ⅔ cup brown sugar | 1½ tablespoons milk |

Thaw dough and roll to 18x6 inch rectangle. Brush with butter or margarine. Combine sugar, nuts and cinnamon. Sprinkle evenly over dough. Roll up jelly roll fashion, moisten edges with water and seal. Cut into about 20 slices. Place rolls, cut side down in a 13X9X2 pan. Let rise until double — about 1½ hours. Pour cream over rolls and bake at 350° for 25 minutes. Combine powdered sugar and milk and drizzle over rolls while warm. These can be made the day before needed; they freeze well.

## MONKEY BREAD

| | |
|---|---|
| 1 package of Rhodes Enriched Frozen Bread Dough (no substitutes) | ½-¾ stick margarine, melted |

Set one loaf out on a well greased cookie sheet. Let thaw until you can push all the way down thru the center, but do not let it begin to rise. Roll out in a rectangle about 6x9 inches. Cut lengthwise into four strips. Then cut across forming little squares. Cut each square across forming a triangle and dip into melted margarine. Arrange in layers in a well greased angel food pan. Pour any remaining melted margarine·over triangles in pan. Place in a warm spot and let rise. It will almost triple in volume. Bake at about 350° for 25 to 30 minutes. Let cook and turn out. This keeps well in a plastic sack in the refrigerator. Place in warm oven before serving.

Pulls apart with fingers and is *Heavenly.*

## ALL BRAN RAISIN MUFFINS

2 cups Bran Flakes or 1 cup All
  Bran
¾ cup milk
1 egg
¼ cup shortening

1 cup sifted flour
2½ teaspoons baking powder
½ teaspoon salt
¼ cup sugar
1 cup raisins

Combine bran and milk and let sit until milk is absorbed. Add egg and shortening and beat well. Add flour, baking powder, salt, sugar and raisins to mixture. Bake in greased muffin tins or paper muffin cups ⅔ full. Bake at 400° for 20 minutes, Yields 12 muffins.

## APPLE MUFFINS

2 cups sifted flour
3 teaspoons baking powder
½ teaspoon salt
2 tablespoons sugar
1 egg
1 cup milk
¼ cup butter or margarine, melted

*Topping:*
½ cup apple, peeled and finely
  chopped
¼ cup sugar
½ teaspoon cinnamon
¼ teaspoon nutmeg

Mix and sift flour, baking powder, salt and sugar. Beat egg until frothy; stir in milk and butter. Make a well in flour mixture; pour in milk all at once. Stir until just mixed. Batter will be lumpy. Fill large muffin tins ⅔ full. Combine topping ingredients and spoon on top of batter. Bake at 425° for 25 minutes or until cake tester inserted comes out clean. Loosen muffins and tip in pans to prevent steaming. Makes 8 large or 12 medium muffins.

Can be made several hours before serving, then reheat — but not as good — unless you have a microwave, which makes them taste fresh-baked.

## ORANGE BLOSSOM MUFFINS

*Having a brunch? Have these made up in advance. The batter is also good for holiday gifts.*

1 egg, slightly beaten
¼ cup sugar
¼ cup water
¼ cup orange juice
2 cups packaged biscuit mix (not
  Bisquick)

½ cup orange marmalade
½ cup pecans, chopped
2 tablespoons vegetable oil

Combine first four ingredients. Add biscuit mix and beat vigorously for 30 seconds. Stir in marmalade and pecans. Grease muffin pans or line with paper baking cups. Fill ⅔ full. Bake at 375° for 20 to 25 minutes or until golden brown on top. Makes 1 dozen. Batter will keep for two weeks in refrigerator.

## REFRIGERATOR MUFFINS

*Every refrigerator should have these!!*

1 cup Oatmeal
1 cup All Bran
1 cup Grape-Nuts
1 cup boiling water
2 eggs
1½ cups sugar

½ cup shortening
1 pint buttermilk
2½ cups flour
½ teaspoon salt
2½ teaspoons soda

Soak the Oatmeal, All Bran and Grape-Nuts in boiling water until cool. In a large bowl, blend the eggs until frothy. Add sugar and shortening. Add buttermilk to cooled cereal mixture, then combine with egg mixture. Blend in flour, salt and soda. Fill muffin tins ½ to ¾ full. Bake at 400° for 15 to 20 minutes. Mixture may be kept in refrigerator up to a month. Makes a lot!!

*P.S.* You can use Raisin Bran instead of Grape-Nuts, if you prefer, and even toss in blueberries.

## NOURISHING PANCAKES

| | |
|---|---|
| 1 cup sour cream | ¾ cup flour |
| 1 cup cottage cheese | 1 tablespoon sugar |
| 4 eggs | ¾ teaspoon salt |

Mix all ingredients in a food processor. Pour batter on a hot, lightly greased griddle. Serve with pure maple syrup. Serves 4.

## YOGURT BREAD

*A little treasure for you folks who are really into health food. Tastes good, too!!*

| | |
|---|---|
| 1 envelope active dry yeast | 1½ cups rye flour |
| 2 cups warm water | 5-7 cups whole wheat flour |
| 2 tablespoons honey | 1 egg, slightly beaten |
| 1 cup plain yogurt | 2 tablespoons water |
| 2 teaspoons salt | Cracked black pepper |

Grease a cookie sheet. In a large mixing bowl, combine yeast and water. Allow yeast to dissolve, about 5 minutes. Stir in honey, yogurt, salt and rye flour. Slowly add wheat flour until dough pulls away from side of bowl.

Turn dough out on a floured board and knead until it feels smooth and elastic, about 5 to 7 minutes. Let rest. Divide dough into three equal parts and shape each into an 8 to 9 inch strip with tapered ends. Place on cookie sheet in horseshoe shape. Slash outer edge every inch and brush with beaten egg and water mixture. Press cracked pepper tightly into slashes. Let rise until double in bulk. Bake at 350° for 45 minutes or until done.

This only rises once. To test — stick finger way into bread and if dent stays it is ready to bake. If it closes back up, it's not ready.

## STRAWBERRY NUT BREAD

1 cup margarine
1½ cups sugar
1 teaspoon vanilla
¼ teaspoon lemon extract
4 eggs
3 cups sifted all-purpose flour

1 teaspoon salt
1 teaspoon cream of tartar
½ teaspoon baking soda
1 cup strawberry jam
½ cup sour cream
1 cup nuts, broken

In mixing bowl, cream margarine, sugar, vanilla and lemon extract until fluffy. Add eggs, one at a time, beating well after each addition. Sift together flour, salt, cream of tartar and soda. Combine jam and sour cream. Add jam mixture alternately with dry ingredients to creamed mixture, beating until well combined. Stir in nuts. Divide into five greased and floured 4½x2¾x2¼ inch pans, or use five clean cans from vegetables. Bake 350° for 35 minutes or until tester comes out clean. These make cute round loaves and fit into small baskets.

## ROSEMARY'S WAFFLES

*Light as a feather, as waffles should be.*

2 cups flour
3 teaspoons baking powder
1 teaspoon soda
1 teaspoon salt

1 cup buttermilk (more, if needed)
4 eggs, separated
1 cup butter, melted

Sift dry ingredients together. Combine buttermilk, egg yolks and dry ingredients. Beat by hand until fairly smooth. Do not overbeat. Add butter and fold in beaten egg whites. Bake in a hot waffle iron. Makes 5 waffles.

# VEGETABLES

# VEGETABLES

## ARTICHOKES AND MUSHROOMS

4 tablespoons butter
1 14 ounce can artichoke hearts,
 drained
1 pound mushrooms, sliced
1¼ teaspoons salt

¼ teaspoon freshly ground black
 pepper
¼ teaspoon thyme
½ cup dry sherry

Melt the butter in a skillet. Sauté the artichoke hearts for 3 minutes. Add the mushrooms and sauté for 2 minutes. Season with salt, pepper and thyme. Add the sherry and cook over a high heat for 3 minutes. Serves 6 to 8.

## ASPARAGUS CASSEROLE

*This can be fixed days ahead and frozen.*

2 3-ounce packages chive cream
 cheese
½ cup Pet evaporated milk
1 11¾ ounce can cream of shrimp
 soup

2 tablespoons lemon juice
3 15-ounce cans asparagus,
 drained
Paprika

Soften cheese. Place in a double boiler and add milk slowly. Add soup and blend. Remove from heat and add lemon juice. In a 1½ quart casserole, layer sauce between asparagus and sprinkle paprika on top. Heat at 350° until bubbly. Serves 6 to 8. Can be frozen.

## ASPARAGUS WITH NUTS

2 10-ounce packages frozen
  asparagus spears (or fresh)
⅓ cup butter or margarine
2 tablespoons pecans, chopped
1 tablespoon lemon juice (fresh if
  possible)

¼ teaspoon salt
Freshly ground pepper
Toast points (optional)
Pimiento, sliced (optional)

Steam asparagus until tender, but not limp. Melt butter or margarine. Stir in next four ingredients. Spoon over asparagus. Arrange asparagus on toast points and garnish with sliced pimiento (optional). Serves 8.

## HARRIET'S ASPARAGUS AND MUSHROOMS

2 bunches of fresh asparagus
2 tablespoons Wesson oil
1 cup fresh mushrooms, sliced

½ cup chicken broth
2 tablespoons corn starch
¼ cup water

Wash and cut asparagus diagonally in one inch pieces. Heat oil and sauté asparagus for 1 minute at a high heat, stirring constantly. Add mushrooms and cook 1 minute. Add chicken broth, cover and cook 1 minute. Mix corn starch and water and add to asparagus. Cook until clear. Season to taste. Serves 8.

# ASPARAGUS SOUFFLE

*Do in a minute in a food processor.*

4 eggs
1 cup Cheddar cheese, shredded
1 cup mayonnaise
1 10¾-ounce can cream of
  mushroom soup, undiluted

1 teaspoon salt
1 15½-ounce can asparagus
  spears, drained

Using plastic blades for food processor, beat eggs. Then add remaining ingredients one at a time. Blend well and pour into a greased 1½ quart casserole. Place in a pan of water and bake at 350° for 55 to 60 minutes. After baked, it will hold in the oven for 55 to 60 minutes — just turn off the heat. Serves 6.

# BAR-B-Q GREEN BEANS

*We like to serve this with grilled polish sausage on the patio in the good old Summertime.*

1 medium onion, chopped
6 slices of bacon, chopped
1 10¾-ounce can Tomato soup

½ cup brown sugar
2 16-ounce cans French style
  green beans, drained

Brown onion and bacon. Add remaining ingredients and mix. Place in a casserole dish and bake at 350° for 1 hour. Serves 6.

## GREEN BEAN CASSEROLE

2 9-ounce packages frozen French cut green beans
1 8-ounce can water chestnuts, sliced
1 8-ounce can mushrooms, sliced
1 10¾-ounce can Campbell's celery soup
½ soup can of milk
1 3-ounce can French's Fried onions

Blanch beans. Make two layers of beans, chestnuts and mushrooms. Combine soup and milk and pour over vegetables. Bake at 350° for 15 minutes. Remove from oven. Crumble French's Fried onions on top. Put back in oven to warm.

## GREEN BEANS HORSERADISH

*Delicious served cold.*

2 #303 cans whole green beans, undrained
1 large onion, sliced
Small amount of ham, bacon or salt pork
1 cup mayonnaise
2 hard boiled eggs, chopped
1 heaping tablespoon horseradish
1 teaspoon Worcestershire sauce
Salt
Pepper
Garlic Salt
1½ teaspoon parsley flakes
1 lemon, juiced

Simmer beans with onion and meat for a half hour. Blend the remaining ingredients and let sit at room temperature. When the beans are ready, drain and spoon mayonnaise mixture over them and serve. Serves 6 to 8.

## BROCCOLI CASSEROLE

2 10-ounce boxes frozen chopped broccoli
¼ cup onion, finely chopped
6 tablespoons margarine
2 tablespoons flour
½ cup water
½ cup cracker crumbs
3 eggs, well beaten
1 8-ounce jar Cheese Whiz

Cook broccoli until just tender; drain, Sauté onions in 4 tablespoons margarine until soft. Make a paste with the flour and water. Add this to the onions and stir until thick. Add the broccoli. Add ¼ cup cracker crumbs, eggs and Cheese Whiz. Put in a small greased Pyrex dish. Top with the rest of the crumbs mixed with the remaining margarine. Bake at 325° for 20 to 25 minutes. Freezes, but leave crumbs off until ready to bake. Serves 6-8.

## BROCCOLI CORN CASSEROLE

*The combination of this twosome is a winner!!*

1 10-ounce package frozen chopped broccoli, thawed
1 16½-ounce can cream style corn
1 egg, beaten
4 tablespoons butter or margarine, melted
1 tablespoon onion, chopped
Salt
Pepper
1 cup Pepperidge Farm herb dressing
2 slices bacon, chopped and cooked.

Mix together broccoli, corn, egg, 2 tablespoons butter, onion, salt and pepper. Put in a baking dish. Combine herb dressing and remaining butter. Spread over top of casserole. Add bacon. Bake uncovered at 350° for approximately 1 hour. Serves 4-6.

## GOURMET CABBAGE

| | |
|---|---|
| 1 head of cabbage | 1 tablespoon sugar |
| 1 teaspoon salt | 1 tablespoon vinegar |
| 2 tablespoons margarine | 1 cup sour cream |

Cut the core from a head of cabbage and slice the cabbage. Place in a sauce pan with 1 inch of water. Add the salt and boil for 5 minutes. Butter the bottom and sides of a casserole. Place the hot cabbage in the casserole. Add the margarine and toss. Add sugar, vinegar and sour cream and toss well. Bake at 350°, uncovered, for 20 minutes.

## CARROT LOAF

*Very different; even your non-lovers of carrots will love it!!*

| | |
|---|---|
| 1 cup carrots, cooked and mashed | 4 tablespoon cracker crumbs |
| 2 egg yolks, slightly beaten | 1 tablespoon parsley, chopped |
| ½ cup milk | 1 tablespoon green pepper, |
| ¾ teaspoon salt |   chopped |
| ¼ teaspoon pepper | 2 egg whites, stiffly beaten |
| 1 tablespoon onion, chopped | |

Combine all ingredients and mix well. Place in a greased mold. Set in a pan of water and cook in a 350° oven for 30 minutes, or until a straw comes out clean. Serves 4.

# CARROTS TARRAGON

*This recipe is especially good if you like a sweet-sour taste and the tarragon flavor.*

1 stick butter
1 cup sugar (more for sweeter
 taste, if desired)
¼ cup tarragon vinegar
Parsley flakes (fresh is best)

Salt
Onions, minced
Green onion tops, minced
2 16-ounce whole style small baby
 carrots

Melt butter. Add sugar and remaining ingredients, except carrots. Cook until well mixed, smooth and hot. Drain carrots and add to butter mixture. Serve hot. Serves 8

# COMPANY CAULIFLOWER

1 medium head cauliflower
Salt and pepper to taste
1 cup sour cream

1 cup sharp American cheese,
 shredded
2 teaspoons toasted sesame seeds

Rinse cauliflower and break into flowerettes. Cook, covered, in a small amount of boiling salted water for 10 to 15 minutes. Drain well.

Place half of cauliflower in a 1 quart dish and season with salt and pepper. Spread with ½ cup sour cream and sprinkle with ½ cup cheese. Top with 1 teaspoon sesame seeds. Repeat layer. Bake at 350° until cheese melts and sour cream is hot. Serves 6.

To toast sesame seeds, place in a shallow pan in a 350° oven for 10 minutes. Shake often.

# CORN POT LUCK

*A fine side dish to serve with left over roast or chicken.*

6 slices bacon
1 cup milk
2 17-ounce cans cream style corn
2 cups bread crumbs, firmly
  packed
¾ teaspoon salt

½ teaspoon chili powder
1 cup Cheddar cheese, grated
1 4-ounce can mushrooms, drained
  and sliced (optional)
½ cup onion, finely minced

Fry bacon until crisp and drain well. Break into bits. Mix with the milk, corn and bread crumbs. Add the salt, chili powder, cheese, mushrooms and onions. Mix all ingredients well and bake uncovered in a 350° oven for 50 minutes, until puffy. Sprinkle more bacon on top, if desired. This must be served within one hour. Serves 6 to 8.

# MARGO HENRY'S EGG PLANT CASSEROLE

*This casserole could be divided into two 1½ quart casseroles. Use one and freeze the other.*

1 package dry chicken flavored
  Stove Top Dressing
1 large egg plant, peeled and
  sliced
1 onion, sliced
1 1-pound can tomatoes, chopped
  (save juice)

1 6-ounce can ripe olives, pitted
  and sliced, with juice
1 8-ounce package Cheddar
  cheese, shredded
1 teaspoon celery salt
1 teaspoon garlic salt
1 teaspoon oregano

Layer the ingredients in the order listed in a 3 quart casserole and season with the three seasonings as you are layering the casserole. Pour the juice from the tomatoes over all ingredients. Bake covered at 350° for 1½ to 2 hours. It will be juicy, but it enables the vegetables to steam in their own juices. Serves 6 to 8.

# NEW ORLEANS EGG PLANT

*A great, distinctive addition for a buffet with beef or lamb.*

1 large egg plant
Salt
1 large onion, chopped
1 large green pepper, chopped
½ stick margarine
1 3-ounce can oysters, with juice
1 cup sharp Cheddar cheese,
   grated

1 tablespoon flour
1 cup shrimp, cooked
¼ teaspoon celery seed
1 teaspoon freshly ground pepper
1 teaspoon Accent
Buttered bread crumbs

Peel and slice egg plant and boil until tender. Drain well and add salt and pepper. Sauté onion and green pepper in margarine until tender. Chop the oysters. Mix all of the ingredients, except bread crumbs, in a large bowl. If the mixture seems a little dry, add a small amount of cream. Pour into a greased casserole and top with buttered bread crumbs. Bake at 300° for 45 minutes. Serves 12 to 15.

This will freeze. If you freeze it, leave out the oysters until it thaws and is ready to bake. Then gently stir in the oysters.

# HOMINY CASSEROLE

*A southern touch and it freezes!! So simple to do and appetizing.*

1 11¼-ounce can cream of
   mushroom soup
½ cup coffee cream
¼ teaspoon cayenne pepper
1 teaspoon celery seed

½ teaspoon pepper
1 teaspoon salt
1 20-ounce can hominy
½ cup toasted almonds
½ cup buttered bread crumbs

Simmer first six ingredients. Pour over large can of hominy in a casserole dish. Sprinkle with almonds and bread crumbs. Bake at 350° for 30 to 40 minutes. Serves 6 to 8.

# 9 HOUR MUSHROOMS

*Once you prepare this we promise it will become part of your repertoire forever!!*

2 pounds medium to large
   mushrooms, whole, cleaned
¼ pound (1 stick) butter (no oleo)
2 cups Burgundy
1 teaspoon Worcestershire sauce
½ teaspoon dill seed

½ teaspoon ground pepper
1 teaspoon MSG
½ teaspoon garlic powder
1 cup boiling water
2 beef bouillon cubes
2 chicken bouillon cubes

Combine all ingredients. Bring to a slow boil and reduce heat to simmer. Cook 4 to 5 hours covered. Remove lid and cook another 3 to 4 hours until liquid barely covers mushrooms. Taste and salt lightly if necessary. Serve in chafing dish with toothpicks for an appetizer or as a side dish with rare beef. Freezes well.

# SOUTHERN FRIED OKRA

2 cups fresh okra, thinly sliced
1 cup green tomatoes, thinly
   sliced
1 medium onion, sliced
Salt

Pepper
⅛ teaspoon garlic powder
¼ cup corn meal
¼ cup flour
½ cup cooking oil

Mix all ingredients together and fry in ½ cup hot oil until brown. Stir frequently during cooking. Serves 4.

# BLACK-EYED PEAS

*Now, friends, everybody who lives in Texas eats black-eyes, or if they don't, they should. They are tasty when properly prepared, nutritious, and it's un-Texan not to like them. So pay attention while we instruct you on how to prepare your native dish.*

**Shelled, or dry, black-eyed peas**
**Meaty ham hock or bone**
**1 very authoritative onion, chopped**

**Green chilies, chopped (optional)**
**Salt and pepper**

Cover peas with water in a heavy kettle with a lid. Bury the onion and ham bone or hock in the center of peas. Cover and bring to a boil. Lower heat and allow to simmer for 3 hours. Check periodically. More warm water may need to be added. Always add warm water, never cold. At the end of the cooking period, use a fork to get off all bits of ham that are still clinging to the bone. Also dig out marrow of bone and add to pot. Add salt and pepper to taste. Add green chilies if you like. Taste and enjoy, the eyes of Texas are upon you!

# CREAMED PEAS WITH WATER CHESTNUTS

*An elegant way with peas!*

**1 large package (approximately 1 pound) frozen green peas**
**½ cup hot water**
**2 teaspoons chicken stock base**
**1 cup light cream**

**3 tablespoons butter**
**1 tablespoon Arrowroot**
**1 5-ounce can water chestnuts**
**1 teaspoon Mei Yen seasoning**
**⅛ teaspoon white pepper**

Cook peas in hot water and chicken stock base until just tender, but still firm. Drain, reserving liquid. To the liquid add enough cream to make 1½ cups of liquid. Melt butter in a sauce pan. Remove from heat and blend in Arrowroot. Add liquid. Cook over low heat, stirring constantly, until thickened and smooth. Drain and slice water chestnuts. Add to cream sauce along with cooked peas. Season with Mei Yen and pepper. Heat thoroughly, but do not boil. Serve very hot. Serves 6.

# PEAS AND ASPARAGUS

*This is a good party recipe. It serves a bunch. Easy to put together in the morning, and bake in the cool, cool, cool of the evening.*

3 17-ounce cans English peas,
 drained
3 14½-ounce cans cut asparagus,
 drained
1 8-ounce can mushroom stems
 and pieces, drained

1 pound New York cheese, grated
*White Sauce:*
6 tablespoons flour
6 tablespoons butter or margarine
3 cups milk
Salt, pepper and paprika to taste

In a 3 quart casserole, put layers of peas, asparagus, mushrooms, white sauce and cheese ending with cheese on top. Bake at 350° for approximately 30 minutes until bubbly. Serves 14 to 16.

# CHEDDAR BAKED POTATOES

*A good reliable item for a buffet dinner. Can be done days ahead and frozen. They are great to have in freezer in ziplocs for that hurry-up dinner.*

3 large baking potatoes
½ stick of butter
1 cup sour cream
1 tablespoon onion, grated
1 teaspoon salt

½ cup Cheddar cheese, grated or
 ¼ cup blue cheese, crumbled
3 tablespoons Cheddar cheese,
 grated
Paprika

Bake potatoes for 1 hour at 400° or until done. Cut hot potatoes in half lengthwise. Scoop out potatoes and save the shells. In a mixing bowl, mash the potatoes with a potato masher to get out the largest lumps. Add butter, cream, onion and salt. Beat until fluffy. Mix in ½ cup cheese. Divide into shells and sprinkle with cheese and paprika. Serves 6.

These can be frozen. Put on a tray in freezer to harden. Then pop into ziploc bags. To serve, bake in preheated 375° oven for 40 to 45 minutes.

# POTATO SURPRISE

*Can be easily divided to serve 4 to 6.*

2 pounds frozen hash brown
  potatoes
1 pint sour cream
1 cup onion, chopped

1 11½-ounce can mushroom soup,
  diluted
1½ cups Cheddar cheese, grated
Salt generously

Thaw potatoes approximately 15 minutes. Mix all ingredients and place in a 3 quart casserole and bake at 350° for 2 to 2½ hours. Serves 10 to 12.

# ROASTED POTATOES

*Potatoes never had it so good!*

½ to ¾ cup butter or margarine
1 teaspoon garlic powder
4-6 baking potatoes

1 cup bread crumbs
½ cup Parmesan cheese
Lawry's seasoning salt

Approximately ½ to 1 hour before you plan to roast potatoes, melt butter or margarine, add garlic powder. This will allow butter to assume garlic flavor. Peel potatoes and slice lengthwise into four quarters. Combine bread crumbs and cheese. Roll potatoes in butter mixture, then bread crumbs and cheese. Sprinkle with seasoning salt. Roast in 350° oven until golden brown and fork tender, approximately 35 to 45 minutes. Serves 6 to 8.

## ZANY, BUT GREAT POTATOES

*Your teenagers may become addicted to this dish.*

1 pound package frozen french
   fries
1 cup onions, thinly sliced
1½ cups thin white sauce
½-¾ cup sharp Cheddar cheese,
   grated

1 tablespoon butter
1 cup cornflakes, crushed
Salt and pepper

In an oven dish, make layers of potatoes, onions, cream sauce and cheese. Repeat. In a skillet, melt butter, stir in cornflakes and cook a couple of minutes. Remove from heat and sprinkle on top of cheese. Bake at 350° for 1 hour. Serves 4 to 6.

## MOCK WILD RICE

*The "What" to serve with doves, ducks or geese.*

¼ stick butter or margarine
2 bunches green onions, chopped
   (include tops)
1 cup raw rice
1 8-ounce can mushroom stems
   and pieces

1 tablespoon oregano
Salt and pepper to taste
2 cups beef bouillon (cubes or
   canned)

In a large skillet, melt butter. Add onions and sauté until wilted. Push onions to the side and add rice. Let rice brown and add a little more butter if it seems to stick. When rice is brown, add mushrooms with their liquid. Add oregano, salt and pepper. Pour into a 2 quart casserole. Add bouillon. Bake at 350° for 1 hour. Stir once or twice as mushrooms and onions float to the top. Serves 6 to 8.

# RICE CAROLINE

*Menfolk always go back for a second helping of this dish.*

3 cups cooked Minute Rice
3 cups sour cream, salted
2 cans Ortega Green Chilies,
   chopped, with seeds removed

¾ pound Monterey Jack cheese
Salt and pepper
½ cup Cheddar cheese, grated
Paprika

Cut cheese in strips. In a 2 quart buttered casserole put layers of rice, sour cream mixed with green chilies, and strips of Jack cheese. Finish with rice on top. Bake at 350° for ½ hour. During last few minutes. add Cheddar to the top and allow to melt. Sprinkle with paprika. Cover casserole with foil while cooking. Serves 12. Will freeze.

# SPINACH CASSEROLE WITH ARTICHOKE HEARTS AND WATER CHESTNUTS

*This can be mixed in the morning, and baked in the evening.*

2 10-ounce packages frozen
   chopped spinach
1 14-ounce can artichoke hearts
1 stick butter
1 8-ounce package cream cheese
1 8½-ounce can water chestnuts,
   sliced

Salt
Pepper
Tabasco
½ cup bread crumbs
Butter

Cook spinach according to directions. Drain artichoke hearts and cut in half. Melt butter in a large sauce pan and add cream cheese. Stir until smooth. Drain spinach thoroughly. Add spinach, water chestnuts and seasonings to cream cheese mixture. Line baking dish with artichoke halves and cover with spinach mixture. Sprinkle with bread crumbs and dot with butter. Bake at 400° for 20 minutes. Serves 6 to 8.

# BAKED SQUASH

6 yellow squash
1 red onion
3 zucchini
1 large tomato
1 tablespoon sugar

2 teaspoons Lawry's garlic salt
¼ teaspoon pepper
1 cup Cheddar cheese, grated
1 stick butter, melted
¾ cup Baby Swiss cheese, grated

Slice the first four ingredients thinly. Layer them in a 2 to 2½ quart casserole. Sprinkle layers with sugar, garlic salt, pepper and Cheddar cheese. Bake at 375° for 30 minutes. Drain. Add melted butter. Bake for 30 minutes more. Place the grated Swiss cheese on the top and bake until the cheese is melted and slightly browned. Serves 6 to 8.

# MIXED SQUASH

*An easy way to prepare that trustworthy vegetable, the squash.*

2 yellow squash
2 small zucchini
½ onion, diced
¼ pound good Cheddar cheese,
    diced

Salt
Pepper
Dill weed

Slice squash and steam with a small amount of water for 8 to 10 minutes. Do not overcook. In a skillet, brown onion in a small amount of butter. Add diced cheese and melt. Add this mixture to drained squash. Add salt and pepper. Sprinkle sparingly with dill weed. Mix and serve. Serves 3 to 4.

# KAKIE'S SQUASH RING

*These portions can easily be halved and put in a small ring mold for a family treat.*

4 eggs
2 cups milk
1 teaspoon salt
⅛ teaspoon pepper
2 tablespoons butter
Frozen chives
Pecans, toasted
⅛ cup bread crumbs

1 teaspoon lemon rind, grated
1 teaspoon onion flakes
3 cups cooked yellow squash, drained well
Brussels sprouts or carrots to fill ring

Mix all ingredients, except brussels sprouts or carrots. Pour into a greased ring mold. Put in a pan of water and bake at 350° for 60 minutes. Remove from oven and let stand 10 minutes before unmolding. Fill center with brussels sprouts or carrots, or fill with your favorite vegetable of a contrasting color. Serves 12.

# FRIED TOMATOES WITH SOUR CREAM GRAVY

*Try this for a summer supper to accompany cold meats.*

4 firm ripe tomatoes
1 egg, slightly beaten
Cornmeal
Salt and pepper

2 tablespoons butter or margarine
1 8-ounce carton sour cream
Paprika
Green onions (optional)

Slice tomatoes in thick slices. Dip slices in beaten egg, then cornmeal, salt and pepper. Brown quickly in butter until they are crisp on the outside, but not too soft on the inside. A little more butter may be necessary. Remove tomatoes to a hot platter while making gravy. Stir in sour cream scraping bottom of pan to get browned bits. Heat thoroughly, but do not allow to boil. Pour over tomatoes. Sprinkle with paprika and a small amount of finely chopped green onions. Serves 4.

# TOMATOES MUENSTER

*These look pretty around a meat platter.*

6 tomatoes
Salt
½ pound Muenster cheese, grated
1 garlic clove, crushed

2 tablespoons white wine
½ teaspoon mustard
½ teaspoon cayenne

Hollow out tomatoes. Reserve pulp for soup or in other vegetable dishes. Sprinkle with salt. Place remaining ingredients in a double boiler. Cook until smooth. Spoon cheese sauce into tomatoes and place in broiler under low heat until bubbly. Serves 6.

# TOMATO PIE

1 9-inch pie shell
2 large semi-ripe tomatoes
¼ cup flour
½ teaspoon salt
⅛ teaspoon pepper
2 tablespoons cooking oil

½ cup ripe olives, sliced
1 cup scallions, minced
2 eggs, slightly beaten
1 cup Cheddar cheese, grated
1 cup cream

Bake pie shell (bought or home made) at 375° for 8 minutes only. Cut tomatoes into 6 slices. Dip each slice in a mixture of flour, salt and pepper. Sauté each slice quickly in cooking oil. Arrange ripe olives and scallions in the bottom of the pie shell. Put tomatoes on top. Stir beaten eggs and Cheddar cheese into cream. Pour in pie shell. Bake at 375° for 40 to 45 minutes. Serves 8.

# ZUCCHINI CUPS

*Zucchini at its finest!!*

6 large zucchini
1 pound fresh mushrooms,
  chopped
¼ cup butter
½ cup sour cream

4 tablespoons parsley, chopped
4 tablespoons fine, dry bread
  crumbs
2 tablespoons butter, melted
Salt and pepper

Cut zucchini into 2 or 3 inch pieces. Steam for 5 minutes. Remove and scoop out seeds leaving ¼ inch at bottom. Sauté mushrooms in ¼ cup butter. Fill centers of squash and top with 1 teaspoon sour cream. Combine parsley, bread crumbs and melted butter. Place on top of zucchini and cover with sour cream. Bake at 350° only until hot. Serves 10 to 12.

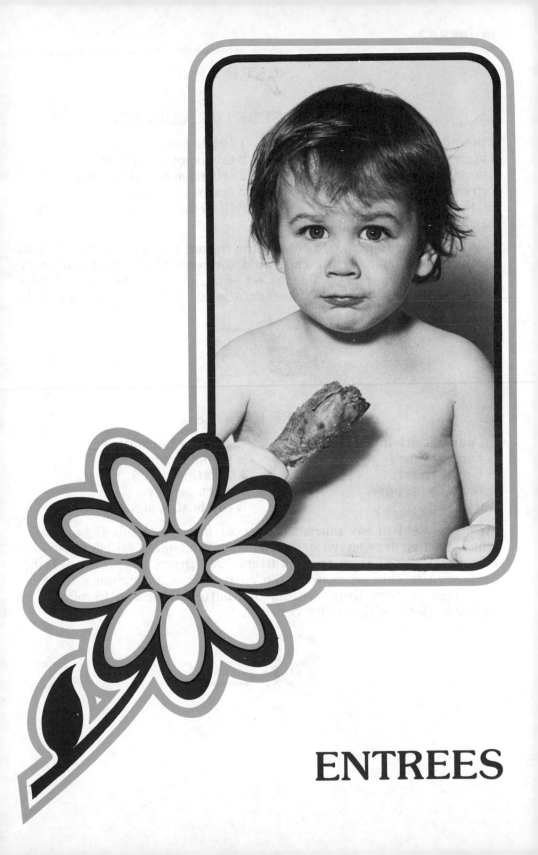

**ENTREES**

# BEEF

## BARBECUED BEEF FOR A CROWD

2 pounds ground beef
3 stalks celery, chopped
4 small onions, chopped
2 green peppers, chopped
½ stick butter
1 teaspoon prepared mustard

1 bottle catsup
2 tablespoons vinegar
2 tablespoons chili powder
2 teaspoons sugar
Salt to taste

Sauté the first four ingredients in the butter, stirring constantly, until the meat is completely browned. Add the remaining ingredients to the meat mixture. Simmer for 30 minutes or until the vegetables are tender. Serve on buns with cole slaw or potato salad. May be frozen. Serves 12-14.

## BEEF KABOBS

1½ pounds sirloin beef, cubed
¼ cup soy sauce
½ teaspoon salt
¼ teaspoon pepper
Garlic salt

12 small whole onions
½ pound mushrooms
3 tomatoes
1 green pepper
¼ cup butter, melted

Marinate meat in soy sauce, salt, pepper and garlic salt for at least 2 hours, turning once or twice. Parboil onions in boiling salted water for 5 minutes. Cut tomatoes into quarters. Cut green pepper into 1 inch squares. Alternate on skewers the meat, onions, mushrooms, tomatoes and green peppers. Brush with melted butter. Broil 5 to 15 minutes on each side. Serve with noodles. Serves 4.

## BEEF WITH SNOW PEAS

½ pound tenderloin or some cut of
   beef, perhaps round steak, that
   can be cut into finger size strips
4 tablespoons soy sauce
1 tablespoon corn starch

2 tablespoons wine
2 tablespoons oil
1 package of snow peas
1 4½-ounce jar mushrooms
   (optional)

After cutting beef into strips, marinate it in the soy sauce, corn starch and wine for ½ to 1 hour. If you have only 10 minutes, that is satisfactory. Brown the strips of beef in the oil. When brown on all sides, add the snow peas that have not been thawed and mushrooms. Stir around for 3 to 4 minutes. Serve immediately over rice, with rice as a side dish or alone. Serves 2 to 3:

## KITCHEN BAR-B-QUE

*Freezes well and children love it.*

2 pounds beef roast (chuck works
   well)
1 bay leaf
1½ cups water
1 medium onion, chopped
Salt and pepper

1 32-ounce bottle catsup
2 tablespoons vinegar
3 tablespoons dark brown sugar
¼ teaspoon celery salt
½ teaspoon garlic salt
½ cup water

Cook meat with bay leaf, onion, salt and pepper in water in a heavy kettle for 45 minutes to 1 hour. Remove meat. Cool broth and skim off fat. To broth add the remaining ingredients. Blend. Add extra salt and pepper, if needed. Shred beef and return to sauce. Simmer for 1 hour or until the mixture thickens. Serve on hamburger buns or other fancy buns. Serves 4.

## QUICK FILETS

**2-8 1½ pound filets (no bacon)**     **2-8 pats of butter**

Brown the filets quickly in a skillet. Remove and set aside until ready to broil. The steaks should not be touching. Top each with a pat of butter. Preheat oven to 325°. Broil the filets 15 minutes for rare and 18 minutes for medium rare.

## LONDON BROIL WITH PEPPER GARNISH

*Our Testers gave this recipe a four star rating!*

**1-1½ pounds beef flank steak**
**½ cup cherry pepper liquid**
**⅓ cup salad oil**
**2 tablespoons lemon juice**
**1 tablespoon brown sugar**
**2 teaspoons Worcestershire sauce**

**1 teaspoon salt**
**Pepper**
**1 small clove garlic, crushed**
**Cherry peppers**
**⅓ cup pasteurized process cheese**
   **spread**

Drain ½ cup liquid from a jar of cherry peppers. Add salad oil, lemon juice, brown sugar, Worcestershire sauce, salt, pepper and garlic, stirring to combine. Score steak with a knife in diamond pattern, ⅛ inch deep. Place steak and marinade in an air-tight container. Marinate in refrigerator overnight, turning several times.

Cut cherry peppers in half lengthwise and remove seeds. Fill with softened process cheese spread and set aside. Remove steak from marinade, reserving marinade, and place on grill so the surface of meat is ¾ inch from heat. Cook on a hot grill approximately 6 minutes per side, brushing with marinade.

Broil stuffed peppers for 2 minutes and use for garnish. Carve steak diagonally across the grain into very thin slices. Serves 4 to 6.

# ITALIAN MEATLOAF

*A new way to treat that celebrated family standby, the meatloaf.*

1 pound ground beef
1 cup bread crumbs
3 eggs
1½ tablespoons parsley, chopped
½ cup Romano cheese, grated
½ cup water
1 small onion, chopped

1 teaspoon salt
¼ teaspoon pepper
2 tablespoons olive oil
2 tablespoons bread crumbs
¾ pound Ricotta cheese
1 15½-ounce jar Ragu Italian
  Cooking Sauce

Mix beef, bread crumbs, 2 beaten eggs, 1 tablespoon of the parsley, Romano cheese, water, onion, salt and pepper.

Brush the bottom of a Pyrex baking dish with olive oil. Sprinkle 2 tablespoons bread crumbs over oil. Place half of meat mixture in dish. Mix the Ricotta with the remaining egg and parsley. Spread over meat mixture. Top with remaining meat. Close edges firmly so Ricotta does not ooze out. Pour Italian Cooking Sauce over meat. Bake at 350° for 1 hour. Serves 6. Will freeze.

# MEXICAN MEATLOAF

*A south of the Border treatment for an old friend.*

1½-2 pounds ground meat
2 teaspoons chili powder
1 onion, chopped
½ cup green pepper, chopped
2 ounces mild green chilies,
  seeded and chopped

1 8-ounce can tomato sauce
1 egg
12 soda crackers, crumbled

Mix together all ingredients. Shape into one large loaf or two small ones. Bake uncovered at 350° for 45 minutes. Serves 6 to 8.

# PASTRAMI

*This is excellent and is worth the effort. An inexpensive cut of meat works well.*

| | |
|---|---|
| 1 3-5 pound steak or roast (boneless) | 2 onions, chopped |
| 4 cups water | 2 teaspoons pickling spice |
| 5 tablespoons salt | 2 garlic cloves, crushed |
| 2 tablespoons brown sugar | 1 teaspoon saltpeter |
| 4 teaspoons parsley | ½ teaspoon black pepper |
| 3 whole cloves | Generous dash of cayenne |

Submerge meat in the mixed ingredients. Store the pastrami in the brine in the refrigerator for one week, turning meat every day. Remove and let the meat stand an hour or so. Sprinkle generously with paprika and dip the edges in cracked peppercorns. Cook for 5 hours on a covered grill or smoker, at the lowest temperature. Slice paper thin to serve. Freezes well.

(*Note:* Saltpeter may be purchased at your local pharmacy.)

# CRAZY CRUST PIZZA

*A special delight for the teenage group.*

**Crust:**
1 cup flour, unsifted
1 teaspoon salt
1 teaspoon Italian seasoning
⅛ teaspoon pepper
2 eggs
⅔ cup milk

**Topping:**
1 pound hamburger meat or
  pepperoni
¼ cup onion, chopped
½ cup green pepper, chopped
1 4-ounce can mushroom stems
  and pieces
1 cup pizza or tomato sauce
4 ounces Mozzarella cheese,
  shredded

If using hamburger meat, brown and season to taste. Drain well and set aside. If using pepperoni, no need to brown. Lightly grease and dust with flour a 12 or 14 inch pizza pan.

Prepare crust batter in a small bowl. Combine flour, salt, Italian seasoning, pepper, eggs and milk. Mix until smooth. Pour batter into pan, tilting pan so batter covers bottom. Arrange toppings of meat, onion, green pepper, mushrooms, sauce and cheese over batter. Bake on low rack of oven at 425° for 25 to 30 minutes. Batter will be runny, but it all bakes together perfectly. Serves 2 to 4, depending on hunger of kids; maybe only 1.

# FLORENTINE PIE

*This will enhance your reputation as a great cook. Super for a dinner party. Fairly inexpensive.*

1 pound lean ground beef
1 10-ounce package frozen
  chopped spinach
1 6-ounce can tomato paste
¾ cup finely crushed soda cracker
  crumbs
¾ cup onion, finely grated

2 eggs
1 teaspoon salt
1 heaping teaspoon oregano
2 tablespoons milk
1 9-inch pie shell
½ cup Cheddar cheese, grated

Cook and drain spinach. In a mixing bowl mix together beef, spinach, tomato paste, cracker crumbs, onion, 1 egg, salt and oregano. Press firmly into pie shell. Bake at 425° for 50 minutes. Cover edge of pie shell with a strip of foil to prevent burning. Beat remaining egg with milk and cheese. Pour over pie evenly. Reduce oven to 350° and bake for 5 to 10 minutes or until top sets. Remove from oven and let stand 10 minutes before serving. Serves 8.

# PRIME RIB FOR TWO

*This is delicious and your husband will think you have been in the kitchen all day.*

1 2¼-2½ pound prime rib

2 baking potatoes

Wrap the prime rib in foil and freeze. When ready to cook, remove from the freezer, unwrap and preheat oven to 400°. Wrap the potatoes in foil. Stand the frozen rib roast on the bone in a flat pan and place the potatoes on either side like book ends. Bake for exactly 1 hour and 15 minutes.

## POLISH RING SAUSAGE

2 Polish sausage rings
Juice of 3 lemons
1 can beer

¼ cup Lea and Perrins
Worcestershire sauce

Preheat oven to 425°. Place sausage and remaining ingredients in a baking dish. Bake for 30 minutes. Slice in 1 inch pieces and let marinate in juice for a few minutes before serving. Serves 5 to 6.

## ROQUEFORT STEAK

*In East Texas this would be termed "Larrupin' good", a great compliment!*

6 10-ounce strip steaks, trimmed
of all fat (or chopped sirloin
patties)
¼ cup oil

¼ pound (½ cup) butter
¼ pound Roquefort cheese,
crumbled
Salt and pepper

Sprinkle steaks very lightly with salt and pepper, remembering that Roquefort is somewhat salty. Put oil and 2 tablespoons butter in a skillet. Sauté steaks over a fairly high heat (5 minutes on each side for rare, 7 minutes for medium and 10 minutes for well done). Remove steaks to serving platter and keep warm. Pour fat from pan and replace pan over reduced heat. Add remaining butter and let it melt. Stir Roquefort throughly into melted butter, pour over steaks and serve. Serves 6.

## STEAK ITALIAN

½ cup flour
½ cup grated Cheddar cheese
1½ pounds round steak, cut into 6 serving-size pieces
1 egg, beaten
½ cup of oil
1 large onion, chopped

1 6-ounce can tomato paste
1 clove garlic, minced
Salt and pepper
2 cups hot water
8-ounce package Mozzarella cheese

Combine flour and cheese. Dip steak into egg, and coat with flour mixture; brown in hot oil. Place in a shallow baking dish. Sauté onion in remaining oil. Stir in tomato paste, garlic, salt, pepper, and water. Simmer 10 minutes. Pour sauce over steak and top with cheese slices. Bake, covered, at 350° for 1 hour. Serve over noodles. Serves 6.

## CAVENDER'S TENDERLOIN

*This is a very special company dish to prepare only if the IRS has made an error in your favor. Wonderful flavor!*

1 beef tenderloin
1 pound butter

1 3½-ounce jar Cavender's Seasoning

Line pan with foil. Cream together thoroughly butter and seasoning. Ice tenderloin on all sides with seasoned butter. Bake uncovered at 400° for 40 minutes. This may be frozen after it is iced. Serves 6-8.

# CHICKEN

## AQUATIC CHICKEN
### (Pollo del Mar)

*Well, if you had a recipe with chicken and clams what would you call it?*

1 3-pound fryer, cut up
¼ cup vegetable oil (maybe more)
1 cup onion, chopped
1 6½-ounce can minced clams with
    the liquid

1 10¼-ounce can mushroom soup
½ cup water
¼ cup white wine

Salt and pepper chicken. Dredge in flour and brown in oil. Remove chicken. In fat left in skillet (may have to add a bit more) add onions and cook until golden brown. Add clams, soup, water and wine. Mix well, then add chicken. Cover and simmer for 30 minutes or until chicken is tender. Serve over rice. Serves 4.

## ARTICHOKE CHICKEN

4 large chicken breasts
1 teaspoon seasoned salt
1 6-ounce jar marinated artichoke
    hearts (reserve marinade)
3 tablespoons margarine
1 tablespoon flour

1 4-ounce can sliced mushrooms
    (reserve juice)
1 chicken bouillon cube
¼ cup dry white wine
1 tablespoon fresh parsley

Sprinkle breasts with salt. Drain artichoke hearts and save the marinade. Heat margarine and brown the chicken breasts. Drain butter off and add artichoke marinade to pan. Heat, adding the flour, mushroom juice mixed with water to make ½ cup, bouillon cube and wine. Cook until thickened and bubbly. Add the mushrooms, artichokes and chicken. Cover and cook slowly for 20 minutes or until tender. Top with fresh parsley. Serves 4.

# BAKED CHICKEN

*This is an ideal dish to take to sick friends, etc.*

1-2 chickens, cut up (amount
   depends on number to be
   served)
1 cup uncooked rice
1 10¼-ounce can chicken and rice
   soup
1 soup can water

1 teaspoon oregano
1 teaspoon onion flakes
1 teaspoon parsley flakes
Dash of celery salt, salt and
   pepper
Mayonnaise

Mix all ingredients, except the chicken, in a roasting pan. Place cut up chickens on top and brush with mayonnaise. Sprinkle with black pepper. Bake covered at 300° for 3 hours or 325° for 1 hour and 15 minutes.

# CHICKEN CASSEROLE I

*The gravy in this dish would melt the hardest heart, bring about peace treaties, or even get your teenager to clean his room!!*

1 chicken
1 stick butter
1 4-ounce (8 ounces if you *love*
   mushrooms) can mushrooms,
   drained
1 tablespoon flour

2 tablespoons Worcestershire
   sauce
1 bay leaf
2 tablespoons lemon juice
1 11-ounce can beef bouillon

Cut chicken in serving pieces and season with salt and pepper. Melt butter and brown chicken in butter (not too fast, or it will burn). Remove chicken to oven casserole dish. Brown mushrooms in pan in which chicken was browned. Add flour and mix well. Stir in the remaining ingredients, making sure to get all brown bits from bottom of pan stirred into mixture. Pour flour mixture over chicken. Cover and bake for 1 hour. Discard bay leaf. Serve over mashed potatoes, rice or whatever. This is a stupendous dish to do the day before and reheat.

# CHICKEN CASSEROLE II

*This may be prepared a day ahead. Gravy is superb, especially over mashed potatoes.*

5 pounds chicken breasts, thighs
  and legs
Salt
Pepper
4 tablespoons butter or margine
⅓ cup cubed salt pork
1 cup fresh mushrooms, sliced
2 cups onions, finely chopped

1 cup carrots, finely minced
1 cup sour cream
1 bay leaf
½ teaspoon thyme
¼ teaspoon tarragon
¼ cup celery, finely chopped
1 teaspoon garlic, minced
1½ cups dry white wine

Season chicken with salt and pepper. Heat butter and salt pork in skillet. Add chicken pieces and brown on all sides. Transfer chicken pieces to large casserole with tight fitting lid. Lightly sauté mushrooms and onions in skillet (you may have to add a bit more butter). Add mushrooms and onions to chicken pieces, stir in remaining ingredients. Cover casserole tightly and bake at 350 oven for 1 and ½ hours. Serves 8.

# CHINESE CHICKEN

3 tablespoons margarine
1 medium onion, chopped
½ pound fresh mushrooms, sliced
  (optional)
2 5-ounce cans boned chicken or 2
  cups diced, cooked chicken
1 cup celery, sliced diagonally
1 8½-ounce can water chestnuts,
  sliced

1 can bamboo shoots
1 cup chicken broth
3 tablespoons soy sauce
2 tablespoons corn starch
¼ cup water
1 16-ounce can bean sprouts
  (fresh if available)

Sauté onions and mushrooms in margarine until tender. Add chicken, celery, water chestnuts, bamboo shoots, broth and soy sauce. Heat until boiling. Reduce heat and simmer for 5 minutes. Mix corn starch and water. Add to chicken mixture, stirring constantly, until thickened. Add bean sprouts and heat thoroughly. Serve over rice or Chinese noodles. Serves 6.
*P.S.:* For a sweet twist, add a 5¼-ounce can drained pineapple chunks.

# LIME-BROILED CHICKEN

*This is a good family offering that all ages seem to like.*

Fryer chicken quarters, 1 per
person, fairly large
2 teaspoons salt
⅓ cup fresh lime juice
2 tablespoons salad oil

½ cup white onion, coarsely
chopped
2 cloves garlic, minced or pressed
1 tablespoon sugar

Salt chicken. Place skin side down in foil-lined broiler pan. Mix remaining ingredients. Some bottled lime juice may be used, but most should be fresh. Spoon half of mixture over chicken. Broil in hot, preheated broiler on top rack (about six inches from broiler). Broil until very brown and crisp — approximately 10 to 15 minutes. Sugar makes it very dark. Turn chicken and spoon on remaining sauce. Broil the same as before. If pieces are very large or if breast quarters are used, then turn to Bake and cook at 400° until the juice is clear when pierced with a fork — about 10 to 15 minutes. This amount of sauce will be sufficient for 6 to 8 servings, depending on size of chicken pieces.

# CHICKEN HUNTINGTON

1 tablespoon butter
1 tablespoon flour
1 10¾-ounce can mushroom soup,
undiluted
1 4-ounce can mushroom stems
and pieces
½ pound Velveeta or sharp
American cheese, grated

1 2-ounce can pimiento, chopped
2 cups chicken broth
4 cups diced, cooked chicken
1 8-ounce package elbow
macaroni or noodles

Cook macaroni according to directions. Mix all ingredients and put in a casserole. Bake at 325° for 45 minutes or until bubbly. Serves 8. Freezes well.

# OLIVE CHICKEN GIRALDA

*Our Tester really went into orbit over this dish.*

3 tablespoons flour
¾ teaspoon paprika
2 whole chicken breasts
2 tablespoons butter
2 medium onions, sliced
1 clove garlic, minced
⅔ cup sherry

1 cup water
2 chicken bouillon cubes
1¼ teaspoons basil
1½ tablespoons lemon juice
⅛ teaspoon pepper
¾ cup green olives, sliced
1 10-ounce can artichoke hearts

Remove bone and skin from chicken breasts and split. Mix flour and paprika and coat chicken. Brown chicken in butter and remove. Sauté onions and garlic. Stir in sherry, water, bouillon cubes, basil, lemon juice and pepper. Bring to a boil. Add olives, artichokes and chicken. Cover and simmer for 25 to 30 minutes. Remove chicken and vegetables. Thicken sauce. Serves 4.

May be served with saffron rice or plain rice.

# CHICKEN OROBIANCO

*We hesitate to use the overworked word "different", but it is.*
*Try it, you will be pleased!*

¼ cup olive oil
2 garlic cloves, quartered
4 whole medium chicken breasts,
   boned and cut in half, or a like
   amount of chicken thighs
2 pounds hot Italian sausage links

2 cups Orobianco or medium-dry
   white wine
½ pound mushrooms, sliced
1 teaspoon salt
¼ cup water
2 tablespoon corn starch

Begin about 1¼ hours before serving. In a 12 inch skillet over medium heat, cook garlic in hot olive oil until golden. Remove garlic from oil with a slotted spoon and discard. Cook chicken and sausages, a few pieces at a time, in drippings in skillet until browned on all sides. Spoon off all but 2 tablespoons drippings. Stir in wine, mushrooms and salt. Heat to boiling. Return chicken and sausages to skillet. Reduce heat to low, cover skillet and simmer for 30 minutes or until chicken is fork tender, basting occasionally with liquid in skillet. Arrange chicken and sausages on a warm platter.

In a cup, blend water and corn starch until smooth. Gradually stir into hot liquid and cook over medium heat, stirring constantly, until mixture is thickened. Spoon some of the sauce over chicken. Place remaining sauce in a gravy boat. Serves 8.

## SOUR CREAM MARINATED CHICKEN BREASTS

*Company tomorrow night? Do the chicken breasts today, add a salad, bread and our Butter Rum Cake tomorrow, then wait for the applause.*

| | |
|---|---|
| 5 split chicken breasts | 2 teaspoons paprika |
| Salt | 2 cloves garlic, minced |
| 1 8-ounce carton sour cream | 2 teaspoons pepper |
| 2 tablespoons lemon juice | Bread crumbs |
| 2 teaspoons Worcestershire sauce | ½ cup butter |
| 2 teaspoons celery salt | ¼ cup Crisco |

Sprinkle chicken breasts with salt. Combine sour cream, lemon juice, Worcestershire sauce, celery salt, paprika, garlic and pepper and blend well. Coat chicken with sour cream mixture. Cover and refrigerate overnight in a 13x9 inch baking dish.

Roll chicken in bread crumbs and return to the baking dish. Melt butter and Crisco and pour half over chicken. Bake at 350° for 45 minutes. Pour remainder of butter over chicken and bake for 15 minutes more.

(*Note:* An artichoke heart may be placed on top of each breast before baking.)

## CHICKEN SUPREME

*Can be made the day before. Best served with rice. The gravy is scrumptious.*

| | |
|---|---|
| 2 broilers | 1 cup sour cream |
| 1 stick butter (no substitutes) | 2 tablespoons grated Parmesan cheese |
| 2 tablespoons hot brandy | 1 teaspoon lemon juice |
| 1 tablespoon tomato paste | Salt, cayenne and black pepper to taste |
| 2 heaping tablespoons flour | |
| 1 cup chicken bouillon | |

Brown chicken slowly in hot butter. Warm the brandy and pour over the chicken after it is browned. Remove chicken to oven dish. Stir tomato paste and flour into pan. Add bouillon, sour cream, cheese, lemon juice, salt, pepper and cayenne. Stir until thickened. Pour around chicken in oven dish. Bake uncovered 375° for 40 minutes. Place on serving dish and serve with rice and gravy. Serves 4 to 6.

## GRILLED TURKEY SANDWICHES

*This makes four great tasting grilled sandwiches. A really super way to use up leftover turkey.*

1 cup coarsely ground turkey or
   chicken
½ cup toasted almonds, chopped
1 teaspoon onion, grated
⅔ cup Hellmann's mayonnaise (no
   substitutes)

¼ cup sweet pickle relish
½ teaspoon salt
¼ teaspoon pepper

Combine all ingredients and chill overnight. Spread on buttered bread, and grill sandwiches.

# GAME

## WILD DUCK

4 wild ducks
1 apple
1 onion
2 stalks of celery
1 bunch of leeks

Thyme
Salt and pepper
1 bottle dry red wine
Arrowroot

Rub salt into ducks, inside and out. Cut apple and onion in quarters. Cut celery stalks in half. Place apple, onion and celery inside cavity. Sprinkle with thyme and pepper. Roast, uncovered, breast side up, at 450° for 20 minutes. Roast for 15 minutes on each side at 400°. Clean leeks and split lengthwise. Put leeks over breasts of ducks and pour wine on top. Cover and cook at 300° for 1 hour. Remove birds and keep warm. Strain juice and thicken with arrowroot for gravy. Serves 4 to 6.

## WILD DUCK OR GOOSE

*When the fragrance of WD 40 permeates your household this should become one of your favorite finds of the year. A new way to prepare your Nimrod's birds. Try it — you'll like it!!*

3 ducks or geese
1 bottle Good Seasons Creamy
   Italian dressing
Onions
Apples

Beaumond seasoning
Garlic salt
Salt and pepper
Bacon

Marinate birds in dressing for at least 8 hours, better overnight. Place in roaster. Quarter onions and apples and stuff birds. Sprinkle with seasonings. Place bacon strips across birds. Cover and bake 350° 1 to 1½ hours until they are tender when you fork them. Remove cover and bake approximately 30 minutes or until brown.

## CORNISH HENS

2 Rock Cornish hens (about 12
   ounces each)
¼ cup garlic-flavored sour cream
   dip

1 cup crushed cheese crackers
   (about 20)
¼ teaspoon dried thyme
Dash of pepper

Ask your butcher to split hens in half lengthwise. Wash and pat dry. Coat with sour cream dip, combine crumbs, thyme and pepper. Roll hens in crumb mixture; place skin up in shallow baking pan. Bake at 350° for 45 to 60 minutes. Serves 4.

## QUAIL SUPERB

*The name for this dish couldn't be more apropos! Superb!*

4-6 quail
8 shallots (or green onions)
4 tablespoons butter
½ cup Cognac or Sauterne

Salt and pepper to taste
1 10½-ounce can chicken broth
1 cup whipping cream

Clean quail. Chop shallots. Brown quail and shallots in butter. Pour Cognac over quail and light. Stir over low heat lightly until Cognac stops burning. Place quail and shallots in an oven dish. Pour broth into skillet and stir to get brown bits. Pour over quail and cover. Cook at 350° for 45 minutes, then pour whipping cream over it and cook for 30 minutes more. Serve with wild rice using gravy from this dish. Serves 4 to 6.
(*Note:* This gravy is perhaps a little thin. If you like when the quail is done, remove birds and thicken the sauce with a little flour or cornstarch.)

# PORK

## SMOKED CANADIAN STYLE BACON

⅓ of a whole roll of Canadian style
   bacon or about 3-4 pounds
3 tablespoons or more of honey

3 tablespoons or more of mustard
Soaked hickory chips

Make several ⅛ inch gashes along the top of the bacon. Add soaked hickory chips to fire. Place bacon in smoker. Brush on honey and mustard. Smoke for 4 hours or more. (If your smoker can be opened during the process, after 2 hours add more chips and brush again with honey and mustard.) Remove and add honey and mustard. Let cool to room temperature. Slice thin and serve 2 or 3 slices per person. Serve with salads, rolls and fruit for a summer supper.

Use the leftovers for sandwiches, quiches, etc. or on toasted English muffin.

Suggest cooking a sausage ring at the same time.

## APRICOT GLAZED HAM

½ cup apricot preserves
2 tablespoons mustard
1 tablespoon water
2 teaspoons lemon juice

1 teaspoon Worcestershire sauce
⅛ teaspoon cinnamon
1 center slice of ham 1 inch thick

Combine first six ingredients and heat until preserves melt. Pour sauce over ham in a shallow dish. Refrigerate overnight turning a couple of times. Grill ham over charcoal for 5 minutes on each side, brush with marinade and grill 5 minutes more on each side. Serve sauce with ham. Serves 4 to 6.

## BAKED PORK TENDERLOINS

2 pork tenderloins
½ cup soy sauce
¼ cup sherry

¼ cup brown sugar
¼ teaspoon ginger, sliced very
  thin or chopped

Place the tenderloins in a baking dish. Combine remaining ingredients and pour over tenderloins. Marinate for 1 hour, turning meat several times. Preheat oven to 325°. Place in oven and bake for 1 hour. Do not overcook. Slice very thin. Leftovers make excellent sandwiches. Serves 2-4, possibly 6.
(*Note:* Ginger may be kept by storing in a jar and covered with sherry.)

# BEDEVILED BACON

*This is something special for a Sunday brunch. Has lots of zip!*

1 egg
½ teaspoon dry mustard
½ teaspoon cayenne pepper

1 teaspoon vinegar
8 slices of bacon
¾ cup cracker crumbs

Beat egg. Add mustard, cayenne pepper and vinegar. Slip bacon into egg mixture, remove and coat with cracker crumbs. Bake in oven at 400° on a broiler rack for 20 minutes. Watch carefully, as this burns easily. Allow 2 to 3 slices per person.

# ITALIAN PORK CHOPS

*Our Tester piled the chops on rice, poured the sauce on top, and pronounced the dish first rate!!!*

4-6 pork chops depending on size
Onion
Brown sugar

1½-ounce package spaghetti sauce mix
1 16-ounce can of tomatoes

Brown pork chops. Put in a long Pyrex dish. Top each with a slice of onion. Sprinkle each with a little brown sugar. Put package of sauce mix in drippings and add can of tomatoes. Pour over chops and cover with foil. Bake for 45 minutes at 350°. Uncover and continue cooking for 15 minutes. Serves 4.

## PORK CHOPS IN SOUR CREAM

*Need to have something a little extra special, and time is critical? This is the R.*

**4 pork chops, 1 inch thick**
**3 tablespoons Madiera wine**

**¾ cup sour cream**
**Salt and pepper**

Pan broil chops slowly until tender and brown. Remove chops from pan and pour off any fat. Add wine and sour cream. Stir and scrape up all particles of meat. Return chops to pan and cook for another 5 to 10 minutes. Serve over cooked noodles. Serves 4 hungry folks.

## PORK ROAST

*If you plan to pull weeds, prune shrubs, etc., this is one dish you can tend to in the yard while doing the green scene.*

**4-5 pound pork roast**
**1 bottle of Good Seasons Italian**
**  dressing**

**1 2-pound package of frozen,**
**  peeled potatoes or 3 cups of**
**  small whole new potatoes**

Marinate the pork roast in dressing for at least 3 hours. Cook in pan with dressing over covered charcoal grill, basting every half hour. Allow 2½ to 3 hours on grill on a slow fire. During the last 45 minutes of cooking time, place potatoes around roast making sure you spoon the drippings over them so they will turn a beautiful brown color. If new potatoes are being used, increase cooking time a bit. Check for doneness by piercing with a fork. The new potatoes may be peeled; however, some like them just scrubbed, not peeled.

# VEAL

## VEAL AND WATER CHESTNUTS

*Are you so in debt dinner party-wise you have had to change grocery stores, switch hairdressers? Help is at hand. This recipe is a freeze ahead marvel and tastes grand! Salad, rolls, a fancy dessert, and you are back in good graces socially.*

¾ pound butter
8 pounds boneless veal
4 cloves garlic, minced
3 medium onions, grated
3 teaspoons salt
1 teaspoon pepper
Dash of cayenne
3 pounds mushrooms, sliced

3 cups consommé
1 tablespoon corn starch
½ teaspoon nutmeg
4 bay leaves
3 cups heavy cream
3 8½-ounce cans water chestnuts, sliced
3 tablespoons parsley

Preheat oven to 350°. Cut veal into bite size pieces. Melt half of the butter in a heavy skillet or skillets. Brown the veal on all sides. Add garlic and onion toward the end. Season with salt, pepper and cayenne. Divide mixture between two greased casseroles. Melt remaining butter in the same skillet and sauté mushrooms quickly. Add to meat. Mix corn starch with 2 tablespoons consommé. Pour enough consommé into skillet to scrape up juices, along with the corn starch mixture to thicken slightly. Divide between the casseroles. Add nutmeg, bay leaves and consommé to cover ⅔ of the meat. Mix and cover. Bake until meat is tender, approximately 4 hours. Add cream and water chestnuts. Cook uncovered for 15 minutes. Sprinkle with parsley and serve. Serves 14 to 16.

This may be cooled and then frozen for six weeks or more.

To serve, defrost at room temperature and reheat in a 300° oven for 45 minutes or until hot. Serve with steamed rice to which 3 tablespoons of parsley has been added.

# VEAL ON TOAST

*This fantastic entreé takes about 20 minutes, but tastes as if you have slaved for hours. We won't tell if you don't. A stunner!!*

| | |
|---|---|
| 8 thin slices of veal scallopini (not cutlets) | 1½ cups heavy cream |
| 6 tablespoons butter | 2 egg yolks |
| 8 slices of white bread, toasted | Salt and pepper |
| ⅓ cup sherry | Chopped parsley |

Dust veal slices with flour. Sauté veal in butter until well browned. Season with salt and pepper. Place each slice of veal on a piece of buttered toast. Arrange them on a platter and keep warm.

Add sherry to the skillet and scrape up all the brown bits. Mix cream with egg yolks and pour into skillet. Cook over a low heat, stirring constantly, until it is thickened. Do not let boil. Season with salt and pepper and spoon over veal. Sprinkle with parsley. Serves 8.

# VENISON

## TEXAS FRIED VENISON

*Okay gentlemen hunters, this is just for you.*

| | |
|---|---|
| 2 pounds venison steak cut 1-inch thick | 1 piece of celery, cut up |
| ¼ cup flour | 3 medium onions, sliced |
| 1 teaspoon salt | 1 tablespoon Worcestershire sauce |
| ½ teaspoon pepper | 2 cups tomatoes |
| 3 tablespoons bacon drippings | 8 ounces noodles |

Cut venison steak into serving size pieces. Mix flour with salt and pepper. Coat venison with flour mixture. Heat bacon drippings in skillet and brown venison on both sides. Add celery and onion and brown. Add remaining ingredients and cook, covered on low temperature 1 to 2 hours, or until tender. Serve over noodles to 4.

## VENISON FONDUE

**Hindquarters or back strap of venison**
*Marinade:*
**2 parts vinegar to 1 part soy sauce**

**At least 1 teaspoon each of garlic powder, paprika and black pepper**

Cut the venison into 1 to 2 inch cubes, removing the fat and gristle. Marinate the pieces in a large bowl for at least 2 to 3 hours, longer if possible.

Allow 12 to 15 pieces of meat per person. It may be cooked with other items on the fondue fork, such as cherry tomatoes, artichoke hearts, chunks of onion, chunks of green pepper, or canned button mushrooms. In a standard size electric fondue pot, heat approximately 24 ounces of peanut oil until it is bubbly. Heat on a medium setting, not the highest. Put fondue fork with meat and/or vegetables in and cook approximately 2 minutes. Adjust accordingly for other pots, but be sure oil is deep enough to allow threading 3 or 4 items at a time on the fork.

# SEAFOOD

## ARTICHOKE STUFFED WITH CRABMEAT

*A luncheon entreé or great as an Hors d'oeuvre. Serve with Melba rounds because there is always too much stuffing, and you will need the rounds as a scooper-upper.*

**For each artichoke:**
**½ cup crabmeat, fresh or canned**
**½ cup Italian bread crumbs**
**½ cup Swiss cheese, grated**
**1 tablespoon sour cream**
**2 tablespoons mayonnaise**

**Tabasco**
**Salt and pepper**
**Lemon juice**
**Worcestershire sauce**
**Small amount of garlic powder**

Trim artichoke. Cook for 30 minutes in boiling water. Remove choke. Mix first six ingredients and season to taste with the next five ingredients. The stuffing should be the consistency of "cornbread dressing". Stuff the center of the artichoke and use the remainder to stuff the leaves. Place in a small amount of water, cover and bake at 400° for 20 minutes. Remove from oven and squeeze a little lemon juice over the whole artichoke.

# CRAB BURGERS

1 tablespoon lemon juice
⅓ cup mayonnaise
Minced green onions or onion
    flakes

1¼ cups Swiss cheese, diced
1 cup canned crab meat
¾ cup ripe olives, chopped
6 hamburger buns

Mix all ingredients together. Fill the six buns. Wrap securely in foil. Bake at 350° for 25 minutes. You could substitute 1 cup of chicken for the crab meat.

# MEETING STREET CRAB

*A loan from the bank would help finance this one, but it is a real impressive company dish.*

4 tablespoons butter
4 tablespoons flour
½ pint cream (or Half and Half)
Salt and white pepper to taste

4 tablespoons sherry
1 pound crab or shrimp
¾ cup sharp cheese, grated

Make a cream sauce with butter, flour and cream. Add salt, pepper and sherry. Remove from stove and add crab. Pour into buttered casserole (sea shells could be used). Sprinkle with grated cheese and cook in hot oven until cheese melts. Serve hot! Serves 4.

## LOBSTER OR KING CRAB CONGA

*If your IBM stock has split two for one, or you have suddenly inherited Uncle's oil well this is a great way to celebrate!! Simple, but simply super.*

Lobster or lump crab meat, one
  can per person
4 ounces cream cheese

2 ounces Roquefort
4 ounces butter
4 filets of anchovies

This is better with lobster. Canned lobster may be used. If canned is used, drain well. Put bite size pieces on a piece of foil that has been buttered and rubbed with garlic. Mix cream cheese, Roquefort and butter to form a paste. Spread over lobster. Place anchovies on top. Wrap foil tightly around lobster. Bake at 350° for 20 minutes. It is most important to serve it with saffron rice (Quiggs is a good brand). Serves 2.

## SEAFOOD QUICHE

*To be served only for: Chairman of the Board, Foreign Diplomats or Presidential Hopefuls.*

2 9-inch pie shells
1 6-ounce package frozen king
  crab
1½ cups shrimp
1 cup natural Swiss cheese, grated
½ cup celery, finely chopped

½ cup onion, finely chopped
1 cup mayonnaise
2 tablespoons flour
1 cup dry white wine
4 eggs, slightly beaten

Bake pie shells for 5 minutes before filling. Thaw and drain crab. Cook, shell and chop shrimp. Combine crab, shrimp, Swiss cheese, celery and onions. Divide between pie shells. Combine mayonnaise, flour, wine and eggs. Divide mixture, pouring evenly over seafood. Bake in preheated 350° oven for 35 to 40 minutes. Serves 6-8.

## SHRIMP IN CHEESE SAUCE

*This works very well for buffets and large numbers of people.*

1 pound shrimp
½ pound fresh mushrooms, sliced
1 roll Kraft Jalapeño cheese

1 can cream of mushroom soup
1 jar chopped pimiento

Cook shrimp in salt and pepper water — no crab boil. Peel shrimp and set aside. Sauté mushrooms in butter and set aside. In a double boiler, melt cheese and add soup, mushrooms, pimiento and shrimp. Heat until very hot. Serve over rice. Serves 4.

# CASSEROLES

## BAKED APRICOTS

*This is unusual and always brings lots of conversation.*

2 29-ounce cans apricot halves,
    drained very well
2 1-pound boxes light brown
    sugar

1 16-ounce box Ritz crackers
Butter

In a buttered 3 quart baking dish, put a layer of apricots. Cover with brown sugar, then crumble a layer of Ritz crackers on top of sugar and dot generously with butter. Repeat to top of dish. Bake at 300° for 1 hour. It will have a crusty top. Excellent with pork or chicken. Serves 6-8.

## STRING BEAN CASSEROLE

6 16-ounce cans vertical-packed
  string beans
2 large onions, minced
3 tablespoons butter
Salt and pepper
6 10¾-ounce cans cream of
  mushroom soup

2 cups white almonds
2 cups (at least) cracker crumbs
1 stick butter
Paprika

Cook string beans briefly with onion, butter, salt and pepper. Drain. Place string beans in a Pyrex rectangular casserole in careful order. Make one layer of beans. Make a mushroom sauce from the label on the can of soup and add almonds. Stir and pour over layer of beans. Add cracker crumbs, another layer of beans and another layer of sauce. Top with dots of butter and sprinkle with paprika. Bake at 325° until bubbly, approximately 30 minutes to 1 hour. Serves 8 to 12, generously.

## CORNED BEEF CASSEROLE

1½ cups cooked noodles
1 10-ounce can cream of chicken
  soup
½ cup evaporated milk
1 12-ounce can Libby's corned
  beef, cut up

1 cup Cheddar cheese, grated
⅓ cup onion, finely chopped
½ cup crumbled potato chips

Preheat oven to 425°. Cook noodles in unsalted water. Combine all ingredients except potato chips. Put in a greased 1 quart casserole. Top with potato chips. Bake for 15 minutes. Serves 4 hungry people.

If this is to be frozen, do not add potato chips until just before baking.

# FRENCH BEEF AND VEGETABLE CASSEROLE

6 slices bacon
1 pound beef chuck about ½ inch thick
½ cup flour
1 teaspoon salt
1 cup red wine
2 tablespoons parsley
½ clove garlic

½ teaspoon thyme
1 10½-ounce can beef broth
6 medium potatoes, peeled and halved
12 small white onions, peeled
3 carrots, sliced lengthwise
1 cup (4 ounces) mushroom stems and pieces, finely chopped

Cook bacon until crisp and drain on a paper towel. Save drippings. Cut beef into cubes. Shake cubes, a few at a time, in a sack containing flour and salt. Brown in drippings. Remove to a 2 quart casserole. Pour wine into blender. Add parsley, garlic, thyme and beef broth. Blend until pureéd. Pour over meat. Cover and bake at 350° for 1 hour. Stir in potatoes, onions and carrots. Cover and bake another hour or until vegetables are done. Stir in mushrooms. Crumble bacon on top with additional chopped parsley. Serves 4 to 5.

This can be made the day before and reheated. If so, sprinkle bacon bits on just before reheating.

## CHICKEN SENTER

*Six hungry people will love you for this dish!!*

2 cups diced cooked chicken
1 cup undiluted cream of chicken
  soup
⅔ cup mayonnaise
1 cup celery, diced
1 tablespoon lemon juice
4 ounces fresh or canned
  mushrooms, sliced

½ teaspoon salt
1 teaspoon onion, grated
2 tablespoons margarine
½ cup slivered almonds
1 cup crushed cornflakes

Mix all ingredients except margarine, almonds and cornflakes. Pour into buttered casserole dish. Melt margarine in pie pan, add almonds and bake at 325° for approximately 15 minutes or until crispy and brown. Remove from oven and add cornflakes. Stir to coat well. Sprinkle on casserole. Bake at 375° for 30 to 40 minutes or until bubbly in center. Serves 6.

You may add one cup of cooked rice to dish. If so, increase mayonnaise to ¾ cup. This can be prepared the day before and baked the next day.

## CHICKEN AND SPINACH NOODLES

*Do this one on Wednesday; have a party on Saturday. We'll be happy to come.*

1 4-pound hen
1 stick margarine
1 cup onion, chopped
1 cup celery, chopped
1 cup bell pepper, chopped
1 10¾-ounce can undiluted cream
  of mushroom soup

½ pound processed cheese,
  preferably Old English
6 ounces of salad olives, chopped
6 ounces of mushroom stems and
  pieces
Salt and pepper to taste
1 package spinach noodles

Boil hen in seasoned water, saving stock. Remove chicken from bone and cut into bite size pieces. Sauté onion, celery and bell pepper in butter. Stir in soup, cheese, olives, mushrooms, salt and pepper. Cook noodles in chicken stock.

Fold chicken, cheese-vegetable mixture and noodles together and place in casserole. Makes approximately 4 quarts. Freezes well. Excellent with fruit salad and french bread. Bake at 350° until hot and bubbly. Serves 8-10.

## CHICKEN ENCHILADAS

1 2½-3 pound chicken
1 cup chicken broth
1 onion, chopped
2-3 tablespoons butter or
 margarine
1 10¾-ounce can condensed cream
 of mushroom soup, undiluted

1 10¾-ounce can cream of chicken
 soup
1 4-ounce can green chilies,
 chopped
1 package Taco flavored Doritos
1 pound Longhorn cheese, grated

Cook chicken until tender in broth seasoned with celery, onion, salt and pepper. Allow to cool in broth before boning. Cut into bite size pieces.

Sauté onion in butter in a large kettle. Add soups, broth and green chilies. Stir until well combined. Add chicken and mix well. In a large baking dish, place a layer of Doritos, a layer of chicken mixture and a layer of cheese. Repeat layers until dish is filled. Bake at 350° for 30 minutes or until bubbling. Serves 8.

This can be frozen, but turns out better if only the sauce is frozen, then thawed and combined with fresh Doritos and cheese.

## SPECIAL ENCHILADAS

*This can be made the day before.*

1 package tortillas
2 pounds ground beef
2 large onions, chopped
Salt
1 10¾-ounce can condensed cream
 of chicken soup, undiluted

1 10¼-ounce can onion soup
1 4 ounce can enchilada sauce
1 can Rotel tomatoes
½-1 pound Cheddar cheese, grated

Dip tortillas in hot fat and drain. Cook ground beef and onions until tender. Season with salt. Combine soups, enchilada sauce and tomatoes. Grease a large casserole with butter. Cut tortillas in quarters. Place a layer of tortillas in bottom of casserole. Add a layer of cheese and sauce. Repeat. Cover with cheese and foil. Bake at 350° for 45 minutes. Serves 10.

# STACKED ENCHILADAS

6-8 tortillas
2½ cups Cheddar cheese, grated
1 10-ounce can enchilada sauce
*Filling:*
2 cups of browned, crumbled
  ground beef or chopped chicken

1 cup sour cream
½ cup green onions, chopped
½ teaspoon salt
¼ teaspoon cumin

Combine filling mixture. Heat enchilada sauce and taste. You may wish to add more chili powder, dash of garlic salt, etc. Using a 1½ quart casserole, layer the bottom with tortillas dipped in enchilada sauce. Do not skimp with sauce. Then layer filling mixture, cheese and more tortillas dipped in enchilada sauce, ending with grated cheese on top. Bake at 350° for approximately 40 minutes. Serve with a tossed salad and more tortillas. Serves 4 to 6.

# BAKED CURRIED FRUIT CASSEROLE

*Great for Holidays in winter.*

2 bananas, sliced
½ cup pitted black cherries
1 #303 can cling peaches
1 #303 can pineapple slices
1 #303 can pear halves

1 small jar maraschino cherries
⅓ cup butter
¾ cup light brown sugar, packed
4 teaspoons curry powder

Prepare the day before needed. Drain fruit on paper towels. Cut in bite size pieces. Arrange in 1½ quart casserole. Melt butter and add brown sugar and curry powder. Spread over fruit. Bake uncovered at 325° for 1 hour. Cool and refrigerate. Reheat at 350° for 30 minutes. Serves 12.

## HOT FRUIT CASSEROLE

*Excellent for a brunch.*

1 16-ounce can pears, sliced
1 16-ounce can peaches, sliced
1 8-ounce can chunk pineapple
1 16-ounce can apricot halves
3 oranges

1 cup sugar
2 tablespoons flour
¾ stick butter
½ cup dry sherry
Cherry halves for color (optional)

Thinly slice oranges, cut in half and boil in water for 45 minutes. Drain all fruits and put in a large cooking pot. Combine ½ cup sugar and flour. Pour over fruit. Cook slowly until thick. Add butter, remaining ½ cup of sugar, sherry and cherry halves. Place in a 3 quart casserole and heat before serving. Serves 10 to 12.

## GNOCCHI

*A new look for grits, and it looks good!!*

1 quart milk
½ cup butter
1 cup grits (not instant)
1 teaspoon salt

1 teaspoon pepper
1 cup Gruyere cheese, grated
⅓ cup Parmesan cheese, grated
Butter

Boil milk and ½ cup butter. Add grits. Remove from heat and beat with hand mixer for 5 minutes. Add salt and pepper and pour into buttered casserole dish. Refrigerate. When cold, cut into 6 sections and sprinkle each with the grated cheese, dot with butter. When ready to serve, reheat in 325° oven for about 25 minutes. Serves 6.

## EASY HAMBURGER CASSEROLE

2 tablespoons margarine
½ onion, chopped
1 pound hamburger
1 tablespoon chili powder
1 teaspoon Lea and Perrin's
  Worcestershire sauce

1 15-ounce can Ranch Style beans
1 16-ounce can stewed tomatoes
  (undrained)
Sprinkle of sugar
1 16-ounce package cornbread
  mix

Cook onion in margarine until soft. Add remaining ingredients, except cornbread mix. Prepare cornbread mix according to directions. Spread over top of hamburger mixture in a 2 quart casserole. Bake at 425°, uncovered, for 30 minutes. Serves 6.

## HAMBURGER CASSEROLE

*This can be doubled and redoubled, and it will win you a grand slam, particularly with the younger set.*

2 tablespoons butter
1 pound ground round
1 clove garlic
1 teaspoon salt
Dash of pepper
1 teaspoon sugar
2 8-ounce cans tomato sauce

1 package flat noodles
6 scallions, tops included, chopped
1 3-ounce package cream cheese,
  softened
1 cup sour cream
1 cup Cheddar cheese, grated

Preheat oven to 350°. Melt butter and brown chuck or ground round. Add garlic, salt, pepper, sugar and tomato sauce. Cover and cook on low heat for 15 to 20 minutes. Cook noodles, drain and blanch. Mix onions, sour cream and softened cream cheese. (In a pinch, cottage cheese may be substituted.) Butter a casserole dish. Put half of the noodles in the dish, then half of the onion/sour cream mixture and half of the meat mixture. Repeat. Top with grated Cheddar cheese. Bake for 20 to 30 minutes. Serves 6.

## MUSHROOM CASSEROLE

1 pound mushrooms, sliced
¼ cup butter
½ cup celery, chopped
½ cup green pepper, chopped
½ cup onion, chopped
½ cup Hellmann's mayonnaise
¾ teaspoon salt

Pepper
6 slices white bread
2 eggs, slightly beaten
1½ cups milk
1 10¾-ounce can mushroom soup
½ cup sharp Cheddar cheese, grated

Sauté mushrooms in butter. Remove from heat and add celery, green pepper, onion, mayonnaise, salt and pepper. Remove crusts from bread, butter and cut into 1 inch cubes. Place half of bread cubes in the bottom of a 3 quart flat casserole. Pour mushroom mixture over cubes. Add remaining bread cubes. Combine eggs and milk and pour over mushroom mixture. Refrigerate several hours. Spoon mushroom soup over top and bake at 325° for 50 minutes. Sprinkle cheese over top and return to oven to allow cheese to melt. Serves 4 to 6 as a luncheon dish.

## MUSHROOM PILAF

½ cup butter
1½ cups rice, raw and any kind
1 10½-ounce can condensed onion soup, undiluted
1 10½-ounce can condensed beef consomme, undiluted

½ pound fresh mushrooms, trimmed and sliced
1½ cups shredded Cheddar cheese

Melt butter in a 2 quart casserole; stir in the rice to coat grains with butter. Add soups and mushrooms; mix well. Cover and bake in pre-heated 325° oven about 55 minutes, or until rice is tender and liquid is absorbed. Stir occasionally during the baking period. Remove cover, top with Cheddar cheese and return to oven for 5 minutes. Serves 6-8. This recipe is good with almost every kind of meat dish. It can be doubled for a large crowd. If baked in one large casserole, extend baking time.

# ONION RICE

1 10¾-ounce can onion soup
1 cup Uncle Ben's converted rice
1 4-ounce can mushrooms
(optional)

1 3-ounce can onion rings (for
company)

Add enough water to 1 can of onion soup to make 2½ cups. Bring to a boil, add Uncle Ben's rice and cook over low heat until liquid is absorbed. Add a little butter and mushrooms if desired. Pour in oven dish. For company, place onion rings on top. Bake 350° for 30 minutes. Serves 4 to 6.

# OYSTER AND ARTICHOKE CASSEROLE

*This is expensive, but divine!! A special dish for company, Thanksgiving or Christmas dinner.*

2 sticks butter
1 cup flour
3 cups milk (maybe more)
½ pint cream
6 dozen oysters, drained
2 teaspoons salt
1 teaspoon pepper

Dash of Tabasco
2 teaspoons Worcestershire sauce
½ cup sherry
8 artichoke hearts, frozen or
canned (cook frozen)
Buttered bread crumbs

Melt butter. Blend in flour. Remove from heat and slowly add milk and cream which have been combined and heated. Stir until slightly thickened. Heat oysters gently to remove excess liquid. Add to cream sauce. Simmer for 5 minutes. Add seasonings, sherry and finely chopped artichokes. Place in a casserole dish. Cover with bread crumbs. Bake at 350° for 10 minutes. Serves 8.

This can be prepared in the morning for baking in the evening. It is best to leave off bread crumbs until ready to bake.

# PIZZA SANDWICH

*A simple supper dish that most youngsters can really relate to.*

1 pound ground meat
3 tablespoons onion, finely
 chopped
2 8-ounce cans tomato sauce
1 teaspoon oregano
2 cups Bisquick baking mix
1 egg

⅔ cup milk
8 slices American cheese
1 2-ounce can sliced mushrooms,
 drained
¼ cup grated Parmesan cheese
6-8 slices Pepperoni (optional)

Cook and stir meat and onions until brown. Drain and mix in 1 can of tomato sauce and oregano. Simmer uncovered for 10 minutes. Meanwhile, stir baking mix, egg and milk into a soft dough. Spread half of dough in a greased 9x9x2 inch pan. Pour remaining can of tomato sauce over dough and spread evenly. Layer 4 slices of cheese, then meat mixture, mushrooms, remaining cheese slices, Parmesan cheese and top with pepperoni. Spread remaining dough over top and seal edges. Bake at 400° for 20 to 25 minutes or until golden brown. Serves 4 to 6.

# GREEN RICE

¼ cup onions, chopped
½ package (1 pound) fresh
 spinach, chopped
1½ cups sharp Cheddar cheese,
 grated

⅓ cup melted margarine
2 eggs, slightly beaten
2 cups milk
½ teaspoon garlic salt
1 cup Minute rice

Mix all ingredients, put in Pyrex dish and bake for about one hour at 325°. Serves 4-6.

# RICE AND SAUSAGE CASSEROLE

*We love this as a companion to the Lime Broiled Chicken recipe.*

1½ cup raw rice
1 pound of pork sausage
1 4-ounce can mushrooms,
  undrained

2 10¾-ounce cans mushroom soup
2 teaspoons Worcestershire sauce

Fry, crumble and drain the sausage. Mix with rest of ingredients. Bake at 350 for 45 minutes or until rice is tender. Serves 6 to 8.

# ROUND STEAK CASSEROLE

*At first glance this looks like a lot of trouble; not so, it is one of those make-ahead jewels we all love so well. With a salad and simple dessert you have a winner for family fare.*

1 pound round steak
¼ cup shortening
1½ cups onion, chopped
1 6-ounce can tomato paste
1 cup water
1 tablespoon sugar
1½ teaspoons salt
¼ teaspoon pepper
1 teaspoon Worcestershire sauce
1½ cups mushrooms, canned or
  fresh
¾ cup sour cream

*Sour Cream Puffs:*
1¼ cups all-purpose flour
2 teaspoons baking powder
½ teaspoon salt
¼ cup shortening
¾ cup sour cream
Sesame seeds or Poppy seeds

Cut meat in ½ inch strips. Brown in shortening, stirring constantly. Add onion and cook until tender. Add tomato paste, water, sugar, salt, pepper and Worcestershire sauce. Cover and simmer 1½ hours, stirring occasionally. Add mushrooms and sour cream. Cook 5 to 8 minutes and place in casserole. May be refrigerated at this point until the next day, then heat slowly and continue. Top with Sour Cream Puffs, sprinkle puffs with sesame or poppy seeds. Bake at 425° for 20 to 25 minutes. Serves 6 to 8.

*Sour Cream Puffs:* These can be done in food processor. Sift flour with baking powder and salt. Cut in shortening until particles are fine. Add sour cream. Stir until dough clings together. Place on a well floured surface. Roll out to ½ inch thickness, cut into 6 or 8 biscuits, place on casserole and bake.

# SPINACH ARTICHOKE CASSEROLE

*Wonderful!! A snap to put together!*

2 10-ounce packages frozen
chopped spinach
½ cup white onion, finely chopped
1 stick butter
1 pint sour cream

1 10-ounce can artichoke hearts,
drained and cut in half
¾ cup Parmesan cheese
Salt and pepper
Buttered bread crumbs

Cook spinach as directed on box and drain well. Sauté onion in butter. Mix all ingredients together and put in buttered casserole. Sprinkle a little more Parmesan cheese on top. Cover lightly with buttered bread crumbs. Bake at 350° for 25 to 30 minutes. Serves 8 to 10.

# SPINACH LASAGNA

*A great prepare ahead viand.*

1 large box lasagna noodles (12-14
pieces)
1 tablespoon oil
3 eggs
2 pounds ground chuck
1 medium onion, chopped
1 teaspoon oregano
3 teaspoons garlic salt or 1 clove
garlic, minced
2 tablespoons parsley
1 teaspoon pepper
2 teaspoons salt (cut down on salt
if you use garlic salt)

1 15-ounce can tomato sauce
2 6-ounce cans tomato paste
3 6-ounce packages grated
Provolone cheese
2 cups cottage cheese
¾ pound Mozzarella cheese,
grated
2 10-ounce packages frozen
chopped spinach, thawed
completely

Cook noodles according to directions on package. Drain and mix with 1 egg. Cook meat and spices. Drain excess fat. Mix in tomato sauce and tomato paste and simmer. Mix two eggs with the Mozzarella cheese. Then mix all cheeses and spinach together. In a large oblong pan or two small dishes, layer noodles, meat and cheese mixture. Make as many layers as desired, ending with cheese. Bake at 350° for 45 minutes. Serves 12-15.

# EGGS, CHEESE, PASTA

# EGGS/CHEESE/PASTA

## BASIC CHEESE PUFF

*This is one of your basic no fail dishes that you have the fun of jazzing up. You could add green chilies, Worcestershire, a cup of mushrooms, or use your imagination and have fun!!*

5 slices bread, cubed
½ pound sharp cheese, grated
2 cups milk
3 eggs
½ teaspoon salt
½ teaspoon dry mustard

*Add 1 of the following:*
1 pound fried, crumbled, drained
  sausage
2 cups cubed ham
2 cups shrimp, coarsely chopped
Plus any extras you dream up

Arrange bread and cheese in a 9x9 inch baking pan which has been buttered. Mix the remaining ingredients together and pour over bread and cheese. Cover and let sit overnight in refrigerator.

Bake at 350° for 45 minutes to 1 hour, or until set and golden brown on top. Serves 6 to 8.

## MEXICAN CHEESE

*Viva Mexico!!*

1 pound Monterey Jack cheese
1 pound Cheddar cheese
2 7-ounce jars chopped green
  Ortega Chilies
1 13-ounce can Pet milk

4 eggs
¼ cup corn meal
1 teaspoon Worcestershire sauce
1 teaspoon salt
5 ounces tomato sauce

Grate the two kinds of cheese. Layer in a long casserole half of the cheese. Place chilies on top and add the remaining cheese. Beat the next 5 ingredients together and pour over the cheese. Bake at 350° for 25 to 30 minutes. Add the tomato sauce and bake for 15 minutes more. Serve with a green salad. Serves 8 to 10.

# MONTEREY JACK CHEESE GRITS

*A new view of the Grits game. Good with ham or a buffet.*

4 cups water
1 cup grits
1 teaspoon salt
2 cups grated Monterey Jack
  cheese

¼ teaspoon garlic salt
1 8-ounce carton sour cream
2 ounces chopped green chilies
3 eggs, well beaten

Heat water to boiling; slowly stir in grits and salt. Cook until thick. Remove from heat. Add cheese, garlic salt, sour cream and chilies (more if you like it really hot) and mix well. Add a little of the hot mixture to the eggs, then the eggs to the grits mixture. Pour into a baking dish and bake at 350° for 30 minutes or until set and golden brown on top. Serves 6 to 8.

# CHEESE STRATA

*With a fruit salad and rolls, it's a good ladies' lunch, or a side dish for roast beef or pork instead of your familiar baked potato.*

2 cups sweet onions, thinly sliced
8 slices of bread
8 ounces sharp Cheddar cheese,
  sliced
3 eggs, beaten
2½ cups milk
1 teaspoon salt

¼ teaspoon dry mustard
¼ teaspoon Worcestershire sauce
3 drops (or 6, if you lean to hotter
  taste) Tabasco
Dash of pepper
2 tablespoons butter, melted

Separate onions into rings. Trim crusts from bread. Place 4 slices of bread in bottom of a buttered 9 inch square baking dish. Top with ½ of the cheese and onions. Repeat. Combine beaten eggs and the remaining ingredients, except the butter. Pour over the bread, cheese and onions. Cover and refrigerate several hours or overnight. Uncover. Spoon melted butter over it and bake at 350° for 50 to 60 minutes or until firm. Cut into squares. Serves 6.

## CHILIES RELLEÑOS EASY WAY

*Simple, but a fresh approach for that egg brunch dish.*

2 4-ounce cans green chilies,
  seeded if desired
1 pound Jack cheese, cut in small
  pieces
1 4¼-ounce can chopped ripe
  olives

4 eggs, slightly beaten
½ cup milk
½-1 teaspoon dry mustard
Salt to taste

Grease 2-2½ quart baking dish. Layer chilies, cheese and olives, repeating one time. Mix together eggs, milk, dry mustard and salt. Pour over chilies and cheese. Put baking dish in a pan of hot water and bake at 325° for 35 minutes or until egg custard is firm. Serves 4 to 6.

## CALIFORNIA POACHED EGGS

*Our tester liked this so much she graded this recipe A + + + !! Good for
Sunday lunch or a quick supper.*

1 avocado, peeled and pitted
½ cup sour cream, maybe a bit
  more
Lemon juice
Salt

Cayenne pepper
2 English muffins
4 slices Monterey Jack cheese
4 slices Canadian bacon, sautéed
4 eggs, poached

If using a food processor, use the plastic blade to whip avocado and sour cream. Add lemon juice, salt and pepper to taste. Split muffins, butter and toast in broiler. Top with cheese and melt. Add Canadian bacon and poached egg. Spoon avocado mixture over muffins. Serves 2.

# EGGS DIVINE

8 eggs
¼ cup butter, melted
½ teaspoon mustard
1 tablespoon grated onion
½ teaspoon Worcestershire sauce
1 2¼-ounce can deviled ham

1 teaspoon minced parsley (dried)
*Sauce:*
¼ cup butter
1 cup bouillon
1 5¾ ounce can evaporated milk
1 cup grated Velveeta cheese

Cook the first three ingredients of the sauce and add the grated cheese.

Meanwhile hard boil the eggs; split and mash yolks. Add the melted butter, mustard, onion, Worcestershire sauce, deviled ham and parsley to the yolks. Arrange the egg halves, stuffed with the above mixture, in a baking dish. Pour the sauce over them and bake at 325°, uncovered, for 40 minutes.

# JALAPEÑO STUFFED EGGS

*These are good to put on a large dish surrounding potato salad.*

6 eggs
Hellmann's mayonnaise
Salt to taste

3 teaspoons jalapeño peppers,
   chopped (or more if you wish)
Chopped parsley

Hard boil 6 eggs. Halve the eggs and mash the egg yolks with enough Hellmann's mayonnaise to make a smooth paste. Add salt to taste, then the chopped jalapeños. Stuff the egg whites and sprinkle top with chopped parsley.

## ORIENTAL EGGS

6 eggs
2½ teaspoons soy sauce
¼ teaspoon dry mustard
1 tablespoon minced parsley

¼ cup mayonnaise
3 teaspoons Worcestershire sauce
Paprika

Hard boil the 6 eggs. Mash the yolks with the soy sauce, dry mustard, parsley, mayonnaise and Worcestershire sauce. Spoon into egg whites. Top with a little chopped parsley and sprinkle with paprika.

## HUEVOS RANCHEROS CASSEROLE

*For brunch*

1 4 ounce can Ortega peppers, chopped
1 medium onion, chopped medium fine
3 tablespoons cooking oil
1 clove garlic, or to taste, chopped and mashed fine

2 8 ounce cans tomatoes
½ pound Cheddar cheese, grated
½ pound Monterey Jack cheese, grated
12 eggs

Sauté peppers and onion in cooking oil. Add garlic. Add canned tomatoes and cook until flavors are blended well — approximately 15 minutes. Fold cheeses into the sauce and heat until melted. Be careful to avoid sticking. Place sauce in a casserole dish. Gently break eggs into the mixture. Bake at 350° until set. Serve over toasted tortillas spread with refritos (refried beans). Serves 10 to 12 generously.

# BAKED LASAGNA

*You can make this ahead and freeze half if you like, and you will like.*

*Sauce:*
3-ounces tomato paste
½ cup hot water
4 tablespoons olive oil
2 cloves garlic, crushed
1 stalk celery, diced
1 9¼-ounce can plum tomatoes
Salt and pepper to to taste

*Filling:*
¾ pound Italian sausage
1½ pounds lasagna noodles
1½ cups grated Parmesan cheese
1½ pounds Ricotta cheese
1½ cups cubed Mozzarella
Salt and pepper to taste

Blend tomato paste with hot water. Brown garlic in hot olive oil for about 3 minutes. Add celery, blended tomato paste and plum tomatoes. Boil for 3 minutes. Lower flame to simmer and cover. Continue to simmer for 1 hour. Add salt and pepper to taste.

Broil sausage about 15 minutes, or until brown on both sides. Cut into small pieces. Meanwhile cook lasagna according to instructions on package. Drain.

Pour ½ cup of tomato sauce in baking dish, then layer of lasagna, Parmesan cheese, sauce, Mozzarella cheese, sausage and Ricotta cheese. Repeat layers until all ingredients are used. The top layer should be sauce and grated Parmesan cheese. Bake at 350° for 15 minutes or until firm. Cut into squares and serve with more sauce and grated cheese. Serves 8 to 10. Will freeze.

# LEEK LORRAINE

*Very good. Easy to prepare. Good for luncheons.*

1 9-inch unbaked pie shell
1 package Knorr Leek Soup Mix
1½ cups milk
½ cup light cream
3 eggs, slightly beaten
1½ cups (or 6 ounces) Swiss
   cheese, shredded

1 teaspoon dry mustard
Dash of white pepper
1 4½-ounce can deviled ham
2 tablespoons fine, dry bread
   crumbs

Preheat oven to 450°. Bake pie shell until brown; remove and reduce temperature to 325°.

In a saucepan, combine soup mix and milk. Bring to a boil, then remove from heat and cool. When cool stir in cream.

In a bowl, combine eggs, cheese, mustard and pepper. Slowly stir in soup mixture. Mix deviled ham and bread crumbs and spread on bottom and sides of pie shell. Pour in the soup mixture and bake at 325° for 45 to 50 minutes or until knife inserted in center comes out clean. Cool for 10 minutes and slice thinly. Serves 7 to 8.

# MACARONI LOAF

*Good as a side dish or a meatless dinner.*

1 cup cooked macaroni (about ½ cup uncooked)
1 cup milk
1 cup softened bread crumbs
⅔ cup grated sharp cheese
4 tablespoons butter, melted

1 tablespoon green pepper, chopped
1 tablespoon onion, chopped
1 tablespoon pimento, chopped
3 eggs, well beaten

Mix all ingredients. Bake in loaf or individual custard cups in a hot water bath at 350° for 1 hour. Let set for 5 minutes so it will lift out of pan easily. Place on serving platter and slice. Serves 4.

# NOODLES FETTUCCINI

*Alfredo's — Rome, Italy*

½ pound noodles
1 cup pure cream
½ stick of butter

½ cup Parmesan cheese
Fresh parsley

Cook noodles according to directions on package and drain.

In a double boiler, simmer cream and butter. Stir in cheese in small amounts. Pour sauce over noodles and sprinkle with parsley. (If a thicker sauce is desired, add a small amount of corn starch.) Serves 4.

# SAUSAGE FILLED CREPES

*Weekend house guests? These are an immense help for Sunday brunch or late supper.*

**Crepes:**
3 eggs, beaten
1 cup milk
1 tablespoon cooking oil
1 cup all-purpose flour
½ teaspoon salt
**Sausage Filling:**
1 pound bulk sausage, cooked and
  drained

¼ cup onion, chopped, sautéed
  with sausage
½ cup processed Cheddar cheese,
  shredded
1 3-ounce package cream cheese
¼ teaspoon dried marjoram
**Topping:**
½ cup sour cream
¼ cup butter, softened

*Crepes:* Combine eggs, milk and oil. Beat well. Add flour and salt. Beat until smooth. Pour 2 tablespoons of batter into greased crepe pan or heavy skillet. Cook on one side, flip and cook on other side. Remove to paper toweling until all crepes are done. Makes 16.

*Filling:* Combine all ingredients for filling. Place 2 tablespoons of sausage filling down the center of each crepe. Roll up. Place in an 11¾x7½ inch flat Pyrex dish. At this point, the crepes may be frozen for up to three weeks.

To serve, remove from freezer for 1 hour. Bake covered at 375° for 40 to 45 minutes. Remove from oven and spoon on topping. Serves 6 to 8.

*Topping:* Soften butter and beat until spreading consistency. Add sour cream and mix well.

SWEETS

# CAKES

### APPLE CAKE

*Moist and delicious to serve to a crowd.*

1½ cups Wesson oil
2 cups sugar
3 eggs
3 cups diced apples (cooking
variety)
3 cups flour
1 cup nuts (preferably black
walnuts)

3 tablespoons vanilla
1 teaspoon salt
1 teaspoon soda
*Icing:*
1 stick of butter
1 cup of brown sugar
1 teaspoon vanilla
½ cup milk

Beat the first 3 ingredients well, then stir with a spoon and add the remaining ingredients. Pour into a well greased and floured flat 9x13x2 pyrex pan and bake at 325° for 45 minutes and cool.

*Icing:* Bring all ingredients to a rolling boil and then pour over well cooled cake. GREAT!

Makes 24 squares. Serves 12-24!

### APPLE KUCHEN

*This is really tasty and different.*

½ cup butter (soft)
1 package yellow cake mix
½ cup flaked coconut
1 can pie apples (drained) or 2½
cups sliced baking apples

½ cup sugar
1 teaspoon cinnamon
1 cup sour cream
1 egg

Heat oven to 350°. Cut butter into cake mix until crumbly. Mix in coconut. Pat mixture lightly into ungreased 13x9x2 pan — bottom and sides. Bake 10 minutes. Arrange apple slices on warm crust. Mix sugar and cinnamon and sprinkle on apples. Blend sour cream and egg and drizzle over apples. Bake for 25 minutes.

Also good using canned peaches.

# BUTTER RUM CAKE

*Serves 12 people, who will love it!!*

*Cake:*
1 box butter cake mix
1 3¾ ounce box instant vanilla
   pudding mix
½ cup cooking oil
4 whole eggs
1 cup water
1 teaspoon rum flavoring

*Butter Rum Syrup:*
1 stick of butter
1 cup sugar
⅓ cup water
2 teaspoons rum flavoring

Mix all ingredients well and pour into a greased and floured tube pan or bundt pan. Bake at 350° for 45 to 50 minutes or until done when tested. While cake is still in pan pour syrup over it. Let it set in pan for 30 minutes.

*Rum Syrup:* Put all ingredients except flavoring in a small pan. Bring to a boil. Cook until butter is just melted and sugar is dissolved. Add flavoring. Pour hot syrup on cake.

Try mixing all cake ingredients in your food processor using the plastic blade — so easy!

# RUTH'S CARROT CAKE

*This is a good keeper!! Stays moist for several days.*

1 cup grated carrots
3 cups sifted flour
2 teaspoons cinnamon
3 beaten eggs
1 tablespoon vanilla
2 cups sugar
1 tablespoon soda
1½ cups Wesson oil
1 cup chopped pecans

1 8¼-ounce can crushed pineapple
*Icing:*
1 8-ounce package cream cheese,
   softened
1 stick margarine
1 pound box powdered sugar
1 teaspoon vanilla
½ cup pecans, chopped
1 7½-ounce can Angel Flake
   coconut

Mix all ingredients and bake in greased and floured tube pan for 1 hour at 350° or 2 layer pans for 35-45 minutes.

*Icing:* Cream cheese and margarine, add remaining ingredients and spread on cake.

If you choose not to ice cake, it is great sliced, buttered and toasted for breakfast.

# CHOCOLATE ANGEL FOOD CAKE

*A nice light dessert!*

1 package Angel Food Cake mix
  (Duncan Hines does well)
1 cup sugar
¾ cup cocoa
1 pint whipping cream

Mix cake according to package directions. Bake.

Mix well sugar, cocoa and whipping cream and refrigerate. The secret to the whipping cream is to refrigerate *at least* 3 hours or overnight, if possible, before whipping. Whip. Slice cake in half and spread the bottom half generously with whipped cream mixture. Replace top and finish icing cake with remainder of whipped cream. Keep refrigerated. Serves 10-14.

# CHOCOLATE CAKE

1 Duncan Hines yellow cake mix
1 4½-ounce package chocolate
  instant pudding
½ cup Crisco oil
4 eggs
¼ cup water
1 cup sour cream
1 cup chopped pecans (optional)
1 6-ounce package chocolate chips
*Icing*
1 8-ounce package cream cheese
1 box powdered sugar
1 stick of margarine
1 teaspoon vanilla

Mix thoroughly all ingredients except the chocolate chips. Then fold in the chocolate chips. Bake in greased and floured bundt pan or angel food cake pan at 350° for 50-55 minutes.

Blend icing ingredients and ice cake when cooled.

Sprinkle cake with colored sugar sprinkles for the holidays!! Pretty!!

## PICNIC CHOCOLATE CAKE

2 cups sugar
½ cup cocoa
½ teaspoon salt
2 cups flour
2 teaspoons soda

1½ cups boiling water
½ cup butter
2 beaten eggs
1 teaspoon vanilla

Mix first five ingredients. Add butter to boiling water to melt. Stir water and butter into sugar-flour mixture; add eggs and vanilla. Bake in ungreased 9x13 inch pan (which has a lid) at 350° for 35 minutes.

Ice with favorite icing and cut in squares.

Covered pan travels well to picnics or lake, etc.

## CHOCOLATE POUND CAKE

*So wonderfully good AND fattening! Darn it!!*

2 cups sugar
1 cup margarine
2 eggs
2 squares chocolate or ½ cup
   cocoa
2½ cups flour
1 cup buttermilk

1 teaspoon soda dissolved in
   buttermilk
2 teaspoons vanilla
½ cup strong, hot coffee
*Icing:*
1½ Hershey (8-ounce) bars
1 stick margarine

Cream sugar and margarine. Add eggs and chocolate that has been melted. Add flour alternately with buttermilk, to which soda has been added. Add coffee last. Bake in greased, lightly floured bundt pan or angel food cake pan for 40-50 minutes at 325°.

*Icing:* Slowly melt Hershey bars with margarine. Ice cake.

# COCONUT POUND CAKE

*This is the kind of cake that medals, plaques and ribbons are given for.*

| | |
|---|---|
| 3 cups sugar | 6 eggs (separated) |
| ¾ cup shortening | 3 cups flour |
| ¼ cup margarine | 1 teaspoon almond flavoring |
| 1 cup milk | 2 cups coconut |

Mix sugar, shortening, margarine and egg yolks. Add flour and milk to mixture. Add coconut. Beat egg whites. Fold in beaten egg whites. Cook in a large greased and lightly floured tube pan for 1 hour and 15 minutes at 300° or until done.

Can be baked the day before or frozen.

Serves 10-15.

# EGGNOG CAKE

*Adult fare — particularly appropriate for the Holidays.*

| | |
|---|---|
| 1 box Pillsbury Angel Food Cake mix | ¼ cup brandy or more for stronger flavor |
| 1 cup butter, softened | ¾ to 1 cup finely chopped toasted pecans (reserve 2 tablespoons) |
| 2 cups powdered sugar, sifted | 1 cup whipping cream, whipped |
| 5 egg yolks (use whites to make Peppermint Forgotten cookies or meringues) | |

Bake cake according to directions. Cool.

Cream butter and sugar until light and fluffy. Add egg yolks, one at a time, beating after each addition. Stir in brandy and nuts. Fold whipped cream into butter mixture.

Slice cake into four layers horizontally. Spread each layer with whipped cream mixture. Chill 24 hours. When ready to serve, spread rest of whipped cream mixture on cake and sprinkle with 2 tablespoons reserved pecans.

Serves 12 to 16.

# ICED JAM CAKE

*This cake is good with a 7 minute white icing. The cupcakes are good just as a snack with no icing.*

1 cup margarine
1¼ cups sugar
4 eggs
2 cups plus 2 tablespoons flour
1 teaspoon cinnamon
1 teaspoon ground cloves
1 teaspoon baking powder
1 cup buttermilk
1 teaspoon soda
1 cup blackberry jam with seeds
(use raspberry jam if you
cannot find blackberry)

Cream margarine and sugar. Add eggs one at a time. Sift flour with all dry ingredients except the baking soda. Add the soda to ½ cup of the buttermilk. Add flour mixture and the other ½ cup of buttermilk alternately to the creamed mixture. Finally add the buttermilk with the soda and the jam. Pour into 3 greased and floured 8 inch cake pans or 2 greased and floured pans and 4-6 muffin tins. Bake 325° — bake layers 25-30 minutes — muffins five minutes less.

# JAM CAKE WITH BUTTER SAUCE

3 eggs, beaten
¾ cup blackberry jam or preserves
1 cup buttermilk
1 cup Wesson oil
1½ cups sugar
1 cup nuts
1 teaspoon vanilla
1 teaspoon cinnamon
1 teaspoon allspice
1 teaspoon soda
½ teaspoon salt
2 cups flour
*Sauce:*
1 stick butter
1¼ cups sugar
¾ cup buttermilk
1 teaspoon soda

Combine all ingredients for cake and mix well. Bake at 350° for 50 minutes. Pour hot sauce over hot cake. Sauce is foamy, so spoon a little at a time over the cake.

*Sauce:* Combine ingredients and boil for 3 minutes.

## MAGIC LEMON ICEBOX CAKE

1 cup finely crushed chocolate
   cookie crumbs (about 16 2¼-
   inch wafers)
6 tablespoons sugar
2 tablespoons butter or
   margarine, melted

2 eggs, separated
1 15-ounce can Eagle Brand
   sweetened condensed milk
1 tablespoon grated lemon rind
¼ teaspoon almond extract
½ cup fresh lemon juice

Combine crumbs, 2 tablespoons of sugar and melted butter. Press 1 cup of mixture on bottom and sides of buttered ice cube tray; chill. Reserve remaining crumbs for top. Beat egg yolks until thick; add Eagle Brand milk. Add lemon rind, almond extract and lemon juice, and continue mixing until thick. Beat egg whites; gradually add remaining 4 tablespoons of sugar and beat until stiff. Fold into lemon mixture. Pour into tray. Garnish with remaining crumbs. Freeze until firm — 6 to 8 hours.

This keeps well in freezer and may easily be doubled or tripled.

## LEMON NUT CAKE

*A good holiday cake for those who do not like fruit cake.*

1 pound butter
2 cups sugar
6 eggs
3 cups flour
¼ teaspoon soda

¼ teaspoon salt
2 ounces lemon extract
1 pound white raisins
1 quart pecans — broken in half

Cream butter and sugar. Add eggs. Mix dry ingredients and gradually add to creamed mixture. Then add lemon extract. Dust raisins with a little flour so they will not stick together. Add raisins and nuts. Pour into angel food cake pan or 2 loaf pans that have been greased and floured. Bake for 2 hours at 250°. Cool 30 minutes and turn out to finish cooling.

This cake slices beautifully if made ahead and frozen, otherwise it is a bit crumbly.

## EASY MAHOGANY CAKE

1 package Duncan Hines Cake
  Mix — Chocolate Butter recipe
*Icing:*
½ cup margarine
1 pound box powdered sugar
  (sifted)

4 heaping tablespoons cocoa
4 tablespoons STRONG coffee
Pinch of salt
1 egg yolk

Bake cake in 2 layers according to box directions. Melt margarine and add coffee, sugar and salt. Mix until smooth and add egg yolk. Stir until it is a good consistency to spread. Frost cake.

## ORANGE CHIFFON CAKE WITH RUM GLAZE

*A light, moist, delicate cake. Would be pretty on a buffet table for 10 to 12, or a different birthday cake.*

1 orange
6 eggs, separated (room
  temperature)
½ cup corn oil
2 cups cake flour
1½ cups sugar
3 teaspoons baking powder

½ teaspoon salt
½ teaspoon cream of tartar
*Rum Glaze:*
½ cup light rum or ½ cup orange
  juice (your choice)
2 tablespoons butter
2 cups sifted confectioner's sugar

Grate all the rind from orange; squeeze orange and measure — if necessary add water to make ¾ cup liquid. To the egg yolks add rind, juice and corn oil. Stir to blend.

Sift cake flour, sugar, baking powder and salt together. Make a well in the center. Add yolk mixture and beat until very smooth.

In another large bowl, add cream of tartar to egg whites. Beat until very stiff. Fold very gently into cake batter until just blended. Don't stir. Pour into ungreased 10-inch tube pan and bake in 325° preheated oven for 1 hour or until cake springs back when pressed lightly.

Invert tube pan over heavy glass or bottle until cool. Remove gently. Pour warm rum glaze over top.

*Rum Glaze:* Heat rum and butter. Pour into sugar and stir. Pour over cake.

# PINEAPPLE CAKE

1½ cups sugar
2 cups flour
½ teaspoon salt
2 teaspoons soda
½ cup Wesson oil
2 large eggs
1 20-ounce can crushed pineapple

*Icing:*
1 5⅓-ounce can Pet milk
1 stick butter
1 cup sugar
½ cup brown sugar
1 teaspoon vanilla
1 cup chopped pecans

Mix all cake ingredients together. Mix well. Pour into 9x13 inch Pyrex dish. Bake at 350° for 30 minutes.

*Icing:* Mix all ingredients. Stir over medium heat and simmer for 10 minutes. Pour over cake while hot.

# AUNT ELIZABETH'S POPPY SEED CAKE

*A very different, rich, creamy "custard-y" cake. First rate!!*

2 tablespoons poppy seeds
¾ cup milk
¾ cup butter
1½ cups sugar
2 cups flour
2 teaspoons baking powder
4 egg whites, stiffly beaten

1 teaspoon vanilla
*Custard Filling:*
¾ cup sugar
1 heaping teaspoon corn starch
4 egg yolks, beaten
2 cups milk
1 teaspoon vanilla

Pour milk over poppy seeds. Soak for ½ hour. Cream butter and sugar. Add milk and poppy seeds. Slowly add flour and baking powder you have sifted together. Add vanilla. Fold in stiffly beaten egg whites. Bake in two 8 inch round layer cake pans at 350° approximately 25 minutes or until center springs back when touched. Cool, and cut each layer into two layers lengthwise. Put together with custard filling. Frost with butter icing.

*Custard Filling:* Mix sugar and corn starch in top of double boiler. Stir in beaten yolks and milk. Boil until thick. Cool slightly; spread between layers.

Cake should be refrigerated after frosting.

# PUMPKIN CAKE

| | |
|---|---|
| 2 cups sugar | 2 teaspoons cinnamon |
| 4 eggs | *Icing:* |
| 1 cup Wesson Oil | 1 package (3 ounces) cream |
| 2 cups pumpkin (1 pound can) | cheese |
| 2 cups flour | ¾ box powdered sugar |
| 2 teaspoons salt | 1 stick margarine |
| 2 teaspoons powdered cloves | 1½ teaspoons vanilla |

Cream together the sugar, eggs, oil and pumpkin. Sift together the dry ingredients. Add to the creamed mixture and stir. Pour into a greased and floured bundt pan or angel food cake pan. Bake for 50 minutes at 325°.

*Icing:* Mix all ingredients together and spread on the cooled cake.

For decoration place a few pecan halves on the icing.

# SABELL'S CAKE

*This is a quick cake; the kind you serve warm, at once — not a keeper. Good to serve on the night you play refrigerator Roulette or left overs Bingo.*

| | |
|---|---|
| 1 cup flour | ½ teaspoon vanilla |
| 1 cup sugar | *Frosting:* |
| 1 teaspoon baking powder | 7 tablespoons brown sugar |
| 2 eggs, beaten | 3 tablespoons butter |
| ½ cup milk | 2 tablespoons cream |
| 4 tablespoons butter | ½ cup pecans |

Mix first four ingredients well. Bring milk, butter and vanilla to a boil and add to the first part. Bake at 325° for 20 minutes or until cake testor comes out clean.

Top with frosting while cake is warm.

*Frosting:* Bring frosting ingredients to a boil. Add ½ cup pecans. Pour on cake and run cake under broiler until it bubbles.

# RASPBERRY CAKE

*A lovely shocking pink shade. This would make a grand birthday, Valentine or Easter cake. For Easter use tiny candy eggs, tint coconut green, etc. to decorate. Delightful!!*

1 box Duncan Hines white cake
  mix
1 3-ounce package Raspberry
  Jello
½ cup water
¾ cup vegetable oil

4 eggs (room temperature)
½ package frozen raspberries
*Icing:*
1 pound box powdered sugar
¼ cup margarine
½ package frozen raspberries

Buzz up raspberries in blender or food processor. Measure and divide in half. Use one half for cake and the other half for icing.

Mix first four ingredients of cake carefully and beat well. Beat in eggs, one at a time. Stir in raspberries. Bake in three 8 inch or two 9 inch layers at 350° for 25 to 35 minutes. Serves 12 to 14.

*Note:* You need to test this carefully for doneness because it may need a little extra baking. Poke with a toothpick. If it comes out clean, it's done!!

*Icing:* Combine all ingredients and mix well. Ice cooled cake.

# COOKIES

## CARAMEL GERMAN CHOCOLATE BROWNIES

*Chocolaty, caramely, hopelessly rich, gooey and divine!!!*

1 14-ounce package light caramels
1 cup evaporated milk
1 package German chocolate cake
   mix
¾ cup margarine
1 cup nuts, finely chopped
1 6-ounce package chocolate chips

Combine caramels and ½ cup evaporated milk in top of double boiler. Cook over low heat until caramels melt.* Combine cake mix, margarine, remaining ½ cup evaporated milk and nuts. Lightly grease a 9x13 inch baking pan. Spread half of cake mixture in pan. Bake at 350° for 10 minutes. Remove from oven. Sprinkle chocolate chips over partially baked cake mixture. Then spread caramel mixture over chips. Drop remaining cake mixture by tiny spoonfuls over caramel mixture. Bake for 5 minutes. Remove from oven and spread to make top layer. Return to oven and bake 18 minutes longer. Cool before cutting.

If you choose a firmer chewy cookie, refrigerate them. Otherwise room temperature is fine. These are spelled RICH.

*Melt for 3 to 4 minutes in your microwave, if you have one!

## DELUXE BROWNIES

*A new idea on the brownie scene that you will vote for.*

1 box Family size Duncan Hines
   Brownie mix
½ cup chopped pecans
1 16-ounce package chocolate
   chips
4 tablespoons brown sugar
4 tablespoons margarine

Mix brownies following the directions on the box — substituting milk for water. Stir in pecans and chocolate chips. Melt margarine and brown sugar and drizzle over brownies. Bake according to directions on box. Sprinkle with a few pecans.

# BUTTER COOKIES

*These cookies keep for a long time; good to send to college folks.*

**2 cups butter (1 pound real butter)**
**2 cups sugar**
**3 egg yolks**

**1-2 teaspoons vanilla**
**4 cups flour**
**¼ teaspoon soda**

Cream butter, sugar, egg yolks and vanilla in mixer. Add flour and soda and mix well. Roll out in balls. Use a scant teaspoon for each ball. Press down with a fork. Bake on a greased cookie sheet for about 10 to 12 minutes at 350°. Makes 3 to 4 dozen cookies.

# CHESS PIE COOKIES

*Good to make ahead. Very luscious, rich squares.*

**1 box White Cake Mix**
**1 egg, beaten with fork**
**1 stick (¼ pound) butter**

**1 8-ounce package cream cheese**
**2 eggs**
**1 box confectioner's sugar**

Grease two 1-quart Pyrex baking dishes. Heat oven to 350°.

Mix cake mix, 1 egg and butter. This makes a stiff batter. Press half of this batter in each pan with your fingers.

Mix the cream cheese, 2 eggs and confectioner's sugar well with electric mixer. Pour half of this mixture over each of the baking dishes with the cake batter in them.

Bake 35 minutes. Cool thoroughly before cutting in squares. It is really best to let these stand at least 6 hours before cutting. Makes 50 squares.

# CHOCOLATE, CHOCOLATE CHIP COOKIES

*Chocolate lovers, rejoice!! This recipe should warm your hearts, and satisfy your chocolate cravings!! Good keepers, when stored in tins.*

2 sticks margarine
1½ cups sugar
2 eggs
2½ cups flour
1 teaspoon soda
1 teaspoon salt

2 heaping tablespoons cocoa
1 12-ounce package chocolate
  chips
1 teaspoon vanilla
1 cup pecans (optional)

Cream margarine and sugar. Add eggs. Sift together flour, soda, salt and cocoa. Add to creamed mixture. Mix well. Add vanilla and fold in chocolate chips. Drop by teaspoonsful on a lightly greased cookie sheet. Bake 8 to 10 minutes at 350° — 8 minutes for a soft cookie, 10 minutes for a crisper one.

# CHOCOLATE/COCONUT COOKIES

1 15-ounce can sweetened
  condensed milk
½ pound flaked coconut

2 squares unsweetened chocolate,
  melted

Mix all ingredients. Drop from a teaspoon on buttered cookie sheets. Bake 10 to 15 minutes at 325°.

# CHOCOLATE NUT CUPCAKES

*Quick and easy for a small group of teenagers.*

| | |
|---|---|
| 4 squares semi-sweet chocolate | 1 cup sifted flour |
| 2 sticks margarine | 4 eggs |
| 1¾ cups sugar | 1 teaspoon vanilla |
| Dash of salt | 2 cups chopped pecans |

Melt chocolate and margarine. Place in large bowl and add sugar, salt and flour. Stir in eggs, one at a time, and add vanilla and pecans. Pour in paper cups in muffin tins. Bake at 325° for 20 to 25 minutes. Do not overcook. Makes 20 to 24 cupcakes.

# COCONUT-PECAN SQUARES

*These are very delectable!!*

| | |
|---|---|
| ½ cup butter | 1 cup nuts, chopped |
| ½ cup brown sugar (optional) | 1 teaspoon vanilla |
| 1 cup flour | ¼ teaspoon salt |
| 1 cup brown sugar, packed | 1½ cups coconut |
| 2 eggs | ½ teaspoon baking powder |
| 2 tablespoons flour | |

Mix the first three ingredients and spread evenly on bottom of greased 9x9 inch pan. Bake at 350° for 10 minutes.

Mix remaining ingredients. Spread over baked layer and bake at 350° for 20 minutes.

# GINGER COOKIES

1 cup sugar
½ cup chicken fat, melted (yes, dear friends, chicken fat)
1 egg
½ cup dark molasses

½ teaspoon ginger
1 shake cayenne
2¼ cups flour
1 teaspoon baking soda
½ teaspoon salt

Cream sugar and melted fat. Add the egg and molasses. Sift together the dry ingredients and add to the sugar mixture. Roll into small balls and place two inches apart on greased cookie sheets. Bake at 375° for 15 minutes. Makes 3½ dozen.

# HEATH BRICKLE COOKIES

*Crunchy and just plain good!!*

1½ cups sifted flour
½ teaspoon baking soda
¼ teaspoon cinnamon
½ teaspoon salt
½ cup butter or margarine

¼ cup (packed) brown sugar
1 egg
1 teaspoon vanilla
1 bag of Heath Brickle bits
⅓ cup coarsely chopped pecans

Combine and sift flour, soda, cinnamon and salt. Cream butter or margarine. Add sugar, egg and vanilla; mix until smooth and creamy. Stir in dry ingredients. Stir in Heath Brickle and pecans. Drop by teaspoons 2 inches apart onto greased baking sheets. Bake at 350° for 9 minutes. Remove from baking sheets. Makes 3 dozen.

## ICEBOX COOKIES #1

1 pound margarine
2 cups sugar
2 eggs, beaten

5 cups flour
2 teaspoons vanilla
1 cup chopped pecans or walnuts

Cream margarine and sugar. Add beaten eggs. Add flour, a small amount at a time, vanilla and nuts. The dough will be very stiff. Form into 3 or 4 log rolls and refrigerate or freeze. Slice and bake at 350° on greased cookie sheet for 8 to 10 minutes till the edges are brown. Makes 5 to 6 dozen cookies.

## ICEBOX COOKIES #2

1 cup white sugar
1 cup brown sugar
½ cup melted butter
½ cup melted shortening
4½ cups flour
1 heaping teaspoon baking
   powder

1 level teaspoon salt
1 scant teaspoon soda
3 teaspoons cinnamon
1 cup chopped pecans
3 well beaten eggs

Mix all ingredients together. Shape into rolls and refrigerate at least overnight. Slice and bake at 325° on greased cookie sheet about 10 to 12 minutes until edges are brown.

Will also freeze in rolls. Makes 3 to 4 dozen cookies depending upon thickness.

## ICEBOX COOKIES #3

| | |
|---|---|
| 1 cup butter or margarine | ½ teaspoon salt |
| 2 cups brown sugar | 1 teaspoon cream of tartar |
| 2 eggs | 1 teaspoon soda |
| 1 teaspoon vanilla | 1 cup nuts, chopped |
| 4 cups flour | |

Cream butter and sugar. Add eggs, one at a time. Add vanilla. Sift together dry ingredients and add, a little at a time. Stir in nuts. Roll dough in two rolls about 2 inches thick — use waxed paper. Chill completely in refrigerator. Slice thin — about ⅛ inch thick and bake on greased cookie sheet in 350° oven about 8 minutes.

This dough, wrapped well, will keep in freezer. Another way to get uniform slices is to store dough in empty, 6½ ounce orange juice cans. When you want to bake, just remove end from can and push dough out a little at a time and slice.

## MOLASSES COOKIES

*These cookies are rather sticky, but evidently the stickier, the more children love them.*

| | |
|---|---|
| 1 cup molasses | 1 teaspoon cloves |
| 1½ cups seeded raisins | 2 teaspoons cinnamon |
| 1 cup shortening | 2 eggs, unbeaten |
| 2 cups brown sugar | 1 teaspoon salt |
| 4 level teaspoons soda dissolved in ½ cup water | 4½-5 cups flour |

Bring molasses to a boil and pour over raisins. Add shortening and let cool a little. Add remaining ingredients. Drop by teaspoon or roll into balls and flatten with floured fork on greased cookie sheet. Bake in 375° oven for 10 minutes. Do not overcook. Makes about 3 dozen cookies.

## OATMEAL COOKIES

2 sticks butter or margarine
1½ cups sugar
2 eggs, well beaten
1 cup raisins
1 teaspoon soda dissolved in ⅓
   cup warm water

2 cups flour
2 cups oatmeal
1 tablespoon cinnamon
2 cups chopped nuts

Cream margarine and sugar. Add eggs, raisins and soda dissolved in water. Mix flour, oatmeal, cinnamon and nuts together and add to mixture. Drop by teaspoon on greased cookie sheet. Bake at 375° for 15 minutes. Makes 5 to 6 dozen cookies.

## PECAN SQUARES

*1st layer:*
1 stick butter or margarine
¼ cup sugar
1 egg, beaten well
1¼ cups sifted flour
⅛ teaspoon salt
⅓ teaspoon vanilla
*2nd layer:*
2 eggs, beaten well

1½ cups brown sugar
1½ cups chopped pecans
½ teaspoon baking powder
2 tablespoons flour
½ teaspoon salt
*Topping:*
1½ cups confectioner's sugar
   thinned with lemon juice

Make soft dough from ingredients for first layer. Spread this dough on a greased 9x13x2 inch baking pan. Bake at 350° for 15 minutes. Then spread with ingredients mixed for second layer. Put back into 350° degree oven for another 25 minutes. Remove from oven, let cool, and then spread with topping. Cut into squares. (Servings depend on size of squares.)

If you have a food processor, use to do each layer. Freezes very well and left overs can always be refrozen.

## PEPPERMINT FORGOTTEN COOKIES

*These just melt in your mouth, m-m-m good!!*

2 egg whites
¾ cup sugar
1 pinch salt

¼ teaspoon peppermint extract
6-ounce package chocolate chips

Beat egg whites until stiff and glossy, adding sugar a little at a time until all used. Add remaining ingredients. Drop on cookie sheets lined with foil. Heat oven to 350°, put cookies in, turn off heat, and leave cookies in oven 3 hours or more. Makes about 4 dozen cookies.

## TOFFEE COOKIES

1 stick margarine
1 stick butter
1 cup brown sugar, well packed
1 egg yolk, beaten
¼ teaspoon salt

1 teaspoon vanilla
1 cup flour
6 plain Hershey bars, broken
¾ cup pecans, finely chopped

Cream together margarine, butter, brown sugar and egg yolk. Add salt, vanilla and flour and beat well. Spread thinly on *ungreased* cookie sheet to edges. Bake* at 300° degrees for 30 to 35 minutes. Remove from oven and immediately add broken Hershey bars. Spread to coat when melted and sprinkle top with chopped pecans. When cool, cut into bars. Store in refrigerator. Can be frozen. Makes 2½ to 3 dozen.

*The slow, lengthy baking time is the key to this glorious bit of pastry.

# PIES

## WEIRD, BUT WONDERFUL PIE CRUST

*Pies seem to be on the decline and that's sad, but take heart pie devotees. With these crusts in the freezer, ready to be rolled out, pies may be on the upswing!!*

4 cups flour
2 teaspoons salt
1 tablespoon sugar
1¾ cups shortening (prefer Crisco)

1 beaten egg
½ cup water
¼ teaspoon baking powder
1 tablespoon vinegar

Cut the shortening into the flour mixture with a pastry blender until the size of green peas. Then mix freely into the mixture of egg, water, baking powder and vinegar.

Divide and roll into 4 large or 6 small crust balls, pop into Ziploc bags and store in freezer until ready to use. Keeps up to 3 months. When thawed, the dough is very soft so roll it between heavily floured, waxed paper, then place in pie pan.

Dough can be freely handled, so if your crust needs patting or pinching, do so!!

# PAPER BAG APPLE PIE

*Apple pie with a new baking idea! It's actually baked inside a big brown grocery bag. Apples cook just right — no juices bubble into the oven.*

1 unbaked 9 inch pastry shell
6-8 large baking apples, about 3
  pounds
½ cup sugar for filling
2 tablespoons flour for filling
½ teaspoon nutmeg

2 tablespoons lemon juice
½ cup sugar for topping
½ cup flour for topping
½ cup (1 stick) butter or
  margarine

Make 9-inch pastry shell. Pare, core and quarter apples, then halve each quarter and place in large bowl.

Combine ½ cup sugar, 2 tablespoons flour and nutmeg in a cup. Sprinkle over apples. Toss to coat well and spoon into pastry shell. Drizzle with lemon juice. Combine ½ cup sugar and ½ cup flour for topping in bowl. Cut in butter or margarine and sprinkle over apples. Slide pie into a brown bag. Fold open end twice, fasten with a paper clip or stapler and place on a cookie sheet.

Bake at 425° for 1 hour. (Apples will be tender and top will be bubbly and golden.) Split bag open, remove pie and cool on wire rack.

Serve plain or with cheese or ice cream. This will freeze.

# BANANA PIE

1 6-ounce box instant vanilla
  pudding
1 cup milk
1 cup sour cream
4 bananas (sliced)

1 baked pie shell, regular or
  graham cracker
½ pint whipping cream or Cool
  Whip

Mix pudding mix and milk and beat until thick. Add sour cream and blend well. Add sliced bananas and pour into baked pie shell. Top with whipped cream or Cool Whip. Place in refrigerator until ready to serve. Serves 6 to 8.

# BANANA SPLIT PIE

| | |
|---|---|
| 1 pound box powdered sugar | 5 bananas |
| 2 eggs | 1 20-ounce can crushed pineapple |
| 1 stick margarine or butter | 1 graham cracker crust |
| 1 teaspoon vanilla | Cool Whip |

Beat sugar, eggs, margarine and vanilla for 10 minutes on medium high speed. Spread on graham cracker crust made in a 9x12 inch pan. Cut and lay bananas lengthwise on filling. Drain pineapple and spread over bananas. Spread Cool Whip on top. Chopped cherries and nuts can be added if desired.

This recipe can be made the night before and is delicious. Add Cool Whip just before serving.

Serves 12 to 15.

# BULLFROG PIE

*Rich, dinner party type pie, not for los niños.*

| | |
|---|---|
| 1¼ cups chocolate wafers, crumbled | 20 marshmallows |
| ½ cup melted butter | 1 cup heavy cream, whipped |
| *Filling:* | 1 ounce crème de menthe |
| ½ cup milk | 1 ounce white crème de cacao |
| | 1 ounce brandy |

Mix the crumbled wafers and melted butter and press into a 9-inch pie pan. Chill while you are making the filling.

Heat milk in a double boiler. Add marshmallows and stir until melted. Cool thoroughly. Combine the cream with the flavorings and fold into the marshmallow mixture. Pour into the chilled crust and chill for 2 to 3 hours, until firm. Serves 6 to 8.

## BUTTERMILK PIE

1 9-inch pie shell
2 cups sugar
2 tablespoons flour
1 stick butter or margarine

3 eggs, beaten
1½ cups buttermilk
2 tablespoons lemon extract

Mix sugar and flour; cream with butter until light and fluffy. Add remaining ingredients, mixing well, and pour into crust. Bake at 325° for 45 minutes. Serves 8.

## EASY CHOCOLATE ALMOND PIE

1 graham cracker crust
1 large (4½ ounce) chocolate
  almond bar
16 large marshmallows or ⅔ jar
  marshmallow cream

¼-½ cup milk
½ teaspoon vanilla
2 tablespoons crème de cacao
½ pint whipping cream, whipped

Combine chocolate and milk over low heat in top of double boiler. Melt marshmallows with the milk and chocolate. Cool. Add vanilla and crème de cacao. Fold in whipped creme. Pour into crust and chill. Sprinkle with shaved chocolate or finely chopped nuts. Serves 6 to 8.

## GERMAN SWEET CHOCOLATE PIE

*This is an impressive bit of confectionary, especially if you like a coconut and chocolate combination.*

1 10-inch pie shell
1 4-ounce package German Sweet chocolate
¼ cup margarine
1 13-ounce can evaporated milk
1½ cups sugar

3 tablespoons corn starch
⅛ teaspoon salt
2 eggs
1 teaspoon vanilla
1⅓ cups Angel Flake coconut
½ cup pecans, chopped

Melt chocolate with margarine over low heat. Stir until blended. Remove from heat; gradually blend in milk. Mix sugar, corn starch and salt. Beat in eggs and vanilla. Gradually blend in chocolate mixture. Pour into pie shell. Mix coconut and pecans; sprinkle over filling. Bake at 375° for 45 minutes or until top is puffed. Filling will be soft, but will set while cooling. Cool at least 4 hours before serving.

## COFFEE SUNDAE PIE

*Good for that notable dinner party!!*

*Crust ingredients:*
18 Oreo chocolate cookies
⅓ cup melted butter
*Filling:*
2 squares unsweetened chocolate
½ cup sugar

1 tablespoon butter
⅔ cup condensed milk
1 quart coffee ice cream
1 cup heavy cream, whipped
1 ounce crème de cacao
2 tablespoons shaved chocolate

Crush cookies to fine crumbs, add melted butter, mix well, and pat into a 9-inch pie shell. Chill.

Melt chocolate in double boiler; stir in sugar and butter. Slowly add milk. Cook, stirring occasionally, until thickened and coats spoon. Chill.

Fill pie shell with coffee ice cream and spread chocolate mixture over top of ice cream. Add crème de cacao to whipped cream. Spoon over chocolate and sprinkle with shaved chocolate. Serves 6. May be frozen.

## CRUSTLESS PECAN PIE

2 eggs
½ cup sifted flour
1 cup sugar
¼ teaspoon salt

6 tablespoons melted butter
1 teaspoon vanilla
¾ cup chopped nuts
1 cup coconut (optional)

Beat eggs 1 minute. Add flour, sugar and salt. Continue beating until smooth. Add remaining ingredients and mix well.

Pour into greased and floured 9 inch pie pan. Bake 30 minutes at 325°. Cool, cut in wedges and serve with whipped cream or ice cream.

## PINEAPPLE CHEESE PIE

*Wow — is this a candidate for a blue ribbon!!*

1 unbaked 9-inch pie shell
⅓ cup sugar
1 tablespoon corn starch
1 9-ounce can crushed pineapple
1 8-ounce package cream cheese
½ cup sugar

1 teaspoon salt
2 eggs
½ cup milk
½ teaspoon vanilla
¼ cup chopped pecans

Blend the sugar and corn starch together and add to the pineapple, juice included. Cook, stirring constantly, until the mixture is thick and clear. Cool.

Blend cream cheese, softened at room temperature, with remaining sugar and salt. Add the two eggs, one at a time, stirring well after each addition. Blend in the milk and vanilla.

Spread cooled pineapple mixture over the bottom of a 9-inch unbaked pie shell. Pour in cream cheese mixture and sprinkle top with pecans. Bake at 400° for 10 minutes, then reduce heat to 325° and bake for 50 minutes. Cool and serve. Serves 6 to 8.

## PUMPKIN PIE FOR PEOPLE
## WHO HATE PUMPKIN PIE

1½ cups sugar
¾ stick of margarine
1 can of Milnot milk — on the grocery shelf with condensed milk
1 teaspoon nutmeg

1 teaspoon cinnamon
1 teaspoon vanilla
Dash of salt
3 eggs, beaten
1 tablespoon cornstarch
½ cup canned pumpkin

Cream sugar and margarine. Add the rest of ingredients and blend well. Pour into a 9-inch pie shell. Bake at 375 for 35 to 45 minutes or until knife comes out clean. Serves 6 to 8.

## CREAMY RAISIN PIE

*Try this. It is a real switch on the raisin story, and it is yummy!*

1 cup raisins
1 cup sugar
1 heaping tablespoon flour
1 cup sour cream
3 eggs, separated

1 teaspoon cinnamon
¼ teaspoon cloves
1 teaspoon vanilla
½ cup pecans, chopped
Baked pie shell

Cover raisins with water and cook until all water is absorbed. Add sugar, flour, sour cream, egg yolks, cinnamon and cloves. Cook until thick. Add vanilla and nuts. Pour into a baked pie shell. Use the egg whites to make a meringue. Top pie filling. Brown in hot oven. Let cool completely; refrigerate an hour or so before serving.

# SINFUL SUNDAE PIE

*Oh my, this is so wickedly good, there should be a law prohibiting it!!*
*Easy, too!!*

Vanilla wafers
1 cup evaporated milk
1 cup tiny marshmallows
1 6-ounce package chocolate chips

Dash of salt
2 pints vanilla ice cream, softened
  in refrigerator (don't allow to
  melt)

Line a 9-inch pie pan, bottom and sides, with vanilla wafers. Combine milk, marshmallows, chocolate chips and salt in saucepan. Cook and stir until blended and thick. Cool slightly. Spoon 1 pint of the softened ice cream into wafer shell. Spoon half of chocolate sauce over ice cream. Spoon in other pint of ice cream, then spoon on rest of chocolate mixture. Pop in the freezer right now!! Freeze for at least 4 hours. Serves 8 to 10. Will keep up to two weeks in the freezer.

# DESSERTS

## BAKED APRICOT TRIFLE

| | |
|---|---|
| 1 8-ounce jelly roll | 1 pint half and half |
| 1 15-ounce can apricots | 3 level tablespoons sugar |
| 4 tablespoons brandy | Grated nutmeg |
| 2 whole eggs | 1 10-ounce carton whipping cream |
| 2 egg yolks | Split toasted almonds |

Slice jelly roll into 12 pieces and line base and sides of a 1½ quart oven-proof dish. Drain and quarter apricots reserving 2 tablespoons of the juice. Spoon the apricots into the dish with 2 tablespoons of juice. Pour on the brandy to soak the jelly roll well. Beat the whole eggs and egg yolks together. Add half and half and sugar. Heat sufficiently to dissolve the sugar. Strain carefully into the dish to avoid disturbing the jelly roll slices. Sprinkle on grated nutmeg. Cover with a greased, waxed paper. Bake at 325° for 1 to 1¼ hours or until just set. Cool. Decorate with whipped cream and chill well. Sprinkle with toasted almonds before serving. Serves 6.

## BANANA PUDDING

*You will either love it or hate it. There's no in between, but if you like banana and peanut butter sandwiches, you should love it!*

| | |
|---|---|
| 1 egg | 1 tablespoon butter |
| 2 tablespoons sugar | 1 tablespoon cream |
| 2 tablespoons vinegar | 2 large bananas |
| Pinch of salt | Crushed salted peanuts |

Beat egg. Add sugar, vinegar and salt. Stir and cook slowly until it thickens. When it begins to thicken, add butter. When it cools, add cream. Slice bananas and stir into custard. Sprinkle peanuts on top. Serves 4-6.

# CHEESE CAKE

*If you are dieting, turn the page quick!*

*Crust:*
1⅓ cups mashed graham crackers
  (1 package in a 16-ounce box of
  grahams)
¼ cup sugar
6 tablespoons butter (3/4 stick)
*Filling:*
3 8-ounce packages Philadelphia
  cream cheese (room
  temperature)

4 eggs
1 cup sugar
½ pint sour cream
2 teaspoons vanilla
1 teaspoon baking powder

For the crust, blend all crust ingredients. Butter a spring-form cake pan. Add cracker mixture and pat against bottom and sides. (A large pie pan may be used.)

For the filling, blend all filling ingredients. Pour into the buttered pan and bake in a pre-heated 350° oven for 45 minutes.

# CHERRY BERRY

*Maybe this recipe is the reason old George chopped down the tree — to get the cherries for Cherry Berry.*

1 stick margarine
1 cup flour
1½ cups pecans
1 package Dream Whip

1 8-ounce package Philadelphia
  cream cheese
1 pound box powdered sugar
1 can cherry pie filling

*Crust:* Use a 9x13x2 cake pan. Melt margarine. Sprinkle flour over the melted margarine. Spread pecans evenly over flour mixture. Bake at 350° for 20 minutes and cool completely.

*Filling:* Mix Dream Whip according to box directions. Blend powdered sugar into softened cream cheese. Fold into Dream Whip and pour into crust. Top with cherry pie filling. Cut in squares. Serves 8-10.

## COFFEE CRUNCH DESSERT

1 cup vanilla wafer crumbs (about
   24 wafers)
2 tablespoons butter, melted
½ cup butter
1 cup powdered sugar
3 eggs, separated

2 teaspoons instant coffee
1 1-ounce square unsweetened
   chocolate, melted and cooled
½ teaspoon vanilla
¼ cup sugar
1 package Heath Bar Chips

Blend crumbs and melted butter. Press into bottom of an 8x8-inch pan. Cream butter and sugar till fluffy. Blend in egg yolks, instant coffee, unsweetened chocolate and vanilla. Stiffly beat egg whites with ¼ cup sugar. Fold into creamed mixture. Spread over crust. Top with crushed candy. Freeze until firm. Serves 6 to 8.

## BOILED CUSTARD

1 quart milk
2 heaping tablespoons flour
1 cup sugar

Pinch of salt
2 eggs, separated
1 teaspoon vanilla

Scald milk. Mix flour, sugar and salt together. Beat egg whites until stiff. Add one egg yolk at a time, beat well. Add sugar and flour to eggs and mix with a spoon until blended. Add to scalded milk in double boiler.

Cook 5 to 10 minutes until it thickens. Chill and add vanilla. Serve with whipped cream. Serves 4 to 6.

# BOURBON CHARLOTTE

*BEAUTIFUL!!*

3 eggs, separated
6 heaping tablespoons sugar
½ cup hot milk
½ package unflavored gelatin,
   dissolved in water

1 pint whipping cream
1 package lady fingers
Bourbon

Beat egg yolks with sugar and stir in hot milk. Add dissolved gelatin. Cool. Add stiffly beaten egg whites. Add whipped cream. Line bowl with the lady fingers and sprinkle with bourbon. Refrigerate until serving time. Can be decorated with additional whipped cream and maraschino cherries. Serves 8.

# BUTTERSCOTCH ICE CREAM DESSERT

Crust and topping
½ cup butter or margarine
¼ cup brown sugar
1 cup flour

½ cup chopped pecans
1 6 to 7-ounce jar of butterscotch
   sauce (Kraft)
⅔ of ½ gallon vanilla ice cream

Soften the ice cream. Mix the margarine, brown sugar, flour and pecans and put them on a cookie sheet or pan and heat for 20 minutes in a 325° oven. Stir. Pour ⅔ of the mixture on the bottom of an 8x8 inch pan. Pour ½ of the butterscotch sauce over the crumbs. Then spread the softened ice cream. Pour the rest of the butterscotch sauce and top with the remaining crumbs. Freeze. Serves 9-16 depending on the size of the pieces.

# DIETER'S DELIGHT

*Everyone is on a diet, so try this one at your next gathering when the fresh strawberries are in season.*

½ cup sour cream
½ cup Dream Whip, the already mixed kind — look in the dairy case

1 tablespoon brown sugar
1 tablespoon rum
1 tablespoon orange liqueur
20 large strawberries, with stems

Blend all ingredients except strawberries. Put berries in pretty bowls for 4. Pass sour cream mixture as topping.

# FROZEN LEMON CRUNCH

*Light, lemony and luscious!!*

½ cup butter
¼ cup brown sugar
1 cup flour
½ cup coconut, flaked
3 eggs, separated

½ cup and 2 tablespoons sugar
3 tablespoons lemon juice
1 cup cream
1 teaspoon grated lemon rind

Blend first 4 ingredients. Reserve ¾ cup for topping. Crumble and spread in 9x13x2-inch pan. Bake at 375° for 20 minutes. Cool.

Beat egg yolks until light yellow. Gradually add ½ cup sugar and beat until thick and light. Add lemon juice and rind and beat.

In a separate bowl, beat egg whites until stiff. Add the remaining sugar. Whip the cream and fold into the egg whites. Fold in the egg yolk mixture. Pour into a crust. Add topping and freeze. Serves 8.

# LEMON CHARLOTTE

*So elegant! Whispers of hoop skirts, Southern Belles, and memorable plantation parties.*

2 envelopes gelatin
½ cup cold water
8 eggs, separated
1 cup lemon juice
1 teaspoon salt

2 cups sugar
2 teaspoons lemon rind, finely grated
1 cup whipping cream
20 lady fingers

Soften gelatin in water. In a double boiler, combine egg yolks, lemon juice, salt and 1 cup sugar. Cook over boiling water, stirring constantly, until mixture coats back of spoon. Into custard, stir softened gelatin and finely grated lemon rind. Cool.

In large bowl, beat egg whites until they hold shape. Gradually beat in the other cup of sugar until mixture holds peaks.

Whip cream and gently fold mixtures together. Line sides of a 9-inch spring-form pan with about 20 split lady fingers. Spoon in mixture and smooth on top. Refrigerate 8 to 12 hours. Remove sides of pan and slide onto plate. The top may be decorated with strawberries and mint leaves. Serves 12.

# LEMON ICE CREAM

*This recipe is delicious and rich.*

6 lemons, juiced
4 cups sugar
1 teaspoon grated lemon rind

6 cups whipping cream
3 cups milk

Mix lemon juice, sugar and rind and combine with cream and milk. Freeze in electric freezer. You may wish to add a few drops of yellow food coloring. Makes 5 quarts.

# PEPPERMINT ICE CREAM

*This is a very smooth ice cream and is wonderful
after a heavy meal.*

1 quart milk, scalded
6 eggs, well beaten
2½ cups sugar
14 ounces peppermint candy,
 crushed

1 14½-ounce can evaporated milk
½ pint whipped cream
2 teaspoons vanilla

To scald milk, heat until just below boiling. Add beaten eggs and sugar. Cook until mixture coats the spoon. Add peppermint and stir until candies are dissolved. Cool thoroughly. Strain through large strainer and add evaporated milk, cream and vanilla. Pour into a one gallon freezer container and add enough milk to fill can to within 5 inches of the top. Freeze in ice cream freezer as you would any other ice cream.

# CAPPUCINO PARFAIT

*Sigh! How can anything so simple be so perfect?*

Coffee ice cream
*Butterscotch Sauce:*
½ cup butter
1½ cups light brown sugar
⅛ teaspoon salt

2 tablespoons corn syrup
½ cup heavy cream
½ teaspoon ground cinnamon
1 teaspoon grated orange rind

Melt butter in saucepan; add light brown sugar, salt and light or dark corn syrup. Bring to a boil and cook until sugar is dissolved. Gradually add ½ cup heavy cream, stirring constantly, and bring to boiling point again. Cool.

Stir cinnamon and grated orange rind into 1½ cups cooled butterscotch sauce. Alternate coffee ice cream and sauce in 10 to 12 parfait glasses. Freeze until serving time. Top with whipped cream and grated orange rind if desired. Serves 10 to 12.

## "DELISH" STRAWBERRY DELIGHT

*This is a very pretty dessert. It would be especially attractive served in large wine goblets.*

2 pint boxes strawberries
½ cup sugar
⅓ cup Cointreau

1 pint vanilla ice cream
1 cup whipping cream
½ teaspoon almond extract

Gently wash strawberries in cold water, drain and hull. Turn into a large bowl and sprinkle with sugar and Cointreau. Toss gently. Refrigerate for 1 hour, stirring occasionally. Let the ice cream soften in refrigerator for approximately 30 minutes. Beat cream until stiff. Fold in almond extract. Gently fold whipped cream into strawberry mixture, then mix into ice cream. Serve at once. Serves 8.

## HOT FUDGE SUNDAE CAKE

*Sheer delight to chocolate addicts.*

1 cup flour
¾ cup granulated sugar
2 tablespoons cocoa
2 teaspoons baking powder
¼ teaspoon salt
½ cup milk

2 tablespoons cooking oil (prefer Wesson)
1 teaspoon vanilla
1 cup brown sugar, packed
¼ cup cocoa
1¾ cups hottest tap water

Preheat oven to 350°. In an ungreased 9x9x2 inch pan, stir together flour, granulated sugar, 2 tablespoons cocoa, baking powder and salt. Stir in milk, oil and vanilla with a fork until smooth. Spread evenly in pan. Sprinkle with the brown sugar and ¼ cup cocoa. Pour the hot water over the batter. Bake for 40 minutes. Let stand for 15 to 20 minutes and cut into squares. Invert each square onto a dessert plate. Spoon sauce over each serving. Serves 9. You may wish to put a dip of ice cream on the square, then the hot fudge sauce, but if you do we will tell Weight Watchers!

# FROZEN PEACH TORTE

*Peachy-keen!*

2 cups mashed fresh peaches (or
frozen peach halves)
1¼ cups sugar
1 tablespoon lemon juice
1 cup whipping cream, whipped
stiff

1 cup coarse macaroon crumbs
(you will have to get these from
your bakery)

Combine the mashed peaches, sugar and lemon juice and fold in the whipped cream. Place ½ cup coarse macaroon crumbs in the bottom of a refrigerator ice cube tray or square pan. Pour in the peach mixture. Top with additional ½ cup crumbs. Freeze firm, which should take about 4 to 6 hours. Serves 6 to 8.

# PEACHES AND CHERRIES
# IN PORT WINE

*An adult treat for that special dinner party.*

2 cans pitted Bing cherries
4 large fresh peaches (canned may
be substituted; drain well)
¾ cup Port wine

1 tablespoon sugar
2 tablespoons grated lemon peel
1 inch stick cinnamon
Sour cream

Drain cherries, reserving 1 cup liquid. Peel peaches, halve and remove pits. In skillet, combine cherry liquid, port wine, sugar, lemon peel and cinnamon. Bring to a boil, stirring. Boil uncovered for 1 minute. Add peaches and simmer 5 minutes. Add cherries and simmer, covered, for 5 minutes. Remove cinnamon. Refrigerate until well chilled — overnight perhaps. Place sour cream in separate small bowl and serve. Will serve 8. Can be made a day ahead.

## PEARS AND RASPBERRIES OVER ICE CREAM

*When you want to do an elegant, but simple dessert this is the answer.*

1 cup water
¼ cup sugar
1 teaspoon vanilla
4 medium fresh pears

1 10-ounce package frozen
  raspberries, thawed
2 tablespoons Cognac
4 scoops vanilla ice cream

Cut pears in half and remove core and seeds. In a heavy skillet combine water, sugar and vanilla. Bring to a boil. Add pears, cover and simmer until tender, 8 to 10 minutes, turning pears once. Remove pears with slotted spoon, draining juice back into skillet. In the meantime, drain raspberries and reserve syrup. Add raspberry syrup to liquid in skillet. Boil hard to reduce liquid to about ⅓ cup. Remove from heat and add Cognac. Cool slightly. To serve, place pears on ice cream. Place raspberries over pears and drizzle with raspberry syrup. Serve at once. Serves 4.

## GRAPE-NUT PUDDING

*Good dessert to end a heavy meal.*

¼ cup margarine
1 cup sugar
2 eggs, separated
3 tablespoons Grapenuts

1 cup milk
1 tablespoon flour
Juice of 1 lemon and grated lemon
  rind

Cream margarine and sugar; add well beaten egg yolks. Add the other ingredients. Gently fold in stiffly beaten egg whites. Set in a pan of boiling water and bake at 350° for about 30 minutes. There will be a crust on top of the pudding with a thinner jelly-like mixture underneath. Serve warm with whipped cream.

## WINE JELLY

2 packages unflavored gelatin
½ cup cold water
1⅔ cups boiling water
1 cup sugar

1 cup Sherry
⅓ cup orange juice
3 tablespoons lemon juice

Soak the gelatin in ½ cup cold water. Add to the boiling water and dissolve the gelatin. Add the other ingredients. Pour into individual molds (6 to 8, depending on size) and chill. Serve with our boiled custard recipe.

# CANDY

## APRICOT CANDY

1 pound dried apricots
Juice and rind of 1 orange

2 cups sugar
1 cup pecans, chopped

Chop apricots and rind of orange. Add juice and sugar. Cook 8 minutes, stirring. Add nuts. Let cool in ice box several hours. Roll into small balls and roll in powdered sugar. Makes 3 to 4 dozen.

## BUTTERSCOTCH PECAN FUDGE

5 tablespoons butter
1¼ cups brown sugar
1¼ cups white sugar

1 cup sour cream
1 teaspoon vanilla
1 cup pecans, chopped

Melt butter in heavy pan. Add brown sugar and heat to boiling. Add granulated sugar and sour cream. Cook over low heat; stir until sugar is dissolved. Cook to soft ball stage (234-240 degrees F). Cool to lukewarm, then beat until stiff. Add vanilla and pecans. Pour into greased 8x8 inch square pan and let cool. Cut into squares. Makes 30 small squares.

## ELLEN'S CRUNCHIES

1 12-ounce package of
  butterscotch morsels
1 cup of crunchy peanut butter

5 or 6 cups of Kellogg's
  Cornflakes, or Product 19 or
  Special K

Melt morsels in double boiler, then add peanut butter. Remove from heat, pour over cereal, drop by teaspoonfuls onto cookie sheet. Place in refrigerator for 10 minutes to harden. If you are one of those people who believes there is only one flavor in the world — chocolate — well then, use chocolate morsels.

## TWO FLAVOR FUDGE

1 14½-ounce can sweetened
  condensed milk
1 6-ounce package of chocolate
  chips

1 6-ounce package of butterscotch
  morsels
1 cup pecans, coarsely chopped
1½ teaspoons vanilla

Mix the milk, chocolate chips and butterscotch morsels in the top of a double boiler. Stir occasionally and remove from heat when melted. Add nuts and vanilla. Form one wide flat ring or two small ones or pour into a 9 inch square pan. Chill and place a small sprig of holly on the ring to form into a wreath.

## PEANUT BUTTER CUPS

*If chocolate and peanut butter is your love, this is especially for you.*

2½ tablespoons paraffin
4 Nèstle's chocolate bars
1 6-ounce package of chocolate
   chips

1 scant tablespoon of creamy
   peanut butter
1 cup of crunchy peanut butter

Mix paraffin, Nèstle's chocolate bars and chocolate chips in the top of a double boiler. Add creamy peanut butter into mixture and stir over boiling water until all is melted. Place little bon-bon fluted paper cups in small muffin tins (makes it easier to handle). Use a small spoon to coat the bottom and sides of paper cup with chocolate mixture. When cool, about ten minutes, drop ¼ teaspoon of the crunch peanut butter into each chocolate cup. Top with remaining chocolate mixture in the double boiler over the hot water. Allow to harden several hours before storing. Makes about 24, more if you don't spoon chocolate too thick in cups. Keeps well in a tin for at least a week.

## PEANUT PATTIES

*Peanut patties, moon pies and RC colas, hot dog!!*

2½ cups sugar
1 cup milk
⅔ cup white corn syrup
¼ teaspoon salt

1½ cups raw peanuts
1 tablespoon butter or margarine
1 teaspoon vanilla

Mix sugar with milk and corn syrup. Bring to a boil over medium heat, stirring constantly, until sugar is dissolved. Add salt and raw peanuts and cook, stirring occasionally, until a small amount of the syrup forms a firm ball when dropped into cold water (246 degrees F). Remove from heat. Add butter and vanilla. Beat until mixture begins to thicken. Drop rapidly into buttered muffin pans. Let stand until cool and set.

# TIPSEY TURTLES

*Gosh, this is definitely a winner!! So good and gooey and chocolaty, you can't eat just one!!*

1 pound Kraft caramels (melt this in a microwave if you can)
2 tablespoons butter
2 tablespoons brandy

2 cups pecan halves
8 ounces semi-sweet chocolate squares (or sweet, if you prefer)

Melt caramels in butter and brandy in the top of a double boiler. When thoroughly melted, remove from heat and let stand for about 10 minutes.

Using 4 pecans make a turtle shape. Using a teaspoon, carefully spoon caramel on pecans, covering the center only. Leave the tips showing. Let cool completely — about 30 minutes. Melt chocolate in the top of a double boiler. Cool to lukewarm, spoon over caramel and leave the pecan tips showing. Makes 3 to 3½ dozen.

# KAHLUA TRUFFLES

*We like to use these for a dinner party on a big tray with cheeses, Carr's wafers, fresh strawberries, grapes. It is pretty and to your advantage the truffles freeze. Neat?*

12 ounces semi-sweet chocolate
4 egg yolks
⅓ cup Kahlúa

⅔ cup sweet butter
Ground nuts, pecans, almonds, walnuts, your choice

Melt the chocolate in top of double boiler over simmering water. When melted, remove from heat and cool to room temperature, *this is most important.* Add yolks, one at a time, stirring constantly until thoroughly blended. Mix in Kahlúa and return to simmering water for 2-3 minutes, stirring constantly. Pour mixture into bowl of electric mixer and beat in butter, a tablespoon at a time. Continue beating mixture until it is airy and fluffy in texture. Cover with plastic wrap and refrigerate for 4 to 5 hours or overnight. Roll by teaspoon in nuts. Refrigerate until ready to use. If you wish to freeze the truffles, place them in a container with wax paper between layers. Makes 3 dozen.

# WAVERLY CANDY

*It is yummy and no one can believe it has crackers in the mixture.*

**9 sections of fresh Waverly wafers**　**1 cup pecans, chopped**
**1 cup butter**　**1½ cups chocolate chips (optional)**
**1 cup brown sugar**

Heavily grease a 9x13 inch Pyrex dish. Lay crackers in the bottom of the pan. Melt butter and brown sugar with pecans. Boil 3 minutes. Pour over crackers. Bake at 350° for 10 minutes. Melt the chocolate chips over hot water. Spread on top of crackers 2 minutes after they are done. Let cool before you cut. Makes approximately 1 pound.

# JAMS AND JELLIES

# JAMS/JELLIES/PRESERVES

### CALIFORNIA CONSERVE

*Great for Christmas gifts.*

1 orange
2 lemons
1 pound dried figs (about 20 or 25)
2 cups water

1 1¾-ounce package fruit pectin
5 cups sugar
1 3½-ounce can flaked coconut

Slice oranges and lemons paper thin. Then cut each slice into quarters. Slice figs. Combine oranges, lemons, figs and water. Bring to a boil in a large kettle and simmer covered for 30 minutes. Add pectin and mix well. Stir over high heat until mixture comes to a hard boil. Stir in sugar at once. Bring to a full rolling boil; boil hard 1 minute, stirring constantly. Remove from heat; add coconut. Ladle into sterilized jelly glasses. Fills 10 6-ounce glasses.

### EASY STRAWBERRY JAM

2 10-ounce packages frozen sliced
    strawberries, thawed
2½ cups sugar

¼ of a 6 ounce bottle of fruit
    pectin
Melted paraffin

Combine strawberries and sugar in a heavy saucepan and mix well. Bring to a boil over high heat and boil rapidly 1 minute, stirring constantly. Remove from heat and immediately stir in fruit pectin. Skim off foam with a metal spoon, then stir and skim 5 minutes to cool slightly and to prevent fruit from floating. Ladle into sterilized jars and seal at once with ⅛ inch paraffin. Cool completely. Makes about 3 cups.

You may substitute frozen raspberries if your family prefers.

## FIG STRAWBERRY PRESERVES

*Figs may be peeled, but the texture of unpeeled
figs is good - and different.*

3 cups ripe figs
3 cups sugar
1 6-ounce package of strawberry
  jello (or raspberry, if you
  prefer)

1 tablespoon lemon juice

Put figs through the blender. Mix all ingredients and let stand for 30 minutes, stirring occasionally. Then cook 3 to 6 minutes, stirring constantly. Put in hot, boiled preserving jars and seal. It is best when chilled.

## GRANOLA

*Instead of the usual graham cracker crust, substitute
crushed granola in making pie crust.*

5 cups rolled oats
1 cup sesame seeds
1 cup wheat germ
1 cup coconut
1 cup soy flour
1 cup almonds, chopped

1 cup sunflower seeds
1 cup vegetable oil
1 cup honey
1 cup golden raisins (or regular
  raisins)

Combine the first 7 ingredients. Mix the vegetable oil and honey together and pour over the dry mixture. Mix well. Place in a large pan and cook at 300° for 1 hour. Stir and watch very carefully for the last 20 minutes. Remove and add the raisins. Makes a ton! We like to fill decorative jars with the granola as gifts.

# JALAPEÑO JELLY

¾ cup bell pepper (remove seeds)
¼ cup jalapeño (remove seeds)
1½ cups cider vinegar
6½ cups sugar
Green food coloring
1 6-ounce bottle of Certo

Blend bell peppers and jalapeños in blender or food processor. Mix vinegar and sugar in a sauce pan and then add the pepper mixture. Bring to a rolling boil for 2 to 3 minutes. Remove from heat. Skim and stir for 10 minutes. Add a few drops of food coloring and then the Certo. Mix well and put in sterilized jars. This makes about 7 to 8½ pints.

# PEARS FOR PORK

*This is an unusual accompaniment for pork.*

3 fresh winter pears (can be hard)
½ cup red Spanish onion, finely
   chopped
1 tablespoon margarine
1 cup bread crumbs — any kind
¼ cup plump golden raisins,
   chopped
2 tablespoons drippings from
   pork roast (can substitute 1
   tablespoon bacon grease)
¼ teaspoon salt
Dash of pepper

Core and halve pears. Sauté onion in margarine until soft. Add remaining ingredients and stir until mixed well. Spoon dressing into pear halves. Bake in a buttered pan at 350° for 30 minutes or place around the pork roast for the last 30 minutes of cooking.

If you are not using this with a pork roast and no drippings are available, you can substitute part melted bacon grease and part margarine. Just a little, though, or it will be too greasy.

Serves 6.

## PEAR RELISH

3 pounds pears, peeled and cored
1½ pounds small white onions,
    peeled
7 sweet green peppers, seeded
1 sweet red pepper, seeded
¼ cup salt

2 cups sugar
2 cups vinegar
1 tablespoon mustard seeds
1 teaspoon tumeric
¼ teaspoon cayenne pepper

Put pears through medium blade of food chopper. Measure 4½ cups into a large bowl. Put onions and peppers through medium blade of food chopper. Mix and measure 6½ cups. Add peppers and onions to the pears. Stir in salt and let stand for 4 hours. Rinse pear and pepper mixture three times in cold water draining after each time. In a large preserving kettle, combine sugar, vinegar and spices. Bring to a boil and boil for 5 minutes. Add the pear and pepper mixture and simmer for 5 minutes. Place in hot, sterilized jars and seal with hot paraffin. Makes 10 to 12 half-pints.

## PICKLED BLACK EYED PEAS

*Gotta have black eyes on New Year's to have a prosperous year!!*

2 cans black eyed peas or 2 pints
    cooked dried or fresh black
    eyed peas
1 medium onion, thinly sliced
¼ cup wine vinegar
1 teaspoon pickling spices (tied in
    a small square of cheese cloth)

½ teaspoon salt
½ teaspoon sugar
Freshly ground pepper to taste
1 cup salad oil
1 clove of garlic
1 teaspoon pimiento, finely
    minced

Place peas and onions in a bowl. Heat vinegar, spices, salt, sugar and pepper to boiling. Pour over peas. Add remaining ingredients and mix thoroughly. Pour into a large jar and store in refrigerator at least two days before serving. Remove garlic clove and spice bag after one day.

# SANGRIA JELLY

*Good for Christmas gifts.*

1½ cups burgundy
¼ cup orange juice
2 tablespoons lemon juice

2 tablespoons orange liqueur
3 cups sugar
½ of 6-ounce bottle Certo

Combine wine, juices and liqueur in top of double boiler. Stir in sugar. Place over, but not touching, boiling water and stir until sugar is dissolved, about 3 to 4 minutes. Remove from heat. At once, stir in Certo and mix well. Fill jars with hot syrup to within ⅛ inch of top and seal with paraffin. Makes 4 cups. Serve with hot, buttered flour tortillas and breakfast eggs. Or serve with meat.

# STRAWBERRY/BLUEBERRY JAM

1 quart ripe strawberries
1 quart ripe blueberries (frozen
  ones may be used)

5½ cups sugar
1¾ box powdered fruit pectin

Stem, wash the berries and crush them. Measure the 4 cups into a large, deep pan. Measure and set aside the sugar. Place the berries over high heat and stir until they come to a rolling boil. Immediately add all the sugar, again stirring until a rolling boil is reached. Boil hard for 1 minute, stirring constantly. Remove from the heat and skim off the foam with a metal spoon. Stir and skim for 5 minutes to cool slightly. This prevents floating fruit. Spoon the jam into sterilized jars and cover at once with ¼ inch hot paraffin. This makes about 6 or 7 half pint jars. A pretty and slightly different tasting jam.

# TOMATO AND PEPPER RELISH

8 quarts green tomatoes
12 sweet red peppers
12 sweet green peppers
12 hot green peppers

1 quart small onions
3 quarts cider vinegar
5 cups sugar
½ cup salt

Wash and rinse 12 pint preserve jars. Place in a deep kettle of cold water. Cover and bring to a boil. Boil for 20 minutes. Leave jars in water until ready to use.

Wash, remove stems, and quarter tomatoes. Wash sweet peppers, remove seeds and fibrous portions, and quarter. Cut stems from hot peppers. Peel and quarter onions. Put all these ingredients through a food chopper. Place ground vegetables in a colander and drain off liquid, discarding it.

Put vegetables in a large kettle and add 2 quarts of the vinegar. Boil, uncovered, for 30 minutes, stirring frequently. Again drain vegetables and discard liquid. Return to kettle. Stir in the remaining 1 quart of vinegar, sugar, and salt. Simmer for 3 minutes. Pour immediately into sterilized jars and seal. Makes 12 pints.

# STAFF COOKS

# STAFF COOKS

## AMARETTO CHOCOLATE RUSSE

1 envelope unflavored gelatin
2 tablespoons cold water
3 1-ounce squares unsweetened
  chocolate
¼ cup water
¼ cup Amaretto
4 eggs, separated
½ cup sugar

1 teaspoon vanilla
Dash of salt
½ teaspoon cream of tartar
¼ cup sugar
1 cup heavy cream, whipped
½ cup pecans, chopped
24 double lady fingers, split

Soften gelatin in 2 tablespoons cold water. Melt chocolate in ¼ cup water over low heat, stirring constantly. Remove from heat; add Amaretto and gelatin. Stir to dissolve. Beat egg yolks until thick. Gradually beat in ½ cup sugar; add vanilla and dash of salt. Blend in chocolate mixture. Cool, then stir until smooth. Beat egg whites, sugar and cream of tartar to soft peaks. Fold into chocolate mixture. Fold in whipped cream and nuts. Set aside about 12 lady fingers for center layer. Line bottom and sides of 10 inch spring form pan. Fill with half the mixture. Layer reserved lady fingers and fill with remaining chocolate mixture. Chill overnight. Serves 8 to 10.

*Marcia Craig, M.D.*

## BOB MOORE'S BISCUITS

### 1 package Pillsbury or Ballard tenderflake refrigerator rolls

Separate each biscuit to make 12. Place on well greased cookies sheet. Brush with Mazola. Bake in a preheated 400° oven for about 3 or 4 minutes, until crisp.

*Robert Moore, M.D.*

## CEVICHE

2 cups fresh fish filets
⅓ cup onion, chopped
¼ cup chives, chopped
2 small hot green peppers
  (chilies), finely chopped
⅓-½ cup fresh lime juice
½ cup V-8 juice
⅓ cup olive oil
1 large tomato, chopped
1½ cloves garlic, pressed
½ teaspoon thyme
1 tablespoon parsley, chopped
1 tablespoon coriander (fresh or
  dried)
¼ cup sweet red peppers, finely
  chopped
Lawry's salt
Black pepper
Tabasco and Worcestershire
  sauce for a hotter taste

Use the freshest fish to be found and rinse thoroughly. Combine all ingredients and refrigerate overnight. Serve with Melba rounds, or Doritos, or as a salad on lettuce.

*George McCracken, M.D.*

## EASY, QUICK CHICKEN CACCIATORE

*Ideal for company since it can be cooked on low for as long as 50 minutes.*

2 tablespoons butter or margarine
½ onion, chopped
1 package boneless chicken
  breasts
1 egg, beaten
½ cup seasoned bread crumbs
1 32-ounce jar Ragú Italian
  Cooking Sauce
¼ cup Mozzarella cheese

In a skillet, on medium flame, sauté onion in butter or margarine. Flatten the chicken breasts with a knife. Dip the chicken into a beaten egg and then into the seasoned bread crumbs. Brown the chicken on both sides. Add the entire jar of Ragú Italian Cooking Sauce. Cover skillet and cook on a low heat for at least 20 minutes. Five minutes before serving, sprinkle Mozzarella cheese on top. May be served on top of spaghetti or noodles. Serves 4.

*Gary Morchower, M.D.*

# MEXICAN CORN BREAD

2 eggs
1 cup sour cream
1 cup cream style corn
⅔ cup salad oil
1½ cups corn meal
3 teaspoons baking powder

1 tablespoon salt
2 jalapeño peppers, seeded and
chopped
2 tablespoons green pepper,
chopped
1 cup Cheddar cheese, grated

Mix all ingredients, except cheese, in the order given. Pour half of the mixture into a hot, well greased iron skillet. Sprinkle half of the cheese over batter. Pour on remaining batter and cheese. Bake at 350° for 1 hour. Serves 8.

*Claude Prestidge, M.D.*

# BRISKET

6-8 pound brisket
Salt
Pepper
Onion powder
Garlic powder

Celery powder
4-5 tablespoons liquid smoke
Red wine
Barbecue sauce

The night before cooking, liberally sprinkle salt, pepper, onion powder, garlic powder, celery powder and liquid smoke on one side. Wrap meat in foil, pouring the red wine over the meat before sealing. Store in refrigerator overnight.

Cook, still wrapped in foil, at 250° for no less than 6 hours (longer if brisket is larger than 8 pounds). Unwrap and pour barbecue sauce over meat. Return to oven for one more hour, at least. Serve sliced with a side dish of warm sauce.

*Dick Morris, M.D.*

# ITALIAN CREME CAKE

*This is even better the second day.*

1 stick margarine
½ cup shortening
2 cups sugar
5 egg yolks
2 cups flour
1 teaspoon soda
1 teaspoon vanilla
1 4-ounce can coconut
1 cup buttermilk

5 egg whites, stiffly beaten
*Cream Cheese Icing:*
1 8-ounce package cream cheese
  (room temperature)
½ stick margarine (room
  temperature)
1 box powdered sugar
1 teaspoon vanilla
1 cup pecans, chopped

Cream butter and shortening well. Add sugar and beat well. Add egg yolks and beat well. Combine the flour and soda and sift twice.

To the first mixture, add the vanilla and coconut. Add the buttermilk and flour alternately and then mix well. Then fold in the stiffly beaten egg whites. Bake at 350° for approximately 30 to 35 minutes in greased and floured pans. Makes 2 layers.

*Icing:* Beat cream cheese and margarine until creamy. Sift in sugar and add vanilla. Beat well and spread between cooled layers. Sprinkle pecans on layers and top.

*Phyllis Pennartz, R.N.*

## MOTHER'S PRUNE CAKE

¾ cup butter
2 cups sugar
3 eggs
1 cup buttermilk
2 cups all-purpose cake flour
½ teaspoon allspice
½ teaspoon cinnamon
1 teaspoon soda
½ teaspoon salt

1 teaspoon vanilla
1 cup cooked prunes
1 cup pecans
*Frosting:*
3 cups powdered sugar
¼ cup cocoa
2 teaspoons butter (or more depending on desired consistency)

Cream butter and sugar. Add eggs, then buttermilk. Sift together flour, spices, soda and salt. Add to butter mixture. Add vanilla, prunes and pecans. Place in greased and floured cake pans (loaf or layers). Bake at 350° until a toothpick comes out clean.

*Frosting:* Combine ingredients and spread on cooled cake.

*P.S. from the editors:* Dr. Sartain's darling Mother is from the old school of wonderful cooks that gauged their baking time by "till it looks done." We suggest you begin testing at the end of 50 minutes.

*Peggy Sartain, M.D.*

## MARINATED CARROTS

5 cups carrots, sliced
1 onion, thinly sliced
1 green pepper, thinly sliced
1 10¼-ounce can tomato soup
½ cup Crisco Oil
¾ cup vinegar
¾ cup sugar
1 teaspoon prepared mustard

1 teaspoon salt
¼ teaspoon pepper (or more if you like)
1 teaspoon celery seed
1 tablespoon crumbled dry sweet basil
1 teaspoon Worcestershire sauce

Boil carrots in salted water until just tender.
Combine the remaining ingredients and pour over carrots. Allow carrots to stand at least 12 hours in the sauce. Keeps two weeks.

*Gladys Fashena, M.D.*

# HAMBURGER GRAVY

1 pound ground meat
1 tablespoon flour

½ cup milk
1 can mushroom soup

Brown the ground meat. Pour off all but 1 tablespoon of drippings. Combine flour and milk and add to meat and drippings. Begin stirring to make a gravy. Add the mushroom soup to the meat and white sauce. Add more milk, if necessary, for a good consistency. Serve over toast, biscuits, English muffins, etc. Serves approximately 3.

*P.S.* "DO NOT tell children about mushroom soup — mine were scared of anything with mushrooms for years — finally one of them became old enough to explain that in one of the Babar books we had faithfully read, the King of the Elephants had died after eating a poisoned mushroom!"

*Dick Morris, M.D.*

# LAMB SHANK STEW

4 lamb shanks
1 cup dry white wine or vermouth
1 16-ounce can tomatoes
1 clove garlic, crushed
1 tablespoon brown sugar
1 teaspoon salt

¼ teaspoon pepper
1 tablespoon dehydrated onions
1 tablespoon Spaghetti Sauce
  Seasoning (Spice Island)
2 zucchini, sliced
2 yellow squash, sliced

Roast shanks in 350° oven for one hour and then place in a large iron casserole. Add wine, tomatoes with juice, garlic, brown sugar, salt, pepper, onions and spaghetti sauce seasoning. Cover and simmer for one hour. Then add zucchini and yellow squash and continue to simmer, covered, for 15 minutes. Serve in large soup bowls accompanied by a green salad and French bread. Serves 4.

*Jo Ann Cornet, M.D.*

# COCONUT ICE CREAM

2 cups sugar
6 tablespoons all-purpose flour
1 teaspoon salt
5 cups milk
6 egg yolks
2 pints half and half
1 pint whipping cream

3 tablespoons vanilla extract
1 8½-ounce can Cream of Coconut milk
½ cup Angel Flake coconut, packed
Rock salt
20 pounds ice

*1.* Early in the day: In a large, heavy sauce pan, combine sugar, flour and salt with a spoon. In a medium bowl, beat milk and egg yolks, with a hand beater or wire whisk, until well blended. Stir into sugar mixture until smooth. Cook over low heat, stirring constantly, until mixture thickens and coats the spoon — about 30 to 45 minutes. Cover surface with waxed paper and refrigerate to cool for about 2 hours.

*2.* Pour half and half, whipping cream, vanilla and cooled mixture into a 4 to 6 quart ice cream freezer. Add Cream of Coconut milk and flaked coconut. Stir to mix well. Place dasher in can, cover and place can in freezer bucket. Freeze according to manufacturer's direction. It will take 35 to 45 minutes to freeze.

*3.* After freezing, ice cream will be soft. Remove dasher, cover can with waxed paper and ripen or put in freezer for 2 to 3 hours. Make 5 quarts.

*Alison Allen, R.N.*

## DOUBLE CHOCOLATE ICE CREAM

*Makes 1 gallon ice cream in electric or hand cranked freezer.*

5 1-ounce squares unsweetened
  chocolate
½ to ¾ cup water
6 eggs
1 13-ounce can evaporated milk
1½ cups sugar
1 box Junket Ice Cream powder,
  chocolate

1 4-serving size box Chocolate
  Instant pudding mix
½ gallon chocolate milk
15 to 20 pounds ice
4 pounds ice cream salt

In a double boiler, melt chocolate squares with ½ to ¾ cup water to a thickened but pourable state. Set aside to cool slightly.

In a large mixing bowl, beat eggs until frothy and continue beating while adding evaporated milk. Add sugar, ice cream powder and pudding mix. Beat until well mixed. Add melted chocolate and mix well. Pour mixture into can of freezer and add chocolate milk to fill to the freezing line. Stir to mix. Insert dasher; close, attach motor and let run for 2 or 3 minutes before adding ice and salt mixture. Freeze according to freezer directions using 1 to 1½ pounds of salt with approximately 10 pounds of ice. Drain brine before packing. After hardening and dasher is removed, pack and let set for 1½ to 2 hours to fully ripen. Pack with the balance of salt and approximately 10 pounds of ice. Cover with a large towel or moisture resistant material.

*Audrey N. Bell, R.N.*

# CREATIVE HOME MADE ICE CREAM

*Basic Ingredients*
4-6 eggs
1 13-ounce can evaporated milk
1-1½ cups sugar
½-¾ gallon milk

1 box Junket Ice Cream powder, 1 box instant pudding mix (4 serving size) or 2 boxes Ice Cream powders; flavor according to other additions

Mix all ingredients, except the milk, with an electric mixer in the order given. Add fruit or other flavors and pour into can of freezer. Add the milk and dasher, top and motor and let run for 2 to 3 minutes before adding the ice and salt. Makes 1 gallon.

*Flavors:*
*Strawberry* — Purée 2 10-ounce packages of frozen sliced strawberries; use strawberry ice cream powders for more flavor.

*Peach* — Purée 2 to 3 cups fresh ripe peaches in a blender, adding a small amount of milk as necessary. Adjust sugar in basic recipe for sweetness. Peach or apricot instant pudding can be used in place of vanilla flavored pudding. Use vanilla flavored ice cream powder.

*Banana Nut* — Mash or purée 3 to 4 very ripe bananas. Use banana instant pudding mix. Add ½ to 1 cup finely chopped nuts.

Almost any flavor of ice cream can be made from the basic ice cream base; vary according to family likes using different flavors of instant pudding mix with fruit, nuts or crushed candy, such as peppermints.

## FREEZING TIPS FOR HOMEMADE ICE CREAM

*1.* I prefer a tall metal can for quicker and harder freezing.

*2.* Crushed ice, such as cocktail, seems to melt slower and provides more chilling; approximately 1 pound of ice cream salt per 8 to 10 pounds of ice for first phase of freezing.

*3.* After disconnecting line cord from wall plug, drain brine from freezer before removing motor and top of container; save unmelted ice.

*4.* Remove dasher from can and push contents down with a long wooden spoon; cover can with aluminum foil and replace top; plug hole in top with cork or aluminum foil plug.

*5.* Repack with ice and salt, using balance of salt or approximately 3 pounds of salt to 8 to 10 pounds of ice. Heap ice and salt mixture 2 to 3 inches above the top of the freezer can.

*6.* Cover freezer with heavy towels or blankets and let set for 1½ to 2 hours to ripen. Check after ¾ to 1 hour to see if more ice is needed.

*Audrey N. Bell, R.N.*

# SHORE LUNCH

*For the fisherman who eats his morning's catch on shore at noontime.*

½ pound thick sliced bacon
½ pound butter or margarine
1 egg, beaten

1 5¼-ounce can evaporated milk
Kellogg's Corn Flake crumbs
Fish filets, 8 to 10

You need a heavy skillet to really fry fish this way. Fry bacon, remove, add margarine or butter to skillet. While it is heating, beat egg. Dip fish in egg and milk mixture, then into the corn flake crumbs. Fry until golden brown.

*Ted Votteler, M.D.*

# MEAT BURRITOS

1 pound stew meat, cut in one inch squares
1 pound ground meat
2 large onions, chopped
2 tablespoons cooking oil

2 8-ounce cans tomato sauce
1 4-ounce can green chilies, chopped
1 pound cheese, grated
Salt and pepper to taste

Cook stew meat slowly in a small amount of water until tender. Brown ground meat and onions in oil. Add tomato sauce, green chilies and stew meat. Cook on low heat for one hour. Add cheese and stir until melted. If mixture is thin, thicken with browned flour, one tablespoon at a time. (To brown flour, put in a dry heavy skillet. Cook over direct low heat, stirring constantly, until golden brown.) Put a heaping tablespoon on a flour tortilla and roll up. Serves 8.

Meat mixture could easily be prepared the day before, reheated and spooned in the flour tortillas.

*Alvis Johnson, M.D.*

## PICKLED MUSHROOMS

1 onion
1 8-ounce can mushrooms
1 4-ounce can mushrooms
*Marinade:*
⅔ cup tarragon vinegar
½ cup salad oil

1 medium garlic clove, crushed
1 tablespoon sugar
2 tablespoons water
4-5 dashes of Tabasco
1½ teaspoons salt
Pepper to taste

Combine marinade ingredients in a blender or processor for 10 to 20 seconds. Slice onion and separate into rings. Add onions and mushrooms to the marinade. Refrigerate and stir several times over 8 hours. Drain to serve.

*Claude Prestidge, M.D.*

## SCRAMBLED OMELET

2 or 3 eggs
Big pinch of salt

Pinch of black pepper
1 tablespoon butter

Mix eggs with a wire whisk until just blended. Place butter in omelet pan and place over high heat. Tilt pan to coat all of it. When butter stops foaming, pour in egg mixture. Hold handle in left hand and slide pan back and forth rapidly. At the same time, fork in right hand, stir the eggs quickly to spread over the bottom of pan as they thicken. Add any filling you prefer, i.e. cheese, ham, bacon, onion, etc. Tilt the pan, slide omelet onto plate. As omelet leaves pan to plate, fold over. If left-handed, reverse process!

*William B. Johnson, M.D.*

## HOT OYSTER HORS D'OEUVRES

2 bunches small green onions, minced
1 cup celery, minced
2 sticks butter
2 pints raw oysters, drained and minced (save liquor)
1 tablespoon Worcestershire sauce
4-6 drops Hot Pepper sauce
1 cup ( + ) Saltine crackers, crumbed

Sauté minced onion and celery in butter until clear, not browned. Add minced oysters. Cook approximately 5 minutes. Add oyster liquor, Worcestershire sauce and hot sauce. Thicken with Saltine crumbs. Serve hot in a chafing dish on toast cups.

*Toast cups:* Trim crusts from fresh white bread slices. Cut each slice into fourths. Press into 1¼ inch muffin pans. Toast in oven at 350°. These can be made ahead and frozen.

*Maurice Adam, M.D.*

## SOUR CREAM PANCAKES

1¼ cups Bisquick
3 eggs
1 16-ounce carton sour cream
¼ pound butter, melted
1 tablespoon sugar
½ tablespoon baking soda
1 teaspoon baking powder
¼ teaspoon salt
¼ cup milk, if batter is too stiff
½ pound crisp bacon, crumbled (optional)

Combine all ingredients and mix well. Cook on hot griddle. Serves 4.

*David Stager, M.D.*

# RUM PIE

*Custard*
5 eggs
1 cup sugar
Pinch of salt
½ cup orange juice
1 tablespoon lemon juice
1 envelope gelatin
¼ cup water

1 tablespoon almond extract
2 tablespoons rum (Bacardi or
  light rum)
*Crust*
1 8½-ounce box of chocolate
  wafers
¾ stick of butter

*Crust:* Crumble wafers and mix with butter. Then pat into a 9 inch spring form pan.

*Custard:* Let ingredients sit out to be at room temperature. Separate the eggs. Beat the yolks with ½ cup sugar, pinch of salt, orange juice and lemon juice. Then heat in a double boiler, stirring with a whisk, until just beginning to thicken. Be careful not to overcook. Meanwhile, dissolve 1 envelope of gelatin in ¼ cup water and put into the custard mixture. Beat egg whites. Gradually add ½ cup sugar, almond extract and rum. Cool the custard. Then fold in the egg whites. Pour all into the crumb crust. Chill 12 hours. Add whipped cream and grate chocolate on top.

*Bob Kramer, M.D.*

# VENISON ROAST

Venison roast
3 tablespoons vinegar to each 6
    cups of water
Salt

Pepper
Butter, softened
Brown sugar
Red wine

If meat is frozen allow to thaw by soaking in water approximately 24 hours. The next day pour water off and cover again with water adding 3 tablespoons of vinegar to each 6 cups of water. Soak roast another 24 hours. (This long process of soaking is not absolutely necessary, but does take away a little of the wild flavor. I quite often start a roast with the following steps immediately upon finishing the processing of the deer.)

Score the roast about ½ inch deep and season with a lot of salt and pepper. Push softened butter into the cuts, covering the top of the roast. Cover butter with a layer of brown sugar and pour enough red wine over the roast to make at least ½ inch of liquid in the pan. Roast in a 325° oven. Baste every 20 minutes for the first 2 hours of cooking and continue to cook slowly until the roast is black. The drippings and wine make a delicious sauce to serve with the venison.

*George E. Hurt, Jr., M.D.*

# BLUEBERRY SALAD

2 3-ounce packages of Raspberry
  Jello
2 cups boiling water
1 15-ounce can blueberries,
  drained
1 8½-ounce can crushed pineapple,
  drained

1 8-ounce package cream cheese
½ cup sugar
½ pint sour cream
½ teaspoon vanilla
½ cup pecans, chopped

Dissolve Jello in 2 cups boiling water. Measure liquid from blueberries and pineapple. Add enough water to make 1 cup and add to dissolved Jello mixture. Stir in drained fruit. Pour into a 2 quart flat dish. Cover and put into refrigerator until firm. Combine cream cheese, sugar, sour cream and vanilla. Spread over gelatin salad. Sprinkle with nuts. Serves 10 to 15.

*Gladys Fashena, M.D.*

# DR. ELGIN WARE'S RECIPE FOR SANGRITA

Juice of 8 oranges
Juice of 3 limes
1 12-ounce can tomato juice
1 teaspoon sugar

Drops (or spoonsful) Tabasco
  sauce to taste
Dash of white pepper
Dash of salt

This delectable concoction from Old Mexico can be mixed with Tequila (like a Bloody Mary) or used as a chaser when drinking Tequila straight. Do not confuse with the sweet Mexican wine drink Sangria. An interesting challenge is to pour equal amounts of Sangrita and Tequila into shot glasses and then chase one with the other, the game being to make the two come out even. Salud! Mix all ingredients and keep chilled.

*Elgin W. Ware, Jr., M.D.*

## QUICK OIL, PARSLEY AND
## GARLIC SPAGHETTI FOR SIX

½ cup of good olive oil
1 pound thin spaghetti
3-4 tablespoons parsley, finely
  chopped

3 medium cloves of garlic
Freshly ground black pepper
Salt
Grated Parmesan cheese

Put oil in a small frying pan and save. Bring 6 quarts of water and 1 to 2 tablespoons salt to a rapid boil on a very high heat. Add spaghetti and stir initially to prevent sticking. Cook, uncovered, at a rapid boil for 6 to 9 minutes. Taste occasionally toward the end. Cook until spaghetti is done but still firm to the bite. Drain spaghetti immediately and put into a large, warm bowl. Toss quickly with chopped parsley. As soon as spaghetti is removed from the stove, place frying pan with oil on fire. When oil is hot, squeeze garlic through a garlic press into the oil and cook according to taste, for about 10 seconds, or longer if desired, even until garlic becomes very brown. The final product will change according to the degree to which the garlic is cooked and one will have to experiment. When garlic is done, quickly add a few gratings of pepper and cook a few more seconds. Then pour oil and garlic onto spaghetti and toss well. Serve in warm plates. Add Parmesan cheese to taste, and additional pepper if desired.

*Guido Currarino, M.D.*

## MY FAVORITE SHRIMP FOR TWO

1 pound large tiger shrimp (have
  split at fish market)
¼ cup parsley, chopped

½ cup olive oil
Garlic juice to taste
Lemon pepper

Mix parsley, oil, and garlic juice. Marinate shrimp, meat side down for several hours in oil mixture. Remove from marinade, sprinkle with lemon pepper. Broil with only the oil mixture that clings to them. Delicious charcoal broiled on outside grill, or approximately 4 minutes on each side in the kitchen broiler.

Serve with melted butter and lemon juice to dip in.

*James McKinney, M.D.*

# YELLOW SQUASH

6 yellow squash, small to medium size

¼ pound grated cheese (or use 1 tablespoon grated Parmesan cheese per squash)

½ tablespoon soft margarine per squash

Cracker crumbs (2 squares per squash)

½ teaspoon dried onion flakes per squash (optional)

1 egg, beaten (optional)

Salt (or onion salt)

Pepper

Boil whole squash until tender, but still firm. (Or use young squash without cooking.) Cut squash in half lengthwise. Trim off ends. Remove center pulp and place it in a small mixing bowl. Add cheese, margarine, cracker crumbs and, if desired, onion flakes and egg, to the pulp. Add salt and pepper to taste. Fill the squash shells. Dot with margarine if broiling. Sprinkle with paprika. Place on a foil covered shallow pan and broil until bubbly (5 to 10 minutes) or arrange on a cookie sheet and bake at 300° until bubbly (about 15 minutes). Serves 6.

*Nancy White, M.D.*

# SUD'S SHRIMP SPREAD

*Make a day ahead. Keeps up to one week in the refrigerator.*

1 pound cream cheese

1 onion, chopped

1 green pepper, chopped

½ pound shrimp, cooked

Salt to taste

Soften cream cheese at room temperature. Blend with the chopped onion and green pepper. Chop shrimp coarsely and add to mixture. Salt to taste. Serves 10 to 12.

*Daniel Levin, M.D.*

## JAPANESE STEAK MARINADE

1 cup soy sauce
1 teaspoon dry mustard
1 teaspoon dry ginger

1 tablespoon vegetable oil
1 to 2 garlic cloves, thinly sliced.

Combine in a bottle and shake well. Marinate meat for 2 to 4 hours. Two tablespoons sugar may be added for chicken or pork.

*Chester Fink, M.D.*

# OUR PATIENTS COOK

# Salad by Brad Fountain

1 pkg. pistachio pudding

1 C. nuts

lg. can crushed pineapple

1 C. small marshmallows

9 oz cool whip

Mix together. Put thin lazer of cool whip on top + sprinkle whith a few nuts.

# Fudge Pie

2 squares of chocolate
¼ lb. of butter
1 ¼ cups of sugar
4 eggs
1 tsp. vanilla
1 heaping tablespoon flour
pinch of salt

Melt chocolate and butter in double boiler. Beat eggs, add sugar to eggs. Add to chocolate mixture. Add vanilla, salt, and flour.

Pour into buttered pie pan and bake 25 minutes at 350° and then 20 minutes at 275°. Put pan of water under shelf.

To Serve: Chill and serve with scoop of vanilla ice cream on top.

Becky Taylor
Tyler Texas

# Bake potatos

1 potata

Butter

Warsh in cool warter, damp dry
wrap in foil and bake for about
30-or half an hour.
When finist let cool and cut
open and put a slice of butter
and net all you have to do is
eat!

Geneva Jones

# caramels

1 cup butter

1 pound ( 2¼ cups) brown sugar
    Dash salt

1 cup light corn surup

1 15-ounce can sweetened
    condensed milk

1 tespoon vanilla

Melt butter in a 3-quart saucepan, add suger and salt stir well. Stir in the corn syrup mix well. Gradually add the milk, stir constantly. Cook and stir over med. heat to firm ball stage (245°), 12-15 min. Remove from heat; stir in vanilla. Pour into buttered 9x9x2-inch pan, Cool and cut into squares.

Heather McDonald

# Jello pops

favorite jello
mix up and
sugar to desire
pour in to icups
cut straws to use
as legs freeze and
eat.

by: Jacki Ridgl

dedicated to: Dr. Kramer & Prestige

---

# Skillet Cookies

1 cup sugar                1 stick oleo
3 eggs                     1½ cups chopped nuts
1 lb dates chopped         4 cups rice crispies
1 tsp Vanilla              1 lb coconut

Mix sugar, eggs oleo and dates
in skillet and cook over low heat for
ten minutes or til thick. Turn off
heat. Add rice crispies nuts, Vanilla.
Mix let cool enough to roll into
balls. Then roll in coconut.
Use lots of coconut and work into
balls. This will fill up a big cookie
Jar.               By James Michael Palmer
This is for Beverly

## STRABERRY CAKE

Once I put a box OR straberry cake and on the top I put piece of nuts on top of the stove it was a button the a put it on 39 high! then it cooked then when it cooked I ated and my family to - with coke and on, top it was candles then I put a match.

Signature, maria Eugenia Urbina

## Crazy Cookies

Antwonetta

grade 3

Age 8

Feb. 20

1979

hope

you

enjoy

cuters them

1 cup of water

1 pack of cookie mix

And some Flour

1 cookie sheet

And some cookies

## Aunt Lil's Applesauce

Apples [6 lb., more or less]     1 1/2 c. water
1 1/2 c. Sugar                            2 T. lemon

Cut up and core apples. <u>DO NOT</u> peel apples. Applesauce retains more vitamins if cooked with skin. (Also gives sauce pretty pink color) Put apples, sugar, water, and lemon juice in large pan (about 6 quart Dutch oven).

Cook until soft, but not loose. Mash apples down in pan while cooking with wooden spoon.

After cooking, run apples through sieve. (This is called a Foley food mill) Put about 1 cup at a time in food mill. Grind through sieve until all of apple has gone 🍎 through. Only skin will be left in food mill. (Skin will be slightly transparent) Remove skin before adding additional apples, and it works better. (Do not drain apples - run all through sieve.)

Makes 3 quarts of applesauce.

Becky Taylor
Tyler, Texas

An Apple A Day Keeps The Doctor Away.

# Pork Chop Deep Dish

6 - Pork Chops
2 - Cans Golden Mushroom Soup
2 - Cans French Green Beans
1 - Cans French Fried Onion Rings

Brown Pork Chops, Place in Casarol Dish add Drained Geen Beans an other ingEDENTs in layFRs. and Top with REmaining Onion Rings. Bake at 300° For 1 HR.

By Donna Guthrie

I D like to dedicate this reciepe to Mrs. Magie Judd Because she was So niee to all off us on dialysis. Before I had my Kidney transplant she use to go to a lot of troubl to fix no salt Pizza and give me regular tomatoe Soup to go with my no salt cheese Sandwish-es. I learned to make this recipe in mpls. Minnesota after my Kidney transplant. I think she will like it. Because she is from Minnesota.

Thank you Mrs. Judd for being so nice to every one. Donna Guthrie

# PumPkin Bread

2½ c. four
3 c. Sugar
2 t. Soda
1 t. ⬛ cinnamon.
1 t. nutmeg
1½ t. Salt
4 egg
¾ c. Mazola oil
½ c. water

2 c. canned pum Pkin
1 c. nuts, chopped

firm. Servers
12 to 14. →

Margaret J. Andreos.

Sift dry ingredients together. Place eggs oil and water. in a lage bowl of Mixer. Gradually add dry ingredients to form smoth batter. Add Pum Pkin, mix well. Fold in nuts. Pour into 2 greased and floured loaf pans. or bake in bundt pan as a cake. Bake at 325° for 1½ hours or until

Pum Pncin bread

Margaret J. Andrews

"Kevin Epperson's Goulash Supreme"

You Need:

1 Lb. ground meat

1 can Water

1 c. grated Cheese

½ t. garlic salt

½ t. onion salt

½ t. salt

½ t. Pepper

1 c. Cooked Noodles

## Procedures

Brown hamburger meat in a skillet.
Add seasonings, tomato sause + water.
Simmer while preparing Noodles. Cook
Nooddes down or remove water.
Add meat mixture + cheese to Noodles

## The End!

### Popcorn Balls

5 cups poped popcorn

2 tbs. CF Butter

40 large marshmellows

put poped popcorn it large pan

Melt margrine in a smaller pan
with marshmellows. After smooth
mix well poring over the popcorn
slowy form in ball wrap with sarain
wrap. make small size balls or for
smaller children.

by: Jacki Ridge

Dedicated to Dr. Kramer

## Tom & Mac

Shell macironi
1 can of stewed tomatoes
2 tb. CF Butter (or <u>without</u>) ~~batter to~~ omit

Cook as much or as little as you
need for you family or child.
Drain macir. heat in pan after draing.
with 1 can of stewed tomatoes untill
warm or desired. Salt & Peper serve.

by: Jacki Ridge

Dedicated to Dr. Kramer

# onion soup
## meat Balls
ground BeeF Meet
Balls

ADD ~~onion soup~~

And wourstior

And water iF Dry

Soup is used

And simmer till

SAuse thickens

Dr. Battles
Dr. Fink
Dr. Hogg

Robbie
Hill

# Chochlate Malt

You will need a blender and some Chochlate icecream. For 1 shake 3 scoops of icecream.

Add some milk. For thick add little milk For thin add more. Turn blender on. Till the malt looks like you like it.

age·10          Tonya Cruze

Chocolate chip Cookies
By Pam 9 years old

1/2 cup of Butter

1 egg

1/2 cup Brown Suger

1/5 white Suger

Mix this togather
then add

1/2 t. Salt

1/5 t. soda

2 cups flower

1/2 t. cinomon
Chocolate chips

bake 350 for
10 min

1 cup of milk and 1\3 of ~~mo~~ milk
2 ~~eggs~~ eggs But only the white
and then one Box of cake mix
and then you mix it
But 2 miunts fast and one
~~Miunts~~ miunt Slow

Name:

~~Sandra~~ Liguroa

---

## Blueberry     Salad

2 packages   Blueberry Jello          Julie
1  cup      miniature   marsh mallows   Vineyard
2  cups     boiling   water
   Mix      together  -  chill
Add:     1 can  blueberrjes  packed  in water - water and all.
1 ½     cups  mashed   bananas   with ½  cup suger
½  cup pecans
Refrigerate   untill   partially   set
Fold in one  small container  Cool Whip

Blueberry
Salad

# FAST FOODS

# FAST FOODS

## BACON CHEESE SQUARES

*With scrambled eggs and soup, that's enough for supper.*

2 tablespoons pimiento, chopped
2 tablespoons parsley, chopped
4 tablespoons onion, chopped
½ teaspoon salt
½ teaspoon Worcestershire sauce
Dash of Tabasco sauce

2 3-ounce packages cream cheese
1 tablespoon mustard
¼ cup Hellmann's mayonnaise
4 slices bacon, finely chopped
8 slices thin bread

Blend all ingredients, except bacon and bread, thoroughly. Trim crusts from bread and cut in 4 strips. Toast bread on one side. Spread cheese mixture on untoasted side. Sprinkle on bacon and broil for approximately 4 minutes. Cheese mixture may be prepared early in the day and then broiled just before serving.

## BACON, TOMATO AND CHEESY SANDWICHES FOR FOUR

8 pieces of bacon
2 tomatoes, sliced
Cheez Whiz
Garlic salt

Salt
Pepper
Hamburger buns, toasted

Fry bacon and drain. Place tomatoes on buns, then bacon. Season, cover with Cheez Whiz and slide under broiler until light brown and bubbling.

Run peach halves with mint jelly under broiler until hot. In the meantime, scramble eggs. Good enough for a simple dinner. Done in 20 minutes.

# THE HOW - TO - MAKE - CANNED - GREEN - BEANS - TASTE - LIKE - GARDEN - FRESH RECIPE

1 16-ounce can green beans, cut
   style
Water

2 teaspoons sugar
1 onion, sliced

Drain beans, dump in strainer, rinse under faucet. Drain well. Pour beans in saucepan, add about ½ cup of water perhaps a tad more, the sugar and onion. Simmer gently 30 minutes. Serves 4.

# BEANS AND WIENERS

6 wieners, cut in pieces
1 8-ounce can pork and beans
¼ cup catsup
1 tablespoon brown sugar
1 can (6 biscuits) refrigerated
   buttermilk biscuits

½ teaspoon margarine, melted
1 teaspoon sesame seeds
(optional)

Heat oven to 375°. Combine first four ingredients and bring to a boil. Simmer for 5 minutes. Spoon this mixture into an ungreased casserole. Top with the six biscuits. Spoon the melted margarine over the biscuits and sprinkle the sesame seeds on top. Bake for 20 to 25 minutes. Serves 3 to 4.

# DRIED BEEF WITH ARTICHOKE HEARTS

*Good brunch or supper dish.*

1 5-ounce package dried chipped beef
½ cup mushrooms, sliced
¼ stick margarine
1½ tablespoons flour
1 pint sour cream
1 4-ounce can artichoke hearts, chopped
¼ teaspoon Worcestershire sauce
2 tablespoons Parmesan cheese
¼ cup red wine
Dash of pepper and Tabasco
English Muffins, split and toasted

Pour boiling water over beef and drain well. Sauté the chipped beef and mushrooms in the margarine. Sprinkle with flour and stir well. Add sour cream. (If too thick, add a little juice from the artichokes). Add remaining ingredients and heat, stirring well. Serve over toasted English muffin halves. Serves 4 to 6.

# QUICK CHEESE BREAD

*Try this with your chili or vegetable soup next time instead of the usual crackers.*

½ cup onion, chopped
1 tablespoon, or a bit more, bacon drippings
½ cup milk
1 egg, beaten
1½ cups Bisquick

*Topping:*
½ cup sharp Cheddar cheese
2 tablespoons butter, melted
Poppy seed

Sauté onions in bacon drippings. Mix milk and beaten egg. Add Bisquick. Mix until well blended. Spread in a greased 9 inch baking dish or muffin cups. Combine topping ingredients and sprinkle on dough. Bake at 400° for 20 to 25 minutes until brown.

# BRUSSELS SPROUTS

*You will not believe how good these taste!! Kids even love them!!*

**Brussels sprouts**          **Parmesan cheese**

Precook firm little sprouts in a small quantity of salted water for 5 minutes. Drain and deep fat fry until almost crisp. Serve at once sprinkled with freshly grated Parmesan cheese.

# SCALLOPED CABBAGE

1 head cabbage
1 cup chicken broth
1 medium onion, diced
½ teaspoon black pepper
1 teaspoon salt

½ stick butter
1 teaspoon Cavender's All
    Purpose Greek Seasoning
2 cups cheese, grated

Cook cabbage with chicken broth, onion and seasonings until done. Place in a casserole dish. Cover with cheese. Bake 350° for 8 minutes or until cheese is melted.

# MANDARIN ORANGE CAKE

*Can be made and baked in 25 minutes. A quickie when needed.*

| | |
|---|---|
| 1 egg | **Topping** |
| 1 cup sugar | ¼ cup sugar |
| 1 cup flour | 3 tablespoons butter |
| 1 teaspoon baking soda | 3 tablespoons milk |
| ½ teaspoon salt | |
| 1 11-ounce can mandarin oranges, plus juice | |

Combine all ingredients including the oranges and beat for three minutes. Pour into a greased 8 inch square pan and bake at 350° for 20 minutes.

Bring the ingredients for the topping to a boil and pour over the cake while it is hot. Serves 4 to 6.

# CALABAZITO

| | |
|---|---|
| 6 slices bacon | ½ cup catsup |
| 1 pound ground beef | 1 cup Rotel tomatoes |
| Salt and pepper | 1 pound zucchini, sliced |
| Garlic | ½ cup Parmesan cheese |
| 1 large onion, chopped | |

Fry bacon until crisp, remove and drain. Season beef with salt, pepper and garlic. Sauté with onion in bacon drippings. Add catsup, tomatoes (mashed), and squash. Cover and cook until tender. Stir in Parmesan cheese and top with crumbled bacon. Serves 6.

## CRUSTLESS CHEESE CAKE

*This is a lovely, light and easy to make cheese cake.*

| | |
|---|---|
| 1 pound cream cheese | 1 pint sour cream |
| 3 eggs | ½ teaspoon almond extract |
| ⅔ cup sugar | 6 tablespoons sugar |
| 2 teaspoons vanilla | |

Beat cream cheese, eggs, sugar and vanilla until very creamy and smooth. Pour into greased spring form or 9 inch pie pan. Bake at 350° for 25 minutes. Cool for 20 minutes.

While cooling, beat remaining three ingredients. Pour sour cream mixture over top and return to 350° oven for 10 minutes. Cool before serving.

## CHICKEN CURRY WITH CHINESE NOODLES

*The apple and curry flavors do a lot for our old steadfast feathered friend, the chicken.*

| | |
|---|---|
| 3 tablespoons butter | 2 cups milk |
| 1½ cups green tart apples, finely chopped (1 large apple) | 1 teaspoon salt |
| ⅓ cup onion, chopped | 2-3 cups cooked chicken, coarsely diced |
| 2 tablespoons flour | 4 cups Chinese noodles |
| 2-2½ teaspoons curry powder | Ripe olives, sliced |

Heat butter in skillet. Add apples and onions. Cook until tender. Stir in flour and curry powder. Add milk slowly and cook until thick. Add salt and chicken. Top with ripe olives and serve over Chinese noodles. Serves 4 to 6.

# EASY CHINESE CHICKEN

*Fast, easy and delicious. Great with a big fruit salad.*

4 chicken breasts, boned and
  skinned
1-2 tablespoons oil
½ cup celery, chopped
1 8½-ounce can water chestnuts
1 10½-ounce can chicken broth

2 teaspoons soy sauce
¼ teaspoon Accent
1 box frozen Chinese pea pods
1 tablespoon corn starch
2 tablespoons cold water
1 large can Chinese noodles

Cut chicken into strips and sauté in oil until white, not brown. Add celery and water chestnuts. Then add chicken broth, soy sauce and Accent. Put frozen pea pods on top. Cover and simmer about 10 minutes. Stir corn starch into cold water and add to chicken. Stir to thicken. Serve on Chinese noodles. Serves 4.

# "HUSH-UP" COOKIES

*This is a sweet treat for little folks when you don't have the time or ingredients to make scratch cookies.*

Pepperidge Farm thin sliced
  bread
Melted butter or margarine

1 cup powdered sugar*
3 tablespoons cinnamon

Trim crusts from bread (electric knife is great) and cut into three strips. Brush sides with melted butter. Place sugar and cinnamon in a paper bag. Drop in bread sticks, shake and place on cookie sheet. Bake at 300° for 10 minutes, turn and bake about 10 minutes longer.

*No powdered sugar? In a blender or food processor, pour 1 cup granulated sugar and 1 tablespoon corn starch. Blend for two minutes — Abbra ca dabra, powdered sugar!!

## ANN SMITH'S COOKIES

*Excellent! And so easy. You can't believe how rich and good these are —
slightly gooey on the inside — but they are supposed to be.*

1 stick butter, melted
1 cup sugar
1 cup flour
1 tablespoon baking powder

1 egg, unbeaten
1 teaspoon vanilla
1 cup pecans

Mix all ingredients together. Put in a 9x9 inch square, greased pan. Bake
at 375° for 20 minutes. It will look undercooked at 20 minutes, but it really is not after it cools.

## INSTANT DESSERT

1 6-ounce package Instant vanilla
  pudding
¼ teaspoon almond flavoring
1 can cherry, blueberry or peach
  pie filling

Cool Whip or Dream Whip
2 or more tablespoons crushed
  nuts (your choice)

Mix instant pudding according to directions, adding almond flavoring.
Using parfait glasses or a deep pretty bowl, make layers of pudding and
pie filling until all is used. Add topping, sprinkle with nuts and eat soon.

## FAST EGGS

6 hard boiled eggs
¼ cup green onion, finely chopped
1 tablespoon minced pimiento

A little milk
Salt and pepper

Mash yolks with remaining ingredients. Stuff whites. Good to fill out a meal of leftovers.

## QUICK ENTREE

3 tablespoons butter
3 tablespoons oil
4 chicken breasts, split and
    deboned, or 1½ pounds veal
    scallops
¼ cup green onions, chopped
1 small pod garlic

½ teaspoon thyme
½ cup Marsala wine
1 small jar mushrooms (juice
    included)
Salt
White pepper

In a heavy skillet, melt butter and oil. Sauté meat for 10 minutes. Push aside in the skillet and add green onions, garlic and thyme and sauté for a minute or two. Add wine and mushrooms, cover and simmer for 5 minutes. Add salt and pepper to taste. Serves 4.

## SOUTH SEAS ICE CREAM SAUCE

⅓ cup apricot preserves
⅓ cup pineapple preserves

1 cup rum
1 quart vanilla ice cream

Heat preserves and rum gently, dear friends — don't boil!! To serve, place ingredients in a chafing dish, take to table and ignite. It is best to have ladled ice cream in dishes before igniting sauce. Light sauce, allow almost to burn out, stir and spoon over ice cream.

## ONION CHEESE MUFFINS

*Good with a soup and salad supper.*

2 cups Bisquick
1 teaspoon onion salt
¾ cup Cheddar cheese, shredded
1 egg

¾ cup milk
1 3½-ounce can French Fried
onions, crumbled

Mix all the ingredients, except the onions, vigorously for 1 minute. Gently fold in onions. Pour into 12 medium greased muffin cups, ⅔'s full. Bake at 400° for approximately 15 minutes. Serve warm.

## LEMON CHESS PIE

4 eggs
1½ cups sugar
¼ cup lemon juice, fresh is better
½ teaspoon lemon rind, finely

grated
3 tablespoons butter, melted
¼ teaspoon salt

Mix all of the above ingredients. Pour into a 9 inch store bought unbaked pie shell. Bake at 350° for 40 minutes. If the top of the pie turns too brown, cover with a piece of foil and bake the remaining time. Serves 6 to 8.

# EASY SHRIMP

1 8-ounce package frozen shrimp
Lump of butter
Dash of sherry
Garlic salt

Salt
Pepper
Dried parsley flakes
Cracker crumbs

Place frozen shrimp in a frying pan with enough water to cover it. Bring to a boil. Immediately pour off all water. Add a lump of butter, dash of sherry, garlic salt, salt, pepper and dried parsley flakes. Crumble cracker crumbs over mixture. Do not stir after cracker crumbs have been added so they form a crust. Cover and cook over low heat for 5 to 8 minutes. Serve over rice. Serves 4.

# SPAGHETTI CARUSO
# OR
# QUICK SPAGHETTI DINNER

*Serve with a green salad, rolls or French bread and you have a quick, delicious meal.*

1 12-ounce package spaghetti
1 stick margarine
1 medium onion, chopped
½ pound fresh mushrooms
   (optional)

2 5-ounce cans boned chicken
¼-½ teaspoon garlic (more if
   desired) salt
Salt and pepper
Parmesan cheese

Cook spaghetti as directed on package. While it is cooking, melt margarine in a skillet. Sauté onion and mushrooms approximately 5 minutes and add the canned chicken. Sprinkle with garlic salt, salt and pepper to taste and continue cooking until heated thoroughly.

Drain the spaghetti. Pour chicken mixture over it and sprinkle liberally with the cheese. Serves 4 to 6.

## SPRING YELLOW SQUASH I

8 to 10 yellow squash, tender,
  young and small
2 tablespoons of margarine
2 tablespoons of bell pepper
1 jalapeño pepper, seeded and
  chopped

1 teaspoon salt
Pepper to taste
½ cup Cheddar cheese, grated

Slice the squash, sauté it with the onion and pepper in the margarine for 8 minutes. *Remove* from heat, stir in jalapeño, salt and pepper, top with cheese, cover with lid allow to sit (without heat) about 5 minutes (until cheese melts) then serve. Serves 4 to 6.

## YELLOW SQUASH II

1 tablespoon butter
1 small onion, chopped
½ green pepper, chopped

1 pound yellow squash, sliced
1 3-ounce package cream cheese
Salt and pepper to taste

Sauté onion and green pepper in butter until limp. Add squash and cook until tender. Add cream cheese and stir into vegetables until melted. Add salt and pepper to taste. Serve immediately or put in a casserole and re-heat when ready to eat. Serves 4 to 6.

# CHICKEN FRIED ROUND STEAK STRIPS

*Good both hot or cold the next day as a sandwich.*

**1 slice or piece of round steak**
**Milk to cover**

**Flour seasoned with salt and pepper**

Cut the round steak into finger size strips. Soak in milk all day. Dip the strips in seasoned flour. Fry the strips in hot Crisco. Do not use too much Crisco, just enough to cover half of the strip. Turn the strips and watch them closely. Drain well and serve with cream gravy made from the milk and seasoned flour.

# YOGURT PIE

**2 8-ounce cartons yogurt**
**1 medium carton Cool Whip**
**1 9-inch graham cracker crust**
  **or**

*For Diet Pie:*
**2 8-ounce cartons yogurt**
**1 1½-ounce package Dream Whip, whipped**
**1 9-inch granola pie crust**

Fold your favorite flavor of yogurt into Cool Whip or Dream Whip and put in pie shell. Refrigerate until ready to serve.

# BAKED ZUCCHINI

**Whole zucchini**          **Butter**
**Seasoning salt**          **Parmesan cheese**
**Pepper**

Allow 1 whole zucchini, medium size, per person. Cut whole zucchini lengthwise in half. With a knife, cut 2 X's in the soft center of both halves. Season with seasoning salt and pepper. Dot butter on top of seasoning and sprinkle heavily with Parmesan cheese. Bake at 350° for approximately 25 minutes or until bubbly.

# DELICIOUS ZUCCHINI

*This recipe is aptly named.*

**½ cup onion, minced**          **½ teaspoon salt**
**2 teaspoons butter**          **1 teaspoon lemon juice**
**2 medium zucchini, grated**          **¼ teaspoon dried dill weed**

Sauté onion in butter. Add remaining ingredients and cook for 5 minutes. Serves 4 to 6.

# CRUSTLESS ZUCCHINI QUICHE

*If your youngsters don't like squash, try this.*
*We think they will ask for more.*

4 zucchini
¼ pound pork sausage
¼ cup onion, chopped
3 eggs, slightly beaten
¼ cup heavy cream
½ cup cracker crumbs

¼ cup Cheddar cheese, grated
¼ cup Parmesan cheese
Pinch of garlic salt
Spaghetti seasoning
Accent

Steam zucchini until just tender. Drain, chop coarsely and drain again. Fry, crumble and drain pork sausage. Mix zucchini and sausage with remaining ingredients. Pour in pie pan. Bake at 350° until firm and brown — approximately 45 minutes. To serve, cut in wedges. Serves 4 or 5.

# HOLIDAY THOUGHTS

# HOLIDAY THOUGHTS

### COFFEE CAN BREAD

1½ cups flour
1 package dry yeast
1 teaspoon salt
½ cup milk
½ cup water

¼ cup Crisco
2 eggs
⅓ cup sugar
1½ cups flour

Grease two one pound coffee cans. Mix together 1½ cups flour, yeast and salt. Have milk, water and Crisco at room temperature. Mix dry and wet ingredients. Add eggs, one at a time, sugar and last 1½ cups of flour. Put in coffee cans; let rise to top of can. Bake for 30 minutes at 325°.

### CROCK CHEESE

1 pound yellow cheese, grated
   (any kind or a variety)
½ pound butter, softened
¼ cup brandy, sherry or beer

Tabasco sauce to taste
2 tablespoons Worcestershire
   sauce

Put cheese in the large bowl of an electric mixer or food processor. Add butter and whip until very light and fluffy. Add brandy (or etc.). Season highly with Tabasco and Worcestershire. Pack into crocks. Serve at room temperature. Keeps in a refrigerator for 3 weeks.

# POTTED CHEESE

1 pound Cheddar cheese
3 tablespoons green onion, chopped
3 tablespoons parsley, chopped
1 teaspoon Dijon mustard

Salt to taste
2 tablespoons softened butter
2 tablespoons sherry
Dash of hot sauce and a dash of Worcestershire sauce

Use food processor to grate cheese using grating blade — Change to plastic mixing blade, add rest of ingredients; whirl until smooth. Store in a jar or crock for a few days, then serve with crusty French bread which you have cut in 2 inch squares. We like to give the cheese and a loaf of bakery French bread as a holiday gift.

# CURRIED PECANS

*Peerless as presents!*

1 pound pecan halves
¼ pound butter
¼ cup peanut oil
2 tablespoons brown sugar

Salt to taste
2 tablespoons curry powder
1 tablespoon ginger
1 tablespoon chutney sauce

Preheat oven to 350°. Place pecans on baking sheet and toast for 10 minutes. Don't let pecans brown. Leave oven on. Melt butter and oil in a large skillet. Add sugar, salt, curry powder and ginger. Blend well. Add pecans and stir with a wooden spoon until well coated. Add chutney sauce and mix. Place pecans on paper towels on a baking sheet and place in oven. With heat turned off, let pecans dry out in oven for about 10 minutes. Remove and salt lightly. Store in airtight containers after cooling.

## EASY EGG NOG

1 quart egg nog mix
Yolks of 3 eggs
2 tablespoons sugar
Few drops of vanilla

¼ teaspoon cinnamon
Dash nutmeg
3 egg whites
4 drops lime juice

Beat the first six ingredients. Beat the egg whites and add the lime juice. Add the whites to the egg nog. When serving add 1 jigger of rum, bourbon, or brandy to cup or glass then fill with the egg nog mix. Serves 4 to 6. Make doubled and re-doubled, which you will probably have to do because it is so creamy and good!

## FROSTED GRAPES

*Want to make a meat tray pretty? Use sprigs of washed mint and frosted grapes.*

Grapes, 5 or 6 small clusters
2 egg whites, slightly beaten

Granulated sugar

Wash and dry bunches of grapes with paper towels. With a soft brush, coat grapes with slightly beaten egg whites. Quickly roll in granulated sugar to coat well. Place on a cake rack. Grapes may need to be redipped and rolled in sugar to coat well. Place in freezer for 3 to 4 minutes.

## INSTANT HOT CHOCOLATE MIX

*Makes a lot of mix. Pour into pretty glass containers, tie with a bow and give for holiday gifts.*

2 pound box Nestles Quick
  Chocolate
1 box (8-quart size) powdered
  milk

1 pound box powdered sugar
1 12-ounce jar powdered non-dairy
  creamer

Mix together in a large container. Use 2 tablespoons for each cup.

## HOMEMADE MUSTARD

*For holiday gifts, put cellophane wrap around jars and tie with a ribbon.*

¼ cup dry mustard
⅔ cup water
½ teaspoon corn starch (maybe a
  bit more)

½ teaspoon salt
3 tablespoons sugar
⅓ cup malt vinegar
Horseradish (optional)

Mix mustard with a small amount of water and let stand. Mix corn starch, salt and sugar with remaining water. Stir until smooth. Add vinegar. Cook on low heat for 8 to 10 minutes, stirring constantly. Remove from heat and cool. Add mustard mixture and blend well. Horseradish may be added at this point, a little at a time, until it suits your taste. Pour into tiny jars. Store in refrigerator.

# BACARDI RUM BALLS

*Gigantic for gifts. Keeps about 100 years!*

2 4¾-ounce packages vanilla
  wafers, crushed
6 tablespoons Golden Rum

½ cup honey
1 pound walnuts or pecans,
  ground

Blend all ingredients thoroughly. Measure 1 tablespoon and roll into a ball. Dip in powdered sugar. Makes about 4½ dozen. Allow to ripen in a tightly covered container for at least ten days before giving as gifts.

# ORANGE LIQUEUR

*Fun to make for Christmas gifts. Can be added to Margarita mix.*

3 oranges
3 cups vodka
1 cup sugar syrup

*Sugar Syrup*
1 cup sugar
½ cup water

Pare, very thinly, the bright-colored rind from the oranges (no white). Blot peel on paper toweling to remove excess oil. Put peel in a large fruit jar and add 2 cups of vodka. Close the jar tightly and store in a cool, dark place for a week.

To make sugar syrup, combine sugar and water and bring to a boil.

Remove peel, add sugar syrup and shake vigorously. Add remaining vodka and shake until thoroughly mixed. Close jar and store in a cool, dark place for another week to mellow. Makes about 1 quart.

# HOT SPICED CIDER

2 quarts apple cider
3 6-ounce cans pineapple juice
3 sticks of cinnamon
1 lemon, sliced paper thin

3 tablespoons brown sugar
5 7-ounce bottles or a 35 ounce
   bottled grapefruit drink

Combine all ingredients, except grapefruit drink, and simmer for 5 minutes. Add grapefruit drink and mix well. Serve warm to 15-20 favored folks!!

# SPICED TEA

*Makes this the day before, then serve next day with a plate of homemade cookies to your neighbors.*

2 oranges
1 lemon
8 sticks of cinnamon
2 tablespoons whole cloves

6 quarts of water
4 small or 2 large tea bags
3 cups sugar

Cut oranges and lemon in half. Juice. Tie orange and lemon rinds, cinnamon sticks and cloves in cheesecloth. Bring the water to a boil and put in all ingredients, except the tea bags and sugar. Simmer for 5 to 10 minutes. Then add tea bags and sugar. Allow to steep 10 minutes, remove tea bags. This can be made a day ahead. Add one half cup of boiling water to clear cloudiness of tea. Serve hot or cold. Makes 15 to 25 servings.

## STEAMED CRANBERRY PUDDING

*Pudding:*
½ cup molasses (or sorghum)
2 level teaspoons baking soda
Hot water
1⅓ cups flour
1 teaspoon baking powder
1 heaping cup cranberries

*Sauce:*
1 cup sugar
½ cup butter
½ cup cream (Half and Half)
1 teaspoon vanilla

Set the cup with molasses in the bottom of a mixing bowl. Add the soda to the molasses. Add boiling water to fill the cup to just running over. Empty the cup and mix. Add 1 cup of flour mixed with the baking powder. Roll the berries in ⅓ cup flour and add to the molasses mixture. Pour into an angel food cake pan or a bundt pan and steam covered over boiling water for 2 hours or more. Serve warm with sauce.

*Sauce:* Mix all ingredients and cook for 5 minutes or a bit longer.

*For Christmas gifts,* grease two 1 pound coffee cans and steam the pudding in them. Remove from the cans when they are cool. Wrap in cellophane and tie with a red ribbon with a sprig of holly. For that extra someone, add a small jar of hard sauce; use baby food jars or pimiento jars for sauce.

# PACKAGING HOLIDAY GIFTS

Inexpensive glass flower pots purchased at chain stores filled with colored cellophane can be used for homemade candies, jams, sauces, etc.

Make calico sacks (buy remnants) for packaging jars of our pickled black-eyed peas; tie with calico ribbon (use your pinking shears); if you are so inclined, a bit of verse attached is fun.

During the year watch for sales on wooden cutting boards, bamboo or woven trays on which to put a variety of cookies. Cover with clear plastic wrap, stick on a bow, and your friends will love you for something good to eat and somethin' good to keep.

Save your empty cardboard cylinders from cheetos, pretzels, chips, etc. Carefully rinse out, dry and cover with red or green contact paper. Decorate the cylinders with gold seals or small lace doilies, etc. Glue a bow on top of plastic snap-on top, and you have a cute container for cookies, candy, or what-have-you, that will also keep them fresh.

When you do your jams, jellies, preserves, etc., in the good old summertime, put up some in the junior size baby food jars, or jars of comparable size. That way you can give two or three different kinds instead of the usual one half pint.

How about a Quiche Lorraine or some other Quiche wrapped in red or green cellophane to be delivered Christmas Eve for the family to serve for Christmas supper? You can make ahead, freeze, then deliver thawed or not.

Bake our Strawberry Nut Bread to pop in a basket lined with strawberry-print material. Add a small jar of our easy Strawberry Jam, and it's "Merry Christmas!!"

Men who like to cook outside love our seasoning salt recipe. Buy one of those aluminum shakers, (holds about a cup), fill with the salt, cover inside of top with foil (so it won't leak), tie a bow on handle and you have a neat gift.

Our Instant Spiced Tea Recipe is fun to put in little jars, slip inside inexpensive ceramic mugs, wrap in cellophane and you have something for the tea drinkers on your list.

For you needlepointers — make round needlepoint medallion pieces that will fit inside your lid top for your jams, jellies for your holiday gift giving. Make a Christmas motif that could be used as an ornament in years to come.

For you crocheters, make a wreath, or a snowflake to tie on to your food gift.

For you knitters, knit a bell to tie on to your jar or loaf of bread.

For any of your gifts of food, remember to label your item with the date you prepared or the date that it is given.

Cookies for little children are easily handled by packing them in dime store toys; e.g. dump trucks, sand pails, doll suitcases, etc.

Most of all, try to spend a little time in some of your favorite stores before the rush of the holidays finding out what is available and how you can adapt it to package something you have prepared from your kitchen with TLC.

## HOLIDAY TABLES

The following are some thoughts for decorating your table for holidays in very simple ways. Most of the things you will have, or you can purchase them at our favorite store, the dime store.

## *CHRISTMAS*

Dip greenery and pyracantha, or holly with berries, etc., in liquid paraffin. While paraffin is still soft, sprinkle with glitter. Use in table arrangements.

Use the non-stick food spray on washed, dried greenery from your yard. The greens will have a nice shine and you can mix them with ornaments or small toys from the dime store; or, you can spray apples, oranges, lemons, etc. to add to your greenery. Consider using velvet bows of yellow, orange, or dark blue as a switch from the usual green and red to mix in with your arrangement.

For a rectangular table that is fairly long, fit carefully washed and dried, flat 6½-ounce cans with a piece of oasis (inexpensive at local florist). Pour water into oasis until it is thoroughly wet. Stick a 12-inch candle in center of oasis; then fill in with greenery, beginning at base of candle. Trim with small, red, shiny Christmas balls and velvet bows. Use a 5-inch wide velvet ribbon down center of table; place candle arrangements at appropriate intervals. If you like your arrangements to have a bit more glamour, spray the greenery with snow, then dust with glitter.

Have a 12- to 18-inch round mirror (depends on your table size) cut at the glass and mirror repair shop (cheapest grade available). Use different sizes of bud vases with single red or pink carnations, filling around the vases with dime store votive candles in clear, glass holders. For an evening holiday dinner, the candles, vases, and flowers reflecting in the mirror are quite lovely. You can use the mirror for any dinner party. Don't save it for just the holidays!

The dime store usually has the tall apothecary jars. Fill with limes and place on the center of your table. Surround with lemon leaves and big bows. Again, don't forget to shine the limes with non-stick food spray. Use the limes after Christmas for our Limed Broiled Chicken.

Soak 6 eight inch pieces of boxwood, holly and ligustrum overnight in water. Using a knife, cut two small holes in the top of a small loaf of unsliced bread (6 to 10 inches long). Cut the holes through to the bottom of the loaf and inset 2 12-inch candles. Stick the greens into the sides of the bread. Make a symmetrical pattern. Start at the base and make a row of boxwood all around. Then make a second row using another evergreen. This method prevents the weight of the branches from tipping the bread. The loaf should be completely covered on all sides and the top. Place the arrangement on a small tray and place on a table. The bread does not get moldy.

For a New Year's party buy some tiny gift cards with envelopes and write funny New Year's predictions on them. Punch a hole in the corners of the envelopes, run a very narrow ribbon through the envelopes, tie them to green floral pics or pipe cleaners, and stick in the plants you received for Christmas. At the end of the evening give each guest an envelope to learn what is in store for him in the New Year. Fortune cookies could be glued to the ribbon instead of using envelopes, if time is limited.

For the New Year's day football game viewing parties, use 4 large brandy snifters to represent each bowl game. Fill one with oranges, one with sugar cubes, one with cotton balls and one with artificial roses. Tie ribbons of the team colors around snifter stems. We like the idea of using those large paper napkins in the colors of all the teams with whatever you are serving.

You can use your brandy snifters again on St. Patricks's Day. Thoroughly scrub Irish potatoes, place in snifters with paper shamrocks, little clay pipes or any other inexpensive items of St. Pat's day that you may find at the dime store.

Children's sand pails filled with wrapped sandwiches, cookies, etc. can be your centerpiece for a children's Easter egg hunt. When they have finished their lunch, the pails become their Easter baskets.

Having 4 tables of six for Easter luncheon? Buy those inexpensive Easter baskets at the you-know-where-store. Tie pretty bows on the handles, use African violets in baskets, and you have centerpieces for luncheon tables. Gently stuff tissue in baskets underneath leaves so plants will fill out baskets.

Tailgate picnic parties before sporting events are very in now. To make yours more festive, wrap your plastic knives, forks and spoons in paper napkins the color of the teams, and tie with narrow, colored paper ribbon. If you don't have a football helmet, borrow one, stick a pot plant in it, tie ribbons of the teams on pipe cleaners, and stick in plant for your centerpiece. Use paper napkins, and plates in like colors, and have fun!!

# OBSERVATIONS

# OBSERVATIONS

Lopsided layer cakes? Cut terry cloth strips to fit around cake pans. Wet in cool water, squeeze, and pin around pan with safety pins.

Sour cream substitute for dieters: 1 carton cottage cheese, ¾ cup buttermilk. Whip in blender or food processor until creamy. Refrigerate. Can be used in cooking when recipe calls for sour cream.

Do you suffer from dull grilled cheese sandwiches? Mix Worcestershire sauce with garlic salt and margarine to spread on both sides of bread. Then grill. Enjoy!!

For brown short ribs, roll in flour and brown in very hot oven. Lower temperature, baste with sauce and cook slowly.

Give your veal cutlets' cream gravy a real lift. Add a pinch of saffron. Saffron is v-e-r-y- expensive, but it lasts about 100 years.

When making cream gravy, never, never add cold milk to flour mixture always warm it a tad.

Keep your calls to Josephine, the plumber, to a bare minimum. Use 2 tablespoons of the following in your kitchen drain about every 10 days: 1 cup salt, 1 cup baking soda, ¼ cup cream of tartar. Follow this mixture with a cup of boiling water. Flush with cold water in one hour.

Use resuscitation method on the taste of canned shrimp — drain shrimp, place in pint jar with 1 teaspoon salt. Fill jar with cold water, and if possible, let it sit overnight. Drain and use.

You say the recipe says "eggs must be room temperature" and you are in a hurry? Don't despair. Plop them in a pan of hot water for five minutes and they are ready!

Cookie tips: Use shiny baking sheets without sides for drop or sliced cookies. Dark finish pans cause heat to concentrate on bottom of cookies and they may burn before they are done.

To fluff up and whiten instant rice, add about 4 or 5 drops of lemon juice to each cup of rice.

Do you just loathe to trim the crusts off of bread when you promised to make 20 sandwiches for the Scout picnic? Smile; use your electric knife to trim crusts. Nothing to it.

To make your fresh string beans cooperate, wash in cold water, then plunge in boiling water for 5 minutes. Cool and the strings will zip right off. Also use boiling water on unshelled pecans. Makes for easier shelling.

To keep your cakes fresh, slip two slices of bread (not stale) in cake box or tin.

To keep your cake plate pretty and neat — slip pieces of wax paper under the cake before you ice it. Whisk it out when done. Neat!!

Do your pies boil over in the oven? Sprinkle salt on the juice to prevent oven filling with smoke until you can clean.

When you are boiling new potatoes, add a few drops of lemon juice to water to prevent them from becoming dark.

Do you have trouble separating ground beef when you are browning it? All righty, just whip out your trusty potato masher and mash the meat several times. Presto, the job is done.

Last minute company's coming and you are behind to begin with. No time to polish silver tableware; do this: Use a large pan, cover bottom with foil, dump in 2 teaspoons of baking soda and about 2 quarts of briskly boiling water. Place silver in the pan, making sure the silver touches the foil. Let it set about 10 minutes. Dry, and set the table. Now, the silver is not going to look as good as if you used the old elbow grease and Wright's silver cream, but gang, it does brighten it up a lot.

In a hurry to thaw meat? Pop in a Ziploc bag and run very hot water on it. In no time, it will be thawed.

If your bacon curls while frying it, cut in half and fry half pieces. It will do less curling. Wrap, pack in freezer. When ready to use run under broiler for a couple of minutes. Makes one less mess to clean.

To slice an angel food cake into layers, use silk or nylon thread with a sawing motion.

You do know that using maple syrup in pecan pies makes them ever so much better. You didn't? Now you do.

Always, but always, cool stewed chicken in its own broth before you debone for chicken salad. The meat will be moist and not stringy.

IMPORTANT — Can weights vary with the brand as well as the contents. If the can you bring home is within an ounce or so of what your recipe calls for, relax; it should not make any difference in your dish — UNLESS — it's a custard, souffle or something that has to jell. If so, it's best to stick to exact measurements.

You love onions, but your tummy doesn't? Soak sliced or chopped in ice water before you use — cools them off!!

Do those plastic produce bags you tear from the roller in the grocery store drive you balmy? After you tear one off, run it back and forth on your sleeve and it opens so easily.

If we seem to be very much in favor of food processors, we confess it's true. Of all the NEW innovations in the culinary world we find this an indispensable aid in cooking. A word of advise — if you buy a food processor, buy a good processor cookbook and then use your machine frequently. Once you begin to use it and become familiar with its charms you will love it!!

We would like to submit a basic list of what we think makes a kitchen well equipped and makes it easy to handle any cooking chore.

2 large mixing bowls
2 sets of measuring cups with measurements clearly marked
2 sets of measuring spoons with measurements clearly marked
A large flour sifter with measurements clearly marked
A heavy rolling pin with ball bearing action
2 large spoons with long handles
A good vegetable peeler (best to buy one in a kitchen shop)
A large wooden cutting board
1 good quality paring knife

2 good quality butcher knives
A portable hand mixer or mixmaster
2 strainers, one large, one small
A large iron skillet
A small heavy skillet
4 saucepans of varying sizes
1 Dutch oven

There are many other wonderful additions such as blenders, food processors, omelet pans, etc. but we believe the above list will meet your needs quite adequately.

We are pleased to acknowledge the generosity of all of the friends of Children's Medical Center, who so graciously entrusted their treasured recipes with us and regret that each recipe contributed could not be included. Thanks also to those who shared ideas and encouragement throughout this endeavor.

Doris Adam
Suegene Addington
Ruth Adler
Alison Allen
Patricia Anderson
Susan Andrews
Marilyn Augur
Tillie Austin
Charles Barnett
Jeanne Bass
Anella Bauer
Kate Belknap
Audrey N. Bell
Mary Lou Bookhout
Mary Brinegar
Irmgard Brooksaler
Deanna Brown
Jane Browning
Janet Burford
Kathy Burnett
Sara Butler
Aline Byrd
Corinne Calder
Joyce Campbell
Linda Clark
Martha Clark
Martha Click
Pat Cline
Anne Coke
Clara Corrigan
Anne Cottingham
Johnnie Mae Crawford
Shirley Craycroft
Ruth Ann Crocker
Marilyn Culwell
Jessica Dalton
Mary Davis
Jean Daywalt
Mary Deaton
Lillie DeGrand
Phronsie H. Dial

Bette Dickinson
Lucile Dragert
Joan Edwards
Thelma Elkins
Jo Jo Ewing
Carla Francis
Virginia Geist
Judy Gibbs
Margot Gill
Toppy Goolsby
Ida Green
Kathryn Greeves
Gloria Hammack
Patsye Hardin
Betty Harlan
Nan Harrington
Linda Harris
Jo Hawn
Velda Heimberg
Jackie Hickman
Judy Holmes
Jean Ann Holt
Jane Houser
Caroline Hunt
Norma Hunt
Jane Jenevein
Patricia Johnson
Phyllis Jones
Louise Jordan
Betty Josey
Jerry Kingery
Lorene Kirkpatrick
Ann Koontz
Joan Kramer
Dorothy Lafitte
Sally Lane
Dale Lawson
Sherry Levin
Donna Linthicum
Margaret McArthur
Grace McCain

Carmen McCracken
Leslie McCracken
Gene McCutchin
Linda McElroy
Vera McGibboney
Shirley McGinnis
Joan McIlyar
Lois McKown
Eula Lee Miller
Rheida Miller
Elizabeth Moore
Betty Morchower
Beverly Muire
Florence Mullins
Nancy Newport
Charlotte Oden
Alice Mae Orr
Pat Owen
Lucy Owsley
Margaret Pace
Ida Pappert
Barbara Paschall
Phyllis Pennartz
Joan Percy
Mae Perkins
Marilyn Perry
Nellie Persons
Kenney Pickens
Ruth Pickens
Helen Pillifant
Lois Pingel
Shirley Pollock
Ruth Powell
Frances Powers
Ancanetta Presley
Gail Prideaux
Carol Reeder

Joy Remson
Estha Roberts
Linda Roberts
Joan Stansbury
Debora Saunier
Peggy Shelmire
Ginny Sillers
Joan Slaughter
Ann Smith
Marilyn Smith
Christine Spencer
Joan Stansbury
Carolyn Stone
Susie Tasker
Dorothy Taylor
Sissy Thompson
Sara Thorpe
Vermelle Votteler
Nancy Underwood
Emily Walker
Becky Wallace
Peggy Wallace
Ruth Wallace
Lucile Walsh
Lee Warren
Nancy Watson
Jean White
Medora White
Nancy White
Phyllis Wilkin
Roberta Williamson
Jane Windrow
Sallie T. Windrow
Mary Wood
Sally Wood
Becky Wooley
Tory Wozencraft
Barbara Zimmerman

# INDEX

## Cookies, 163

## Desserts, 151

### Cakes, 152

## Venison, 123

**Children's Medical Center Auxiliary Publications**
1935 Amelia Street
Dallas, TX    75235

Please reserve _____ copies of **With Tender Loving Care** at 8.95 each, plus 1.05 for handling and postage (Add .45 tax if Texas resident.) Enclosed is my check for _____.

Name_____
Address_____
City_____State_____Zip_____

\*\*\*\*\*

**Children's Medical Center Auxiliary Publications**
1935 Amelia Street
Dallas, TX    75235

Please reserve _____ copies of **With Tender Loving Care** at 8.95 each, plus 1.05 for handling and postage (Add .45 tax if Texas resident.) Enclosed is my check for _____.

Name_____
Address_____
City_____State_____Zip_____

\*\*\*\*\*

**Children's Medical Center Auxiliary Publications**
1935 Amelia Street
Dallas, TX    75235

Please reserve _____ copies of **With Tender Loving Care** at 8.95 each, plus 1.05 for handling and postage (Add .45 tax if Texas resident.) Enclosed is my check for _____.

Name_____
Address_____
City_____State_____Zip_____

\*\*\*\*\*